# CHILDREN
## of ICARUS

CAIGHLAN SMITH

Curious Fox
a capstone company-publishers for children

*To my mom*

*The gods were always jealous of the angels, or so we are taught.*

*They captured the angels, envious of their purity and perfection, but in their haste left one free. This was the youngest of the angels, Icarus. When the gods realized their folly, they bade Icarus come to their land to retrieve his people, and so they opened to him the doors to their realm: the sun.*

*The gods have always been cruel, always tricksters. The sun was no gateway but poor, young Icarus could not have known the gods' plan for him. He flew into the sky until his wings caught fire and he plummeted back to the earth.*

*Death would have become Icarus had he not been discovered in the field where he had fallen. He was found by the great Daedala, who took pity on the beautiful, innocent creature. She built for him a tomb far underground and crafted for him a sarcophagus, in which he might regenerate over the centuries and one day rise once more.*

*Daedala knew she would not live to see Icarus fly again, and so built for him two more gifts, to protect him from the ruthless, relentless gods. She constructed a giant city over the tomb of Icarus, with walls and towers so high they threatened the territory of the gods themselves. And then, around this city, she built a labyrinth that was thought to never end.*

*There is, somewhere, an end to the labyrinth. Every year those young and innocent like Icarus are sent to find this end. If they accomplish this task they are rewarded with entry into Alyssia, land of the angels, where they themselves will become angels and one day welcome Icarus home.*

*Or so we are taught.*

1

# JUDGE

I count every ping in the lift on the way up. Fifteen. Sixteen. I don't look at the number Clara pressed. I don't listen to her or the others now as they chatter about the parade. I just keep counting and praying to Icarus it's not twenty-three, not the balcony floor.

Twenty-three.

The lift doors open with a final ping. The others spill out into the hall. I linger, wondering if I could get away with waiting in the lift. Then Clara comes back for me. She grins and, despite her split lip, it's so pretty. I follow her after the others.

At the end of the hall the door is already propped open, spilling sunlight and a cool breeze inside. Tanner and two of the other boys from my class are already outside, peering off the balcony to the street below.

"Parade started yet?" Clara calls.

Tanner shakes his head. When he looks at Clara, his mouth twists. "What in Alyssia happened to you? Try and rob the bakery again?"

Clara doesn't waste her breath on him. She goes right to the balcony, shoving herself up on the stone ledge. A few of the other girls shriek at her and one of the guys tells her to get down, but Tanner and a few of the others laugh. I wish they wouldn't. It encourages her.

Clara walks along the ledge like it is a tightrope, throwing a grin over her shoulder as she pretends to wobble. I catch my breath, sure today will be the day she slips and falls. She doesn't. Not yet. She makes it out to the spire and sits, one leg on either side of the structure. Then she starts to shimmy out to the very end, so she's right behind the gargoyle.

"How's your boyfriend doing?" one of the guys calls.

"Great!" Clara wraps her arms around the gargoyle's waist. "He's my rock, y'know?"

A few more of the guys laugh. Some of the girls are into it now, but most still look worried or cross with her. Most of the girls don't like Clara. I can hear one of them whisper something about Clara being a show-off who just wants to impress the boys. I don't know if that's true. Rather, I think it's that Clara wants to impress everyone.

Although everyone is somewhat impressed at first, when Clara calls out that she sees the parade coming down the street, they lose interest in her exploits. The balcony's too far back, too far up, to properly enjoy the parade. They all head back to the lift.

"Losers!" Clara calls after them, sticking to her perch. She rests her chin on the gargoyle's shoulder, peering down at the street.

The breeze is slight, enough to rustle my skirt and hair, but not enough to erase the faint ping of the lift closing. Clara and I are alone now.

"Don't you want to see the parade?" I ask her.

"I can't hear you," Clara says, not turning around. "At least come to the balcony."

I do, albeit hesitantly. When I reach the stone ledge and peek down, my head swims. The crowds on the pavement are like one grey blob. We're too far up for details. We're too far up.

I must say this aloud, because Clara says, "Just look at the sky if you can't look at the ground."

Then again, maybe I don't say it aloud, because Clara knows this is what I need anyway. The sky is as grey as the crowds. It makes me wonder, does the sky worship Icarus as well, if it so often wears his colour?

"Deep breaths," Clara says. I don't know if she says it for herself or for me, because that's when she releases the gargoyle. Carefully, she rises to her feet.

I grip the ledge so tightly it hurts. I want to tell her to stop but I'm afraid I'll distract her and she'll fall. I'm afraid she'll fall anyway.

Clara raises her arms for balance as she stands over the city. Between the fluttering wisps of her blonde hair I see her grin. I wonder if she feels like she's flying when she's like that. I wonder if she feels like Icarus.

Finally, Clara starts backing up, off the spire. She tilts at one point and I have to swallow a squeal. She regains her balance and takes the last few steps to safety, then hops down to my level. I feel like I can breathe again.

"Let's go," Clara says. "We'll be just in time for the Dance of the Angels. I saw them coming down the street."

Clara and I hurry to the lift. I don't count the pings this time. They hardly register at all.

"Will you tell me what happened?" I ask Clara. She knows I mean her split lip and the bruise on her cheek.

"I tried to hide them. I borrowed Mum's make-up. Are they really obvious?"

I shake my head, even though they are.

"I went to the temple last night. After hours. Some guards caught me."

Clara knows as well as the rest of us we aren't allowed in the temple after night service. The city is very strict about curfews.

"I just needed some time there alone. I get that if we want to speak to Icarus at night we have to do so before bed, but I figured he'd be more likely to hear me in his own temple. Right?"

I nod because I know that's what Clara wants me to do.

"It's just… I needed to tell him again. I tell him all the time, but I wanted him to know how important this is to me. I'm already sixteen so tomorrow's my last chance. I have to be chosen tomorrow."

Clara has talked to me about this before. It makes me uncomfortable, but I listen anyway. She's my best friend.

"I'm going to be chosen," Clara says, and I know she's saying it more for her own benefit than mine. "I've prayed to Icarus more than anyone. He has to send me into the labyrinth."

*Ping.* We're almost at the first floor.

"I'll miss you," I murmur.

Usually Clara tells me to speak louder, even though she can understand me perfectly. It's her way of trying to get me to come out of my shell, I think. This time she gives me a warm smile.

*Ping.*

"Don't worry," she says, "I prayed that you would get chosen too."

My alarm goes off at seven. The service is at nine, but everyone in our building is expected to arrive at eight thirty. I need to shower and dress and do my hair.

I need to shower. I tell myself this over and over as I stare at my alarm clock. Its alarm is the same chime as the bells at the Temple of Icarus. Instead of turning it off, I lie there, thinking of how those bells have sounded to me on this morning for the past six years.

Children aged ten to sixteen are candidates for the labyrinth trial. Clara is sixteen. So am I. This is our last chance to become Icarii: to enter the labyrinth and become angels.

Clara's older brother became an Icarii when he was twelve and we were ten. Clara cried, but her mother was so proud and her brother was so excited and everyone was so pleased for him that eventually Clara stopped crying. It happened suddenly after her brother had been gone for a couple of months. One night I was helping Clara dry her tears with little grey handkerchiefs and the next I was praying with her for Icarus to send her into the labyrinth. Except that's never really what I prayed for.

Mother comes in for me seven minutes after seven. I close my eyes and pretend I've slept through my alarm.

Mother wakes me with a light shake of my shoulder. "Honey, you have to get up."

The bells go quiet. I open my eyes. Mother smiles at me. Pats my shoulder once more. "We don't want to be late. This is your big day."

My last big day. After today – this morning – I'll never be able to become an Icarii.

The shower is too hot or too cold. My skin is pink all over when I get out. As I dry my hair, I think about the parade. The Dance of the Angels is always so pretty. The dancers wear golden robes that catch the light as they twirl. The robes fan out behind them like wings. The Icarus dancer is dressed all in grey, muted yet striking against the gold. He dances differently than the other angels, movements languid and loose and haphazard. Sometimes it looks like the Icarus dancer is simply throwing himself around the street. Still, it manages to be just as beautiful as the Angels' dance, if not more so. Something about the movements of Icarus are desperate.

Sometimes I fantasize about joining the Dance of the Angels, but all the dancers are over sixteen. I'd have to wait until next year to try out and I probably wouldn't get a role. I love watching dancers, but I can't execute such perfect movements myself. I trip and I stumble and, more than anything, I freeze.

Clara would make a beautiful dancer.

"Are you going to put it up?" Father asks, startling me as he passes by my room. He gestures to my hair. I shake my head and he frowns. He says, "Alright." He leaves.

Father doesn't like it when I leave my hair down. I don't think Mother likes it either. I like it. Having it down makes it easier to hide my face. For the past six years I've hidden the expression I make when I'm not chosen. This is my last year. I won't let anyone find out how I really feel now.

Mother comes in to fuss with my dress. She brushes my hair back behind my ears. "You're so beautiful, dear. It's a pity you don't let others see that more often."

I wonder if Father put her up to this.

"What about that lovely clip you got for Fallen Day last year? It matches your eyes. I'll go get it, shall I?"

I shake my head, but Mother's already gone to the small music box where I keep my jewellery. She opens it and the little golden angel springs up as the Daedalum anthem starts to play. The little golden angel spins slowly. It's just about to meet its reflection in the music box mirror when Mother closes it again.

"It's not there. Where might you have put it?"

I shrug and Mother taps her chin, scanning my room as if her gaze will lure the hair-clip out.

"Mother?"

"Hm? What is it, dear?"

I twist the material of my skirt between my fingers. "If I'm chosen today, will you be happy?"

"More than anything. You know that. I guess we'll have to do without the clip."

Father announces we have to go. It's nearly quarter after eight and if we wait any longer there's going to be a line at the lift. There's a line anyway, when we get there.

Mother and Father socialize with the neighbours until we board. Once inside the lift, Mother gives my arm a squeeze and tucks my hair behind my ears again. She gives my arm one more squeeze, as if this action will seal my hair into place.

*Ping.*

The temple is on the seventh floor. It's the only thing on the seventh floor. I've been told it's the same for every building. The first six floors are for commerce. Nine up to fifteen include commerce and school rooms. Beyond that is housing. There is no eighth floor. The temple takes up two floors with its high ceiling.

I've never been in a building apart from my own, so I wouldn't know for sure what the others look like. There's no point in entering other buildings when we have all we need here.

We get off on the seventh floor and join the line of families streaming into the temple. I hear children whispering excitedly. I hear parents whispering excitedly. Will someone they know get the honour of entering the labyrinth? Do they know a future angel?

Mother, Father and I take our specified seats. I see Clara, two benches ahead, sitting next to her mother. Clara's hair is in two braids on either side of her head, tied by grey ribbons. From here I can't see the ribbons, but I know they're grey. I know exactly what they look like. Clara always braids her hair just like this for special occasions.

More people file into the temple. Mother and Father talk to our bench neighbours, who are also our real neighbours. This is how seating is determined, for the sake of organization. I sit between Mother and Father and don't talk to anyone. Instead I stare up at the mural that covers the entire ceiling: Daedala's labyrinth. I look down, between my feet, where the mural continues over the whole floor. This is the most we ever see of the labyrinth. The mural is so beautiful it almost makes me want to see the labyrinth itself, which is depicted as being made of silver, with sections covered in shrubbery and moss and flowers. Some parts of the labyrinth are even made of gold, while others are wide spaces bearing fountains or gardens. I can't imagine something like this in real life. I can't imagine this existing just outside the city walls.

I press my feet together, obscuring my immediate view of the mural. I look to Clara and focus on her braids, on the way loose blonde hairs curl against her neck. Her head is bowed, I realize. Even now, she's praying.

I look away from Clara.

The priest of Icarus arrives, swathed in grey robes. Over his robes he wears a heavy silver chain, attached to which is the symbol of Icarus: a pair of wings emblazoned against a sun.

As happens every year on Fallen Day, the priest retells the story of Icarus and Daedala. After that we're led through prayers for Icarus and in thanks of Daedala. Then the priest reads the names of last year's Icarii and announces they have all reached Alyssia and become angels. We pray for them too. I notice a woman ahead of us crying, her prayer especially vigorous. One of those Icarii must have been her child.

The priest finally turns to the naming of this year's Icarii. He holds aloft a piece of parchment and I know it contains the list of chosen. It's the shortest I've ever seen the parchment.

The priest reads the first name and my hands knot in my skirt. I don't recognize the name. I don't recognize the second name either. I see Clara is as tense as me, but I know it's for another reason. I realize she's gripping her braids, that she's pulled them taut. This is her last chance to join her brother in Alyssia. If she's not chosen, she'll never see him again. If she is chosen, I'll never see her. I know it's selfish, but every name that isn't hers is a weight off my chest.

The next name isn't hers.

Mother's hand is on my shoulder. She's saying something to me. Father's brushing back my hair, turning my face to make me look at him. He says something too.

*"That's my girl."*

Clara has turned around. She's staring right at me. It's shock first and then it's hatred. She hates me, instantly.

And then they call her name too.

"You did it, darling," Mother says to me, and her nails feel like talons in my shoulder. "You're going to become an angel."

Mother and Father bring me to the temple the next morning. They wait outside with the other parents while the new Icarii and I change into our Icarii robes. They're white with the symbol of Icarus on the back. I help Clara get her robe over her head without disturbing her braids.

For once I want to linger in the temple, but Clara teases my hand from my billowing sleeve and tugs me outside. She leaves me there, among a swarm of Icarii and parents, to go show her mother her robes.

I can't see Mother, but I see Father talking to some neighbours. He doesn't notice me. Nobody does, except the priest. He stands at the edge of the crowd, watching the Icarii. In a moment he will summon us and we will leave our tower and never return.

Panic sends me deeper into the crowd, away from the priest. I freeze when I spot the lift. No one would notice if I slipped inside. I could go back to our floor or even the balcony. Anywhere that I could hide while the Icarii left. Surely, they wouldn't send me into the labyrinth after Fallen Day? And they wouldn't send me next year, at seventeen.

All I need to do is board the lift.

My limbs lock into place. Suddenly, the robes feel so heavy, too heavy to move. Is it the will of Icarus that paralyzes me? He's never intervened before. Doing so now just isn't fair.

"There you are, dear."

It's Mother. When I turn to her and she sees my robes she puts her hands over her mouth and her eyes go misty. She says something into her palms.

"You look beautiful," Father says, as he appears from the crowd. "My future angel."

"She's already an angel," Mother says.

This seems to irritate Father. "Careful," he says. "You don't want to sound like that woman from the thirtieth floor. The neighbours told me she tried to hide her son."

"What happened?" Mother asks.

"They beat her, of course, and the guards brought her son. Can you imagine? What kind of parent would try to stop their child from becoming an angel?"

Mother gives Father a weak nod, and an even weaker smile, but his attention is already back on me. "It's a pity we couldn't find that clip. Do try to keep your hair out of your eyes; you want to show the angels your lovely face."

I brush my hair back in a way that makes the room too wide. I can see more of the crowd like this and more of my fellow Icarii and the priest. My stomach knots even as Father smiles approvingly and says, "I'm proud of you."

It doesn't help. The knot inside me keeps twisting. Then Mother is standing in front of me, blocking the large hall and all the people. She brushes back my hair and rests a hand on my forehead as she smiles down at me. Her smile isn't like Father's. It's like the smile she gave Father when he spoke about the woman on the thirtieth floor. She smooths back my hair again, gently, slowly, and suddenly I want to tell her the one thing I promised I'd never tell anyone.

*I don't want to enter the labyrinth. Please don't make me go.*

"Time to go," Father says, and he replaces Mother's presence, but not with a gentle hand on my crown; his hand is on my shoulder, guiding me towards the priest. The other Icarii have already started to gather.

I try to turn and see around Father, but he keeps pushing me forward. "Mother?"

She's there, standing where we left her. She says, "We're so proud of you, dear."

I think her voice breaks, but the crowd is so noisy it swallows her words. Then the crowd swallows her. Or maybe it swallows me. Either way, I'm with the Icarii now.

I take Clara's hand as we're led from our tower. I've spent the sixteen years of my life in this building. I only ever left it for the Daedalum parades or the New Year's celebration in the city square. I grew up in this building and I was supposed to die in this building. Now I'll never die. Now I'll become an angel.

So why is my heart in my throat?

Clara smiles at me and she's the most joyous I've ever seen her. She squeezes my hand. Then she realizes I'm trying to press something into her palm.

"I was going to give it to you," I whisper, "if you were chosen, so that maybe you wouldn't forget me."

"I'd never forget you." Clara fixes the blue clip in her hair. She takes my hand again. Smiles again. "But now we don't have to worry about forgetting each other. We'll become angels together, just like I always wanted."

I want to tell her it's not what she's always wanted. I want to remind her there was a time when the thought of her brother leaving and becoming an angel made her weep all night. I want to tell her I don't want this and that I never have. But that rare spark of courage I felt with my mother is gone.

"I've got it!" Clara exclaims, then starts to untie a grey ribbon from her hair. Underneath the ribbons I see she has little silver bands, keeping her braids tied tight. She pulls off one of the many bands and holds that and the ribbon up to me. "I always thought you'd look pretty with your hair up. Can I?"

Clara braids her hair for special occasions. Today I let her braid mine.

The priest leads us through the city. I pass more towers than I have seen in my life. They all look just like my tower. I wonder if they're the same inside. I wonder if there's a family just like mine on the twenty-first floor, but the daughter wasn't chosen to become an Icarii. I wonder if she'll be in the Dance of the Angels next year.

Clara catches her breath. I follow her gaze to the wall. I've never been this close to it, and I'm glad. Seeing it like this now almost makes me faint. It's higher than every tower in the city. I've never seen over the wall. I don't think anyone in the city has. Only Icarii have seen the other side.

Only Icarii have seen the labyrinth.

The priest is gone. I'm not sure when he left, but we're being led by city guards now. They wear the symbol of Icarus, as a crest on their jackets, not as a silver medallion. They lead us right up to the wall and then herd us through a door in the structure's side. My grip on Clara's hand tightens as the door shuts behind us, sealing us into darkness. Slowly, my eyesight begins to adjust, but not in time. We're moving again before I can take in our surroundings.

We go down halls and we might go through doors and at one point there are stairs. Then we're in a very cold, very dark room. I can see neither walls nor ceiling in the shadows. I hear a child crying softly. Another child silences them. Someone else starts to cry. Someone coughs. It seems as if there are more people here than our group of fifteen.

After what seems like ages, light appears ahead of us, so bright it's blinding. The light grows as a grinding sound fills the room. Tearing my gaze from the brightness, I see that the floor is actually made of dirt, which continues outside.

There's enough light now to see that the room is shaped as a sort of tunnel, the walls and ceiling made of old bricks. I also see I was right that there are more children here than before. They've come from the other towers. We're all dressed in Icarii robes.

"The guards are gone," I murmur.

"This must be it," Clara whispers excitedly, and I'm not sure if it's in response to my comment or if she even heard me. "This must be the start of the trial."

Others seem to be coming to this same conclusion, for slowly some of the Icarii head towards the exit. Clara pulls me after her. Together, we step into the light.

Into the labyrinth.

# JURY

The air is so fresh it's cutting. Clara takes deep breath after deep breath. I'm sure her lungs have been sliced into pieces by now.

"It's so clear," Clara whispers, and I don't know if she means the air or the sky, because her eyes turn upwards. Mine follow. It's the same sky but, for once, it's not filled with towers. Behind us, I can still glimpse the wall, but if I cover that part with my hand I only see sky. Grey sky and grey clouds and a sun that seems farther away than ever. How did Icarus ever make it up there?

The labyrinth stretches ahead of us, a straight corridor with old stone walls on either side, an open ceiling and dirt floors. Icarii are already moving forward. Others seem hesitant to leave the wall, even though we've all left the room by now.

"C'mon." Clara tugs me after her again. "We can't get through the labyrinth if we don't start."

I follow Clara, but as I do I glance over my shoulder. Just before Clara pulls me around a corner, I see the wall gate start to close.

Wordlessly we Icarii stick together, even when we reach the first crossroads. We all turn left. At the next one, we all turn right. I wonder when we'll see the moss and the flowers and the gold.

The next break in the path has three options. Left, right and forward. The group continues forward. Then, up ahead, I see three girls break away to go right.

"We'll keep going straight," Clara says, before I can ask. "Don't you feel like that's the right way?"

I don't know what I feel. Everything about this is so surreal. Yesterday I was being congratulated. Last night I cried myself to sleep. This morning I don't think I woke up. I think this is all a dream. Even when a rock digs into my heel, ripping through my soft white slippers, I'm sure it's a dream.

The group starts to break down as small parties go different ways. Two boys go off to the right. A girl goes off alone to the left. There are maybe a dozen of us left together now.

"We'll all meet up eventually," Clara says to me. "We're Icarii. We're destined to become angels. Some of us will just become angels more quickly."

"What happens when night falls?" I murmur.

"We'll keep going," Clara says. "You know that Icarii don't get tired in the labyrinth. We won't even get hungry."

She sounds resolved. I guess she isn't tired or hungry yet. Maybe her excitement helps convince her that she isn't. Or maybe it's my paranoia convincing me that I am.

We pass a section of the wall that's caved in at the centre, revealing dirt and bits of crumbled stone inside. There's a plant growing in this crevice, dark green vines leaking out onto the wall and tangling over the ground. The vines are withered at the ends. They're dying.

Nothing dies in the labyrinth, or so we were told.

There's an argument up ahead. The two Icarii leading us, who seem to be around my age, are fighting. The girl wants to take the right and the boy wants to take the left. The girl goes off in a huff and several Icarii follow her. Others follow the boy.

I want to ask Clara which way we should go, but my mouth feels like it's filled with ash. I watch wordlessly as Clara looks to the left for a long time, then to the right. I see her flicking the fingers of her free hand. I don't know if she realizes she's doing it. She usually doesn't.

She's counting how many Icarii have gone each way.

"The left," Clara says. "That must be the way. Don't you feel like it's the way Icarus would want us to go?"

She doesn't want me to answer. She wants me to follow. It's all I can do now. Clara is all I have here.

As we walk I overhear one of the Icarii speaking to her friend. "Birds."

She's pointing to something in the sky. Small shadows, blotted out against the sun, wings flapping up and down.

I wonder what kind of birds they are. I've only seen pigeons and crows in Daedalum, perched on balconies or crowding the streets. Every other bird I know from library books. I wonder if these birds are from library books.

Our group eventually comes out into a large open area. I'm surprised to find myself a little bit excited. Maybe there's a fountain or a garden here.

There isn't. There's only stone walls and dirt. One of the walls has entirely collapsed, but behind it is more wall. There are three exits, one leading to a dirt path and two leading to stone. I hope we take one of the latter. They may have fewer pebbles that cut into my feet.

Our group lingers here, in this area. Nobody asks for a break. Nobody sits down. This would be admitting to growing tired. Nobody suggests we press on either.

"The birds are back..." a girl starts to say, but she trails off. I follow her gaze to the sky, where the birds are flying towards us, still shadows. Their shadows are larger and there's something wrong with the shape. They look more like humans than birds. Winged humans.

"Angels," Clara breathes. "It's my brother. It's got to be. He's here to take us to Alyssia!"

Clara's hand rips from my own as she runs forward, waving and shouting at the angels. Other Icarii do the same. The angels get closer. They're so close I can hear the powerful beat of their wings. Clara jumps up and down and her braids bounce over her shoulders. The clip I gave her comes undone. It pings off the ground. The angel scoops her up, talons piercing through her shoulders and spilling red onto her cloak.

Clara screams.

Suddenly everyone is screaming. The angels are wrong. Horribly wrong and grotesque. Their flesh is grey and pulled taut over their bones, showing ribs and shoulder blades and elbows in vivid detail. From the waist down they are covered in black feathers, and their feet are not feet at all but giant claws. Their arms are large, strong wings made of the same black feathers. They are bald with pointed ears and pointed faces and long, pointed teeth. Their faces are half human, half something else. They open their mouths and their tongues are forked and they screech like something that should be dead.

Clara is still screaming. Everyone is still screaming. I don't know if I'm screaming or not. I know I can't move.

And then an angel attacks the angel carrying Clara. It grips Clara's waist in its talons and Clara shrieks and the angels pull her back and forth and then–

Blood sprays on my face. I can taste it in my mouth. The angels are snatching other Icarii and I know for sure I'm screaming now. I'm screaming and my throat is raw and I'm never going to stop screaming.

Someone runs into me and knocks me down. My head clips off the ground and everything blurs.

Inhuman screeches and childish screams still echo around me. Something slams into the ground in front of me. Something white. An Icarii. I push myself away from it, gasping and sobbing and crying as the rocks bite into my palms. From here I see the collapsed wall again. The way it leans against the other walls provides some shelter. I scramble over to it.

Just as I'm pushing myself in, somebody pushes me out. "There's no room! Go away!"

Through my tears I see two Icarii. They're both boys and both terrified. The one with red hair glares at me, hands out to shove me again.

Something else thumps onto the ground behind me. There are more screeches than screams now.

I throw myself into the shelter. The boy curses at me and tries to push me out again, but I fight against him, grinding my sore heels into the hard ground. I tug the edge of my cloak into the shadows before curling in on myself. The boy pushes at me. Then he grabs one of my braids and pulls on it, hard. Tears spring to my eyes and I cover my mouth to keep back a scream.

"Don't," the other Icarii whispers, grabbing the redhead's arm. "If we make too much noise, they'll find us."

"They'll find us if she stays here," the redhead hisses. The other boy edges farther into the shelter in reply, making himself as small as possible. I'm glared at once more before the redhead shifts in farther as well. I follow.

Outside the shelter the screeching and screaming and thumps continue. Then the screaming stops. The screeches continue, sporadically. Other noises fill the void. Ripping and grinding and gushing. Snapping sounds, scraping sounds, like rock on rock. The Icarii boys jump whenever a screech sounds. I jump too, barely biting back a gasp.

Something is thrown right next to the shelter entrance: the bloody body of an Icarii. I'm about to scream when the redhead clamps a hand over my mouth. He hisses at me to shut up or he'll throw me out. His hand is shaking as much as his voice.

There's screeching just outside the shelter, followed by more screeching and scraping. Black feathers litter the Icarii's body. Then a pair of feather-clad legs are right in front of me, deadly sharp talons digging into the corpse. I'm so terrified there's no way I could scream, but the boy's hand presses harder against my mouth. Then there's a whoosh and the feathered legs and sharp talons and body disappear up into the air. The feathers that had been on the Icarii float gently to the ground. One drifts into the shelter, right next to me.

Time passes. I don't know how much. My muscles are starting to cramp from being tensed for so long. I tense again when a chorus of shrieks sound. Something's happening outside. Then it's over. An eerie silence descends.

None of us move. It starts to get dark. I think about what I was doing this time yesterday. I was sitting at the dining room table for our celebration meal. Father's sister was there with her family. I wanted to ask my parents if they were really happy I'd been chosen. I told myself I couldn't ask in front of the family. Father told his sister how proud he was of me. Mother started to cry. She told me not to worry. She was just happy her daughter was becoming an angel. They were happy tears.

The tears that have dried into my cheeks aren't happy. They make my flesh feel tight, as if it's made of porcelain, as if moving at all will make it crack and make me fall apart. So I can't move, I tell myself. I can't move.

The redhead shoves my shoulder. "Check and see if they're gone."

I gape at him.

"Look!"

I savagely shake my head. He pinches my arm and I flinch. "Check or I'll shove you out there and we'll find out that way."

He keeps twisting the flesh of my arm between his fingers. It hurts through my sleeve. He lets go when I start edging towards the shelter entrance. He hisses for me to hurry up, but I don't. It feels like a whole minute has passed by the time I'm far enough to peek out.

The angels are gone and the clearing is littered with Icarii bodies. Before I can look too hard at the bodies, I notice something moving among them. A woman, wearing tight black clothing and a baggy grey jacket. The dying light picks up the dull brown of her messy hair as she manoeuvres through the Icarii. She crouches down by a body and when she rises I realize she's collecting the white cloaks. Except she's not taking all of the cloaks. She's cutting them apart with some kind of blade. She separates clean rags from bloodied rags and leaves them in two piles in the centre of the clearing.

As I watch, the woman looks up. If my throat weren't so raw I'm sure I'd gasp. There's a large scar in the shape of an X right over her mouth.

Suddenly the Icarii boy pulls me back into the shelter, demanding in a hushed voice to know what I've seen. Unable to formulate words, I just keep shaking my head. I feel like words are too much for what I saw and what I've seen. Maybe words will always be too much.

The boy pushes past me. I have to shove up against the back of the shelter while he half crawls over me to peer outside. His elbow pokes into my chest and then his knee is digging into my thigh but I keep my mouth shut. After a few seconds, he shoots back into the shelter.

"What's out there?" the other boy whispers. As I did, the red-haired Icarii just shakes his head. He isn't pressed further.

We sit in silence for a while longer. Night falls. Eventually I bring myself to check outside again. The person is gone. Hesitantly I start to push myself out of the shelter. My legs cramp up and I can't move.

"What are you waiting for?" the redhead demands.

I try to push myself out again, but I can't.

"Hurry up!"

I look from him to my legs. I can't speak and I can't move.

"Try rubbing them," the other boy says to me. "Your legs. Get circulation back into them if they're asleep."

I do so. After a while rubbing them starts to work. I can move again, albeit weakly. Now that I can move, though, I'm not sure I want to.

When I hesitate again the redhead shoves me outside. I scrape my hands on the ground, reopening cuts from earlier. As I crawl away from the shelter, the boy ducks outside. His red hair looks almost brown in the darkness. The other boy's hair is entirely black. It's the same colour as the angels' feathers.

I push myself up. It takes longer than it should to

find my balance. The red-haired boy has gone over to the closest Icarii body. He starts to kneel by it, then shoots to his feet. He covers his mouth as he backs up right into the black-haired boy.

"What is it?" the black-haired boy asks, trying to get a look at the body. Details can't be seen in the darkness, but even so, I don't look at the shadowy mound very long. I don't want to see what's made the redhead sick.

"Have to get out of here," he says, half to himself. He starts back the way our group came.

"Where are you going?" the black-haired boy asks. "We have to reach the end of the labyrinth."

"And become angels like those?" the boy demands. "No way! No way. I'm not doing this. I don't want this."

"But Icarus chose us!"

"Then you go! You find your way to Alyssia!" The redhead turns away, his voice small. "I'm going home."

*Home.*

I follow him. After a moment, the black-haired boy follows too.

"What's your name?"

I peek at the black-haired boy before going back to hiding my face in my hair.

"I'm Felix," the boy says, "and that's Kyle."

I try to say something, but my voice won't work.

"I'm fourteen," Felix says, then gestures to the boy walking briskly ahead of us. "Kyle's sixteen. Kyle and I are from the same building. We only live a few floors apart. What about you? How old are you?"

Clara and I only live a couple of floors apart. Two pings. She comes to get me and we go to the school floor together. Sometimes she'll have breakfast at my house.

A sob catches in my throat before breaking free. Felix jumps, startled by the noise. I sob again and tears blur my vision.

"Shut up!" Kyle snaps and I feel his hand clamping over my mouth again. I try to pull away from him, but his other hand is at the back of my neck, keeping me in place.

"You're slow and noisy," Kyle says. "And you're annoying. We all had to live through today, but you don't see us breaking down. I don't care that you're a girl; wait until you're back home. You can cry to your mama then."

The tears keep coming, but I don't even whimper

when Kyle lets me go. I keep my lips sealed tight.

"It's better to be quiet," Felix adds, after Kyle's gone ahead, "in case those... those angels come back."

The two boys keep walking, but I don't move. I know they'll leave me if I don't move. I'll be all alone in a labyrinth with dark angels that kill the children of Icarus. I'll never find my way home and I'll never find my way out. I can't. Not without Clara. I can't.

Kyle's just rounded the corner when he stops. Felix bumps into him and is instantly shoved back a few steps, even while Kyle keeps gaping down the next corridor. My feet move on their own towards the boys. There's another boy down the next corridor. This one's very young and it's clear he's been crying. Like us, he wears Icarii robes, but his are stained with blood, which has pooled under him where he's curled on the ground.

Kyle rushes over to the boy and drops down beside him. He tries to roll the boy over, to check the source of the blood, but the boy sobs even louder. I expect Kyle to snap at him to keep quiet, but instead he says, "What happened to you?"

"The wall," the boy cries. "I just wanted to go back home. Why can't I go home? Why won't they let me?"

"Who?" Felix asks hesitantly. "The angels?"

The boy's eyes fill with hope as he clutches Kyle's robes. "The angels will help me, won't they? The angels will make it stop hurting?"

The pool of blood below the boy is getting bigger.

"That's right," Kyle says, smoothing back the boy's hair from his sweaty forehead. Kyle's hand is shaking.

"The angels will protect us."

Felix starts to say, "But the angels we saw–"

A sharp look from Kyle shuts him up. Kyle returns to smoothing back the boy's hair, in a way so similar to what my mother did this morning my heart squeezes. I wasn't sure why she did it, but watching Kyle like this now makes me think she was trying to comfort me. I wish I could go back to that moment and take comfort from it, instead of confusion.

The boy has stopped sobbing and started shivering. Kyle wraps his arms around him and starts rocking him gently, like the workers at the nursery do with babies. Kyle keeps rocking long after the boy has stilled.

"Is he…?" Felix asks.

"Help me roll him over."

I'm not sure if Kyle is saying this to both of us, but I can't bring myself to approach the boy. His blood has pooled so that it's staining the edge of Kyle's robes.

Felix helps turn the boy, but Kyle's careful to keep him lifted off the ground. The back of the boy's robes are dyed red. There is a hole in the material, showing bloodied flesh underneath. The hole distorts the symbol of Icarus, making it look like the gods themselves have reached down to rip apart Icarus's wings.

"Bullet hole," Kyle says. "He was shot."

"Someone brought a gun into the labyrinth?" Felix whispers.

"Not into the labyrinth. You heard him. It was the guards on the wall. They're the only ones with guns."

"No… no, they wouldn't. We're Icarii."

Gaze hooded, Kyle flips the boy over again. He starts dragging him to the far wall of the corridor, out of the blood. This time, Felix doesn't help. He's staring at the city walls in the distance.

"They wouldn't," Felix whispers again, half to himself. "My father was a guard. He never would have–"

"Enough about your father," Kyle snaps. "This kid just *died*."

I tried to ignore it, the amount of blood, the boy's silence, even the way his eyes grew foggy and he stopped blinking. But I can't ignore Kyle's words.

"They said nobody dies in the labyrinth."

I don't realize I'm the one who's spoken until Kyle's glare shoots my way. He marches to me and I back up until I hit the wall, then he grabs my wrist and tries tugging me towards the boy. When I struggle against him he says, "C'mon. Check his breathing. Try to find his pulse. Look at that bullet wound up close and tell me nobody dies in the labyrinth."

I start crying again.

"Kyle…" Felix says.

"Shut up," Kyle snaps, but he lets me go and starts marching away.

Felix catches my gaze and speaks so quietly he basically mouths, "You OK?"

I know he's only asking about what Kyle just did, but I still can't nod it away. Nor can I shake my head. It feels like acknowledging the question at all would open everything up, everything that makes me the opposite of OK, and I'd shut down completely.

Met with my silence, Felix eventually follows Kyle. I'm not far behind. I reach to rub my wrist where Kyle grabbed me, but my fingers come away slick. Glancing down, I'm horrified to find myself wearing a bracelet of blood.

My first instinct is to scrub it off on my robes, but then my robes will stain and I'll never be free of the reminder. So I use my hand to rub it off and try not to gag at the stickiness. I rub and rub until both my hand and my wrist are raw.

We aren't returning to the wall any more. We've turned back round. I keep trying not to think about the boy who died, about the fact people who once guarded us killed him, but it's impossible.

When we reach the open area again, the bodies are in the exact same spots as they were before. We skirt them, hugging the edge of the wall, until we reach the closest corridor. My battered feet meet cool tile. I can feel the cracks in the stone, but no jagged bits.

We all stop when Kyle holds up his hand and looks around. "Do you hear that?"

In the silence is a muted grinding sound. Underfoot there are slight, almost unnoticeable tremors.

Felix says, "I can't hear–"

The floor between the boys and me cracks. We freeze, staring at the spot. There's a thud from underground. Another crack spikes across the surface.

Kyle and Felix start running. I panic. Do I try and cross the crack and follow or do I turn around and–

Stone and dirt explode in my face and I fall backwards. A creature twice my height shoots up from the hole in front of me. It's long and thin with neither limbs nor head. It's covered in greenish-black scales that catch the moonlight as it twists its sickening body towards me. The top of the creature opens to a never-ending mouth filled with thousands of needle teeth that poke out at all angles.

Something hits its side and bounces off, clattering to the ground. An arrow. The creature swivels about, as if searching for its attacker. This is my chance to escape, but my arms and legs are shaking too much. I can't stop staring at the monster in front of me.

Suddenly there's a shout and a boy leaps at the creature. He slams a club into the upper part of the monster's body – where the head would surely be if it had one. The creature jerks taut. Then it crumples in on itself in a heap, the long folds of its body obscuring the hole from which it appeared.

Now that the monster has fallen, I see three new people standing on the other side of the hole, with Kyle and Felix behind them. The people all seem to be my age or older with dirty, ragged clothes and dirty, scratched faces. There's a boy with thick brown hair and a quiver of arrows on his back, carrying a bow. There's a girl wearing a hood that closes at her neck with a wooden clip, obscuring her hair. She's carrying a rusted and chipped short sword. The other boy is tall with spiky black hair. He's inspecting his club, picking something off the nails that are driven through the wood.

"That was smart," he says loudly, "shooting at it."

"If he hadn't shot," the girl in the hood says, while the other boy goes to retrieve his fallen arrow, "the digger would've eaten this kid's face off."

As the boy picks up his arrow, he glances at me. His eyes are a surprisingly light green. I can't help looking away. The boy pushes to his feet, sliding his arrow back into its quiver.

The black-haired boy comes over to me and, even though I see him coming, I squeak when he grabs my upper arm. I unintentionally resist when he tries to pull me to my feet. He raises an eyebrow. "Not coming with us?"

"Don't you want to see your first sunrise in the labyrinth?" the girl in the hood asks.

"You must be hungry, at least," the boy says to me. "We don't have much, but hey, it's still better to eat than be eaten, right? If you don't come with us, you're gonna become something's meal."

I immediately flash back to what happened with the angels. I can't help whimpering, but I don't think anyone except the boy hears me.

"If we don't hurry," the girl in the hood says, "we'll become a very big something's meal. Digger Mama's not gonna take too kindly to us bashing in her progeny. Plus we gotta get these two hoods asap."

I realize the girl is gesturing to Kyle and me.

"What in Alyssia are you talking about?" Kyle demands.

The girl grins and the black-haired boy chuckles. At a dirty look from Kyle, the boy says, "Sorry, I just haven't heard that in a long time."

"Who are you guys?" Felix asks.

"Isn't it obvious?" the girl says. "We're Icarii."

The girl in the hood introduces herself as Andrea and introduces the boy with the bow as Ryan. The other boy says his name is Theo. Andrea says they'll tell us everything on the way home. Then they start heading deeper into the labyrinth. Theo stays at the back, right behind me.

"In case something tries to sneak up on us," Theo says to me. "Trust me, it happens. A lot. You don't want to be at the back unless you have a weapon and very, very quick reflexes."

He smiles after saying this, maybe as an attempt to reassure me after what he's said. I'm not reassured and I don't smile back. I focus on the group ahead. Andrea seems to know exactly where we're going as she hurries us down corridors and around corners. Ryan travels right beside her, arrow notched and waiting in his bow.

"Can you explain now?" Kyle demands, and I can tell by his voice he's as out of breath as I am.

"What's there to explain?" Andrea asks.

"A lot!" Theo calls. Ryan glares over his shoulder at him. When Theo next speaks it's to me. "It's best to be quiet in the labyrinth. You never know what might be nearby."

Up front, Andrea has started her explanation. "We used to be Icarii, just like you guys. Same tacky robes and everything. Then we discovered the unattractive side of the labyrinth. Luckily for us, we were all picked up by Fates. They're a group of Icarii dedicated to teaching new Icarii how to adapt and survive in the labyrinth. Luckily for you guys, Fates just picked you up too."

"How long have you been here?" Felix asks.

"I've been here three years," Andrea says. "Ryan's been here four."

"Five for me," Theo says. "It's practically a record."

"It's not a record," Andrea argues. "You're not even in second."

"Of course I'm in second. Who's had more than six?"

"Would you be quiet?" Ryan hisses. "You're gonna get a flock of screechers down on us. And the record's seven."

"Seven? Who had seven?"

"Sybil." Ryan darts forward. "I'm scouting ahead."

"I thought it was six," Theo whispers to himself before going quiet. I almost want to look back and see his expression, but I'd definitely be caught, so I don't look.

"Why are you guys talking about records?" Kyle asks. "Is that how long it takes you to find the way out of the labyrinth?"

"Nobody's ever made it out of the labyrinth," Andrea says, "but you could say that's how long it takes us to become angels."

We're all quiet for a while after that, but finally Felix says, "Angels attacked us earlier."

"What did they look like?" Andrea asks.

Felix starts to describe them, but Andrea stops him after grey skin and black feathers. "Oh, those were screechers. They usually get to the fresh Icarii first."

"Screechers?" Felix echoes.

"Not their proper name," Theo says, "but it's what we all call them, like diggers. They're one of the labyrinth's many carnivorous attractions. Definitely not angels."

"Maybe not to you, Theo," Andrea says, "but you know some of the others think differently."

"So they *are* angels?" Felix asks.

"Some of us think so," Andrea says. "Some of us think they're what we turn into if we don't make it out of the labyrinth in time. Others think they're the angels the gods kidnapped and that the gods turned them into horrible monsters, before sending them back to Daedalum to hunt down Icarus and his children."

"What do you think they are?" Felix asks.

"I think they're fast and fierce and bloodthirsty. That's what I have to think if I have any chance of taking them down."

"Not that the chances of taking down a screecher are ever very high," Theo adds. "I'd advise avoiding them at all costs. Admittedly, that's easier said than done, but if you know your labyrinth sector well enough there's always a getaway route somewhere."

"By 'always'," Andrea says, "he means 'sometimes' and 'hopefully'. You guys'll be filled in on all of this back at Fates: what monsters are around, how best to avoid them, the best places to collect stuff. First, we gotta get you back to Fates and get you fed and rested, like the others we picked up."

"You found other Icarii?" Felix asks.

"Yep. Not many, but more than last year. Then again, last year was a bit abnormal. There was this huge flock of screechers near the wall come Fallen Day. The flock thinned out after that, thankfully."

As we walk I think about what I've seen and what Andrea said. Do I believe that those monsters were angels? Do I believe there were ever any angels? It's hard to say. My parents were devout, my father especially, but I could never bring myself to share their enthusiasm. I spent more energy pretending to worship Icarus than actually praying to him. Maybe that's why I've ended up in such a horrible place, as punishment for skipping my prayers, but somehow I doubt that's the case. Clara was the most eager, faithful follower Icarus could have ever wanted, and that didn't save her.

When tears start pricking at my eyes again, I focus on something else: the labyrinth. If there are no angels, then maybe there was never a Daedala either. But if that's true, then who could have possibly built this immense, terrifying place? And why?

We reach a section of collapsed wall and Andrea hops over it. Kyle and a very unbalanced Felix follow. The first section of stone I step on tilts under my foot. I back up into Theo.

"It's hard in those robes, isn't it?" Theo says and goes up the rubble ahead of me. He turns and offers me his hand. "We'll get you proper clothes back at Fates. Until then, I'm happy to help, if you'll let me."

Hesitantly I take his hand. It's bigger than mine,

extremely calloused. I wonder how often he's scratched his hands like I did today, escaping monsters I never knew existed.

On the other side of the collapsed wall, Ryan is waiting. We fall back into our earlier formation as we continue down the next corridor.

"So," Theo says after a few minutes of walking, "what's your name?"

That question again. I feel a sweat break at the back of my neck.

"You know my name," Theo continues. "It's only fair."

"Good luck with that," Kyle says. "We could barely get her to move, let alone say anything."

"That sort of response is natural after your first taste of the labyrinth," Andrea says. "It's the shock."

"I was just as bad," Theo says. "Hey, I was even worse. I was twelve at the time, but still. I curled up in this nook in the wall when the screechers attacked. I cried so much my robes soaked right through. Also – and don't tell the others this..." Theo leans in close to me, dropping his voice, "I pissed myself a couple of times."

I pull back, more because of our proximity than what he's telling me.

"Oh, don't worry," Theo says, "it's not a regular thing. My clothes right now are perfectly clean. Er... clean of that, anyway."

Theo smiles at me again, but I still can't return it. As we continue moving, the boys introduce themselves and their ages.

"Can I ask how old you are?" Theo says to me. "I'm not really good with guessing. You could just, uh, hold up fingers, I guess?"

"She's probably fifteen," Andrea says. "Or almost fifteen."

"Sixteen," Ryan says.

"Sixteen?" Andrea asks, "Seriously, you think so?"

Ryan stares straight at me. "Am I wrong?"

After a moment, I shake my head.

"Wow," Andrea says, half to herself. "Er, sorry, I mean. I'm bad with ages too."

"You're already sixteen," Ryan says to me. "You've got a better starting chance than most. Pull yourself together."

"Ryan." Andrea's tone is cautionary. Ryan ignores her and continues on ahead, disappearing around a corner.

"Don't worry about Ryan too much," Theo says to me. "He's been here since he was eleven, so he can be a little tough on older Icarii."

That means Ryan's fifteen. I can't believe someone a year younger than me has survived out here that long. I don't even know how I'm going to survive here, although I have these people helping me. There's only three of them, after all. What do we do if the screechers come back before we reach Fates? There's so many of them and they're so powerful.

I'm consumed with worry the rest of the way. Every little noise makes me jump, even if it's only the scrape of a pebble one of us has accidentally kicked. At one point Theo gives my arm a squeeze. It's quick, so I don't have time to startle or pull away.

"It's going to be OK," Theo says. "We're going to make it back to Fates. Our group always makes it back to Fates."

Despite Theo's reassurances, I'm still jumpy. He must notice, because he starts telling me about himself. He reiterates that he entered the labyrinth at twelve, but skips the part where he and his fellow Icarii were attacked. He describes the members of Fates that found him and some of the others. He talks mostly about the girl named Sybil, who knew more about the monsters in the labyrinth than anyone. Theo says that when he turned thirteen Sybil gave him his club and took him out through some of her routes in the labyrinth. After that they upgraded his club with some old nails they'd found.

"There's tons of stuff in the labyrinth, aside from monsters," Theo says. "Near the wall it's all pretty bland, but the farther in you get, the more treasures there are to find. There's even areas where plants have grown through the stone, and holes that turn into mini ponds when it rains. That's how we get our food and water. Of course, we go hunting too."

"What do you hunt?" Felix asks, having slowed earlier to walk with us and listen to Theo. "Can you… can you actually eat the monsters?"

"Some of them," Theo says. "If you can catch them before they catch you."

"Not the ange– not the screechers, right?"

"Definitely not the screechers. For one, they're too humanoid. It would be really weird. Plus, some people back at Fates actually think they're humans, so that's a whole other can of worms. Speaking of worms, we don't hunt the diggers either. They're venomous, so there's no telling if their meat is even edible; plus apart from baby diggers, they're impossible to fight. No one from Fates has ever beaten an adult digger. Luckily they're rare and usually only show up in certain parts of the labyrinth."

"So the one we saw today was a baby?" Felix asks. When Theo nods, Felix says, "How big is an adult?"

Theo stops walking. He points back the way we came, then down at the distant end of the corridor. All in all it probably measures around twenty feet.

"Longer than this," Theo drops his arms. "About three-quarters the width. I've only ever seen two and, at that, I haven't seen all of them. Despite their size they're super-fast. You can hear them coming from a mile away, although sometimes it's hard to pinpoint what direction they're coming from. My motto is to keep running until you can't hear them any more. That goes for basically every monster in the labyrinth. This isn't the kind of place where you play at being a hero: escape when and however you can."

"That's the best advice anyone will give you," Andrea calls back. "Having said that, if you guys decide to act as scavengers like us when Fallen Day comes around again, you'll be expected to try and help save some new Icarii. But you might decide to do something else."

"Like what?" Kyle asks.

"At Fates the older members can choose between two roles," Andrea says. "You're either a scavenger or a caretaker. You come out with us or you stick around the base looking after the younger kids and doing meal prep and distributing supplies and stuff. Also, if you don't know how to sew already someone will teach you, no matter what role you choose. Caretakers make and mend our clothes, while we scavengers sometimes find ourselves having to stitch up wounds on the quick. But don't worry too much about it all right now. All new Icarii are given a chance to rest and recover before you're expected to pull your weight."

"What if we don't pull our weight?" Kyle asks.

Andrea gives him a confused look. "No need to get defensive, bud. It's just an expression. Having said that, you must understand if we all want to survive out here, we've gotta help each other."

"When I look at how my life was this morning, inside the walls," Kyle says, "I don't understand anything."

Andrea doesn't seem to know how to reply to that. Nobody does. This time Theo doesn't break the silence with his stories. No more questions are asked as we go down corridor after corridor. Without any distractions, I become painfully aware of my sore, tired body and paper-dry mouth. I thought earlier that I would collapse from hunger but now food is the last thing I want. I need a drink.

I notice Andrea and Ryan have flasks attached to their belts. Theo must have one too. I'm sure they all carry water with them, especially if they go through the labyrinth as much as they claim. I'm sure if I asked for some water they'd give it to me. I just have to ask.

I don't know how much longer we walk, but I know we've turned down three new corridors. All the while I've just been repeating to myself what I'll say: *"I'm thirsty. Could I please have some water?"* or *"I'm very thirsty. Do you have any water?"* or maybe just *"Do you have any water?"* I can't decide and it's starting to become stressful.

"I'm kind of thirsty," someone says, and I realize it's not me, but Felix.

"Oh, right!" Andrea unhooks her flask and hands it to Felix. "You guys must be crazy dehydrated by now. Sorry, I forgot."

Ryan passes Kyle his flask, while Theo offers his to me. My fingers shake as I uncork it, then the water's slipping past my lips and down my throat. I've never tasted anything so wonderful.

Licking my lips to catch any stray drops, I twist the lid back on the flask and hand it to Theo. He doesn't take it.

"Keep it for now," he says. "You might get thirsty again."

This time when he smiles at me, I find myself smiling a little back.

As we're walking along, another tremor shakes the corridor. I grab on to the closest thing to balance, which happens to be Theo. Before I can mumble an apology and pull my hand back, he puts his own hand over mine and says, "Don't worry, diggers still surprise me too, after all this time. But don't tell Andrea that."

Theo goes on to assure me that since the tremor was fairly slight, the digger isn't anywhere close and probably won't bother us. Still, the Icarii from Fates fall into what Theo explains is a digger defence formation. This involves Theo and his club being at the centre of the group. Hearing this, I'm terrified I'll end up alone at the back, but ultimately Ryan takes Theo's place.

"We're almost there," Andrea says. She's been saying it every few minutes for the past hour.

I'm exhausted, but I know I can't complain. I'm sixteen and, although I'm scratched and bruised, my legs still work. Even if they feel like they'll give any minute.

Suddenly Ryan shoves me. I stumble forward, but he catches the back of my robe before I can fall. The others don't see and keep walking.

"Too slow," Ryan hisses. He lets me go and gives me another shove. I try to walk faster but it feels like my feet are dragging through mud. My legs threaten to buckle. I wish Theo were still walking with me instead.

Ryan grabs my arm and I tense. Is he going to push me or snap at me again? Instead, he lets out a long, faltering whistle. Andrea and Theo freeze. Felix starts to ask what's wrong and Andrea quickly silences him. She looks at Theo, then back at Ryan, then gives one, clipped nod. She grabs Felix's hand and tugs him quickly down the corridor. Kyle starts to follow but Theo holds out his arm for him to stop. He speaks to Kyle so quietly I can't hear what he says. Then I feel Ryan start to pull me back the way we came. I grind my feet into the ground, confused and unwilling to travel away from the promised safety. Ryan squeezes my arm so hard I'm sure he'll leave a bruise. He glares at me until I follow him.

Instead of retracing our steps, Ryan pulls me down a corridor we passed earlier. He's running so fast I can barely keep up. Then I hear something overhead. A soft whoosh.

Ryan lets go of my hand and I trip up, falling to the ground beside him as he slides to a stop. He already has his bow drawn, arrow notched. The arrow's let loose with a hiss and whistles through the air, disappearing in the night sky. A split second later it clatters to the ground a mile away.

I hear Ryan curse under his breath as he notches another arrow. Just as he fires, a shadow descends from the sky. At first I think it's a screecher because it's humanoid and winged, but then I realize it has no feathers and is covered entirely in dark, leathery skin.

The arrow embeds in its shoulder and the monster lets out a feeble, strangled cry. Ryan quickly reaches for another arrow but the monster drops on him, pinning him to the ground as his bow clatters away. It snaps at him with a pair of massive fangs. Ryan just manages to hold the creature back.

I'm frozen again, staring at this new and horrible monster, except this time I'm closer. I can see that its body is the size of a child's, but its limbs and torso are thick with muscle. Its wings are smaller than those of the screechers, but big enough to support its body. Unlike the screechers, it has arms, and its hands are tipped with black talons that dig into the concrete on one side and Ryan's shoulder on the other. Worst of all is the creature's head, which is a grotesque, hairless mix of a human and a bat.

Suddenly I realize Ryan's yelling at me. "Get me an arrow!"

He keeps yelling but I can't move. It's just like before, with the screechers. But this time there's nowhere for me to hide and when this monster's done with Ryan it's going to come for me.

Ryan stops yelling at me. He braces his arm under the monster's chin to keep it back and, with his free hand, yanks on the arrow in the creature's shoulder until it comes free. The monster makes a sound a cross between a hiss and a wheeze as black blood pours from its wound onto Ryan's tunic. Ryan stabs the arrow into the monster's massive left ear. The creature cries and rips out slices of Ryan's shoulder. Ryan winces as he shoves the arrow in deeper until blood spurts from the ear and the monster goes limp on top of him. He shoves the body aside and backs away, breathing heavily. Ryan looks at his shoulder and touches it tentatively. His fingers come away bloodied. He sighs.

"Get over here."

I know he's talking to me. I try to push myself up. I tell my arms they have to stop shaking.

"Get over here!" Ryan yells. His voice echoes down the corridor.

I'm on my feet in an instant and standing in front of him just as quickly. He reaches into his jacket and pulls out a roll of gauze. "Can you do this much, at least?"

Ryan shrugs out of his jacket and stretches the neck of his tunic over his shoulder as I unwind the gauze. I start looping it over his shoulder and under his armpit, covering the ghastly wound. It bleeds through the layers of gauze immediately. I keep winding.

"That's enough," Ryan says, but it's still bleeding through. I start to add another layer. Ryan shoves me away from him so that I land on my butt and the gauze stretches between us. Ryan rips off the end closest to him and tucks it into the rest of the bandage, then rearranges his clothing. He snatches the gauze from me and slides it back into his jacket before pushing to his feet. He returns to the monster and puts a foot on its head to keep it still while he yanks out his arrow. It takes a few pulls but finally dislodges in a burst of black blood. Ryan half-heartedly wipes the arrow off on the monster's back, making its leathery flesh glisten. He retrieves his bow, then backtracks for the arrow he first fired.

I stare at the monster again. Its wings have curled around its corpse. Its head is turned to the side against the stones, facing me. Its black eyes are wide open and I feel like even in death it can see me. I half expect it to blink.

I hear Ryan returning and quickly get up before he can yell at me again. I turn around to follow him back to the corridor that leads to Fates.

Ryan's free hand splays over my chest, stopping me. I feel my cheeks heat in surprise. I'm not sure he realizes where he's touching, because of the thick, form-obscuring Icarii robe. Before I can back away from him, he's shoving me backwards.

"Not that way," is all he says as he walks past me. I hesitate, glancing down the corridor, back the way we came. Isn't that how we get to Fates? I want to ask him, but I know I won't. He's walking briskly. If I don't follow now it's going to be hard to catch up.

I run after him.

I don't want to stick close to Ryan, but I do. It's difficult. Now that we're on our own he keeps increasing his pace. I'm sure he can hear me panting, even though I try to stay quiet. I wonder if he's going faster because he knows I'm tired. He couldn't be that mean, could he?

As I walk behind Ryan I realize he and I are close to the same height. Then I remember how old he is and I know I shouldn't be surprised by his height. He may not have gone through a growth spurt yet. Tanner and most of the other boys back home didn't start getting really tall until they turned sixteen.

Clara had her growth spurt early, even earlier than the rest of us girls, and she used to tease the boys about being short. When Tanner started getting tall and claimed to be taller than Clara she'd demand we measure their heights. The day finally came when Tanner surpassed Clara by an inch. She blamed it on the shoes he was wearing and refused to believe anyone who said otherwise. She never agreed to a height test with Tanner again. That's when Tanner started teasing her about her inferior height. He wouldn't say anything so much as he would act in ways that would annoy her. He'd balance his arms or chin on her head, or even help hoist her up to reach a book in the library – not that she ever wanted his help. She'd snap at him whenever he did any of that and he'd only grin.

A tear drips off my chin. I wonder how long I've been crying. I wonder at what point today it started to become as unconscious to me as breathing.

When we turn a corner Ryan glances back at me. Seeing my tears he mutters, "Pathetic."

That makes me want to cry even more, but instead I try to quietly sniffle back my tears and rub at my eyes. The moisture from my tears seeps into the cuts on my palms and makes them sting.

Ryan stops halfway down a thin corridor, at a part of the wall that's jagged and half-crumbled. He hitches his bow over his shoulder and starts climbing up the wall. My heart lodges in my throat. I try to say something, but all that comes out is a choked sound. Still, it makes Ryan pause. He starts climbing again. At the top of the wall he stops, one leg on either side, to look down at me.

"This is the way to Fates," he says. "If you don't think you can follow, don't even try."

Then he disappears over the other side of the wall.

My heart is hammering so hard I'm sure screechers will hear it and attack me. A cold sweat has broken out at the back of my neck and I look skittishly around. Ryan's gone. He's left me. I'm alone in the labyrinth.

My gaze returns to the wall. Hesitantly, I curl my hands around the jutting rock Ryan used to climb. I try to pull myself up, to find purchase for my worn feet. I've only just made it off the ground when my robes tangle in the rocks and I find my hold slipping. I let go and my feet hit flat stone.

Back home for every school division – primary, secondary and tertiary – there was a special athletics room. In primary and secondary, physical education was mostly games and lots of fun. When we turned twelve and entered tertiary, physical education changed. We started to have more difficult lessons, like vaulting and obstacle courses and rope climbing. I hated the ropes. The athletics rooms had ceilings two levels high so the ropes were very long and the fall treacherous. Even if the instructor kept mats under the ropes, I was still terrified of falling.

Clara loved the ropes. Whenever we had free days to use the equipment as we pleased, Clara would go right for the ropes. I'd watch her climb, nimble and agile, three-quarters of the way up. Then she'd suddenly start sliding down. When she reached the bottom she'd complain to me of rope burn and show me her beetroot-red hands. Five minutes later, after her hands were back to normal, she'd go do it again.

One day, when we were thirteen, she offered to teach me. "It's not so hard. Once you get the hang of it, it's really fun."

Clara insisted so I let her show me. She positioned my arms and my legs and then got on the rope next to mine to show me the right movements. I hadn't yet moved an inch when Tanner and some of the other boys came over.

"You really think you're the right person to teach someone else how to climb?" he asked Clara. "You haven't even made it to the top yet."

"Neither have you," Clara argued. "Go away, Tannie. This is a private lesson."

"It's a useless lesson," Tanner said. "Climbing's a matter of upper body strength, not style. If you don't have the strength, you won't make it."

"Shows what you know," Clara said. "Scat!"

Tanner and the boys left. I dropped off my rope.

"What are you doing?" Clara asked me. "Don't listen to Tannie. I'm not that strong, am I? That proves it's all about technique."

Clara set to teaching me again after that and I followed her every instruction. As I listened to her and watched her I couldn't help thinking that, like everything with Clara, it wasn't a matter of technique that let her succeed, but of determination. In everything she did, Clara was always one hundred per cent determined and she always pulled through.

In the end, I never made it more than half a foot up the rope. But Clara, before she turned fourteen, made it to the top.

I'm crying again, but this time I don't swipe the tears away. The wall blurs in front of me as I step towards it, searching for a purchase. I try pulling myself up again. My robe tangles. I fall. I try again with the same results. I stare at the wall for a long moment before pulling my robe off over my head.

Without it the wind is biting. It tears right through my thin grey dress and my bare arms and legs are instantly covered in goose bumps. I grit my teeth against the cold and grip the jutting chunk of wall in front of me. I heave myself up.

I get farther before falling, this time. I land on the soft mass of my Icarii robes. My hands and feet are even more scraped than before, thanks to the wall, and old cuts have reopened. I leave dots of blood on the rocks as I climb.

Even as more cuts open I keep pushing myself up. My legs get scraped and my dress catches on jagged edges and rips. I keep climbing. I imagine Clara climbing, first up her rope, then this wall. I imagine how simple it would be for her, how she'd be waiting for me at the top, hand outstretched. She was always waiting for me somewhere we both knew I'd never be able to reach.

Just as my hand grips the top of the wall, I feel my foot sliding. I bite my lip so hard it bleeds as I scramble for a perch. At the last moment, my toes slide into a crack in the wall. Before I can lose this purchase, I pull myself up so that I'm bending over both sides of the wall. Its rough edges dig into my belly, but I barely notice the pain. I'm too giddy at actually making it to the top.

Then I see the distance I have to go down and my stomach drops. I thought I'd made it but I'm really halfway there. I'll be just like Clara, almost reaching the top only to slide down with burns on her hands.

I wiggle around, trying to situate myself on the top of the wall like Ryan did. When I accomplish this I search for a foothold and then slide my other leg over. Carefully, I start easing myself down the other side of the wall. My foot slips and I lose my handhold. As I fall, a scream lodges in my throat.

I land in a pile of something that crunches under my weight. It feels like needles are digging into me all over.

As I crack my eyes open I see that I'm in some kind of dying bush, with more twigs than leaves. It blends into the shadow of the wall, invisible from higher up. I whimper as I push myself up and pain spikes through my back and limbs. I pick my way out of the bush and find a series of tiny twigs sticking out of my arms and legs. Every time I pick one out it stings and leaves a little dot of blood.

When I'm finally free of twigs I start down the corridor, my left leg cramping with every movement. I must have twisted it in the fall. I don't think it's broken. Even though this hurts, I feel like a broken leg would hurt more and wouldn't work as well as this.

I don't see Ryan anywhere, but the corridor is a dead end on one side, so there's only one way I can go. I walk as quickly as I can, terrified that I'll get lost before catching up with him. Or what if he's gone over another wall?

The end of the corridor turns down to another, very long corridor. I hurry down that one, my breath coming ragged and my lungs burning by the time I reach the end. There's a fork here, I realize, and I feel myself start to shake. What way do I go? What way did Ryan go?

I take the right and start running flat out. I'll go to the end and check what's there, then try the left.

I've made it halfway down the corridor when I pass a side alley. I skid to a stop. There's Ryan. Relief crashes into me and for a moment I can't move, then I'm running towards him. Ryan must hear me because he stops.

I've almost reached him when he spins around, aiming an arrow right at me. I almost trip up in my hurry to stop, and barely swallow a scream. Ryan doesn't fire, staring at me with evident surprise. After a moment, he scowls and lowers his bow.

"I did it!" I blurt out. I'm shocked as much at the sound of my voice as I am that I'm able to speak. My voice sounds chalky, like I'm sick or have a sore throat.

"Do you expect praise or something?" Ryan's frown deepens as he looks me up and down. "You ditched the robe."

I nod quickly.

"That was stupid. You're going to freeze before we get there."

I deflate at his words. Ryan turns away and starts walking again. I hurry to follow, unwilling to lose him after working so hard to catch up. I'm starting to feel numb again. Maybe it's because of the cold, like Ryan said. But I've felt numb all day and I was wearing the robe. Only when I reached the top of that wall did the numbness fade.

There's a sound up ahead. Ryan tenses, raising his bow again. I find myself gripping the back of his jacket. We wait in silence. The sound doesn't come again. Ryan relaxes. Then he realizes I'm holding on to him.

He glares back at me, lips parted to snap at me to let him go, when something distracts him. Despite the dark we're close enough for me to see him looking me over again, which prompts me to look down at myself. Between the climb and the fall my dress and I are completely torn up. Scratches and scrapes cover me everywhere. An entire patch of cloth over my left ribs and belly-button has been ripped off at an angle, showing a shallow gash over my stomach. The blood has already clotted and dried but it's disgusting to look at.

"Stop sticking so close," Ryan says, yanking his jacket out of my hold. He's looking away from me now.

Although I don't grab on to him again I can't help sticking close. I wish for what feels like the hundredth time that he and Theo hadn't switched spots. I know I've only just met these people, but I'm sure Theo would have helped me over that wall. He'd look out for me and try and make me feel better and be kind. Andrea would have been better too. Either of them, just not Ryan. He should have gone with Kyle. They'd get along really well.

Despite these thoughts, I'm glad I'm with someone who knows the labyrinth. I know I'd be lost on my own, in every sense of the word.

Ryan stops us in a corridor overgrown with dying vines. He crouches by the left-hand wall that, to me, looks no different from the rest. Laying his bow aside, he starts pulling out chunks of the wall. When he's finished he's revealed a small tunnel, going straight through to the other side.

"You go first," Ryan says, pushing himself away from the hole. When I don't move right away he adds, "Or don't. This is the only way to Fates."

I hesitate barely a second more before falling to my knees in front of the hole. It's big enough for me to crawl through without fear of getting stuck, but I can't see what's on the other side. There's not even any moonlight.

"Get up," Ryan says.

I glance back at him, confused. He's looking away from me, down the corridor. I think he's spotted a monster, but there really doesn't seem to be anything there.

"I changed my mind," he says. "I'll go first. Get up."

I just have time to push to my feet when Ryan's in front of the hole. He hikes his bow up over his shoulder before going onto his knees. "Come through after me."

Ryan disappears into the shadows of the tunnel. I try to keep myself calm after he's gone. This is entirely different than the wall. I can follow him easily. And I do. The tunnel is rocky around me but under my palms I feel softer soil in spots. Is that what's under all the stone and packed dirt of the labyrinth – soil? It's a funny thought to have, but what's even funnier is that it comforts me. It's the one thing I expected of the labyrinth: fresh, fertile soil.

I feel when I come out of the tunnel more than see it. In the darkness I can make out vague shapes, but I have no idea what any of them are. I have no idea where I am.

Then Ryan grabs me under the arms. He hauls me to my feet and I feel his breath tickling my cheek as he says, "Wait *right* here."

A second later I feel something brush past my leg. I realize it's Ryan, going back through the hole. He's gone for a couple of minutes and, in that time, I can faintly hear him putting the wall back together. I know when he returns because I hear his panting, then the scuff of his shoes as he rises. I'm still standing near the hole so when he stands up his arm brushes mine. He jerks away instantly. I see him moving between the shadows of the room. I don't know if I'm supposed to follow. He told me to wait where I am, but was that only until he finished sealing the tunnel?

Light flares to life up ahead, so sudden against all the darkness that it's blinding. When my eyesight finally adjusts I see I'm in a low-ceilinged room with wooden walls and packed dirt floors. The room is full of old crates and bulging cloth sacks. Ryan's standing next to a table scattered with yellowed parchment and matches. He's holding an old brass lantern that contains a half-eaten wax candle, now burning with a little seed of fire that seems to light an impossible distance. The only time we ever used candles at home was when Mother was having a luxurious bath or Mother and Father an anniversary dinner. They always seemed such tiny, faint things in comparison to our light bulbs and torches.

"Come on," Ryan says, moving around the boxes. I follow him and soon find myself in front of a wooden door. Ryan opens it onto a short hall with the same wooden walls and dirt floor as the room. Ryan closes the door behind us before starting down the hall. There's another door at the end, a hook in the wall beside it. Ryan hangs the lantern on the hook.

"Plug your ears," Ryan says. "That or go back down the hall."

Confused, I cover my ears.

"Plug them, I said."

Ryan glares at me until I do. He glares at me a moment longer before turning to the door, blocking it with his body. After a few moments the door opens from the outside. Hesitantly, I unplug my ears.

There's a boy on the other side of the door. He has bristly black hair that's just long enough to cover his whole head. He's tall and broad with a cleft chin and a sort of large nose. He looks like he's older than me, maybe around Theo's age.

"What's with you and coming in the back door?" the boy says to Ryan. Then he notices me and his brown eyes widen. "What did you pick up out there?"

"Fresh Icarii." Ryan opens the lantern and blows out the candle inside. I realize we don't need it any more because the room behind the new boy is lit.

"It's Fallen Day already?" the boy says. "Guess that would explain all the new, petrified faces I've been seeing."

"Are you going to let us in?"

"Alright, alright. Sheesh, try to be friendly with a guy…" The moment the boy steps out of the way Ryan ploughs past him, not looking back. I start to follow, but I find myself arrested by the sight of the room. The walls and low ceiling are wooden, just like the hall, but there are scattered wooden support beams dug into the packed dirt. At the centre of the room is a long wooden table with benches on either side. The table is piled with all sorts of items, from folded cloth to arrows to baskets of green herbs. On the other side of the room are dual hearths made of stone. Neither is lit. To my left are two hallways and to my right is a door with a wooden bar across it.

"Welcome to Fates," the boy behind me says. "I'm guessing Ryan didn't say it, and somebody needs to welcome you. I'm Gus."

I turn to see he's closed the door again and I realize he's also barred it like the other door. There's a chair next to this door and resting on it is a small wooden horse, crudely carved with a fat torso and stubby legs.

"Not the most beautiful toy," Gus says, "but it's the best I can manage with the stuff around here. It's nice to give the younger kids something to play with, to take their mind off... well, off what's outside. Anyway, what's your name?"

The question makes me tense up. At that same moment I notice Ryan going down one of the side halls.

"No name, huh? Don't worry, you're not the first one. Go on, follow him. There's food down there."

Gus sits down and returns to carving detail into the horse's head as I go after Ryan. The hall isn't very long and through the half-opened door at the end is another room. This one is smaller than the one I just left but has its own, lit hearth. The heat from this fire coils throughout the room, making it feel like my ice-cold skin has been wrapped in a blanket.

Kyle and Felix are eating at the one long table in the room, scraping the remains of some kind of porridge from little clay bowls. On the bench with them is a girl with long, curly red hair, who's sorting through a box of medical supplies. Across the table, a girl with black hair in a messy bun is aggressively stitching closed a slash in Theo's right upper arm.

"Where's Andrea?" Ryan asks. Everyone immediately looks at us.

"You made it back," Theo says, relieved.

"You're injured!" the redhead exclaims, pushing herself up from the table.

"Leave it, Cassie," Ryan snaps. The redhead flinches. "Where's Andrea?"

"Relax," Theo says, "she made it back fine. Better than either of us, by the looks of it. She's out getting clothes for our new Icarii." Theo looks to me now. "She'll have something for you too, I'd say. She was adamant you guys would get back soon."

Theo looks me over a moment longer, then grabs his discarded jacket off the table and gets up, even though his wound isn't done being stitched. The black-haired girl doesn't seem to care that her patient's left. She lays aside the thread and needle and turns her attention to something in front of her.

Theo comes over to me and offers his jacket. He says under his breath to Ryan, "You couldn't have lent her yours?"

Ryan scowls at him.

"How did you get like this?" Theo asks, helping me into his jacket before I can do it myself. "You look like you were in a fight with a patch of thorns."

He probably doesn't realize how right he is.

"You were supposed to look after her," Theo says to Ryan.

"We went over the wall," Ryan says. "It isn't smooth – not that you'd remember."

"You know you don't take new Icarii that way. What if you hadn't been able to get her over the wall?"

"She's here, isn't she?" Ryan growls. "Besides, at that point it was better to go that way."

"Is that where her Icarii robe is?" the black-haired girl asks, back still to us. When Ryan confirms this, the girl says, "Go get it for me, if it's still there."

"He can't go out again," Cassie says. "He just got back and he's injured."

"Then I'll patch him up," the black-haired girl replies curtly. "We can't leave it out there. For one, it's valuable material. Two, it may attract unwanted attention to our secret route. If it hadn't been left out there in the first place, recovery wouldn't be an issue."

"Ryan was trying to get the Icarii back," Theo says. "That's hard enough without having to worry about an article of clothing."

"You've been here long enough to know that something as simple as an article of clothing can change everything." The black-haired girl motions Ryan over. "Let's make this quick."

"I'll do it," Cassie says, gauze and thread already in hand. More quietly, she says, "At least I finish my stitches."

Theo glances at his half-stitched arm. "It's good enough, I think. Not bleeding any more, at least."

"If you're content with that," the black-haired girl says.

Ryan draws out one of his arrows as he rounds the table. He holds out the arrow to the black-haired girl. It's the one he used to kill the monster. Dried black blood covers it from the shaft to the arrowhead.

"*Dira* blood?" the girl asks, accepting it and turning it around in her hands. "Hm…"

"C'mon," Theo says to me, "you're hungry, aren't you?"

I follow Theo over to the hearth. A metal pot hangs over the flames, half full of goopy grey porridge. Theo grabs a clay bowl from the table and scoops out a portion for me. Then he grabs a small, flat wooden spoon from the table and holds it and the bowl out with a smile. "Decadent, huh?"

It doesn't smell like anything other than warmth, but looking at it makes my stomach rumble all the same. I blush, worried someone's heard, and accept the bowl. The taste is just like the smell: bland warmth. Still, it's the most delicious meal I've ever had.

I sit on the end of the bench, the side closest to the fire. Felix is next to me, having moved down to make room for Ryan. Cassie is currently unwinding the soaked gauze from his shoulder.

"You should have used more than this," she murmurs, laying the dirty bandages aside. Ryan doesn't reply.

Theo returns to my side with a flask of water. I smile at him in thanks, which seems to please him. He addresses the room, "One more round of introductions."

"Oh, right!" Cassie casts me a brief smile over Ryan's shoulder. She introduces herself and adds, "Welcome to Fates!"

"That's Addie," Theo says, when the black-haired girl doesn't speak. She's staring intently at a small pile of leather in front of her. It looks strangely familiar and for a moment I wonder why. When I realize where I've seen such material before, I cover my mouth. I feel like the porridge is going to come right back up.

Addie notices my reaction. She's unimpressed, but not surprised. "You make do with what's available if you want to survive in the labyrinth. What do you think that jacket's made of?"

I glance down at myself, really seeing the jacket for the first time. It's dark, leathery, just like that monster's flesh. My stomach rolls.

"Don't worry," Theo says. "You'll get used to it, promise."

I feel Theo's hand on my shoulder. He squeezes it and I try not to wince, since he's touching a bruise. Still, I appreciate that he's trying to be reassuring.

The door opens. A girl with short strawberry-blonde hair comes in carrying a bundle of clothing. Seeing Ryan, she breaks into a grin. I realize that it's Andrea, without her hood.

"I told you they'd be back in no time," Andrea says to everyone as she dumps the clothing on the table. "What took you so long?"

"Ryan went over the wall," Theo says. Ryan shoots him a glare.

"Oh?" Andrea looks at me. "You made it over the wall? Good job! Here: a reward!"

Andrea tosses me a bundled-up dress. It lands in a heap on the table in front of me. Laying down my porridge, I tentatively pull it towards me, afraid it's also made of monster hide. Instead it seems to be made of normal, old cloth. It's thicker than my current dress, at least, and all in one piece.

"Did you take down the bat?" Andrea asks Ryan, who

nods as Cassie winds her needle through his shoulder. "I see it left you with a parting gift. Must have been the quick one."

"Hey," Theo says, "why's it a quick enemy when he's hurt but when I get hurt I 'must have been clumsy again'?"

Andrea ignores Theo and tosses a tunic to Felix. "That gonna fit?"

Felix nods, then says, "So there were only three of those things?"

"There's always three," Addie says. "They travel in a trio and work as a trio: that's why whenever you encounter one you have to split up. If you're ever caught alone, your best course of action is to find cover where they can't reach you, which hardly ever works. They're small, so they can claw their way into most places."

"In other words," Andrea says, "don't travel alone. Ever. At Fates no one goes out solo. We won't even let you past the doors if you're on your own."

"Then why are you sending him out alone?" Kyle asks, gesturing to Ryan.

"We're what?" Andrea asks, looking from Theo to Addie.

"To get the robe," Addie explains, then to Kyle, "naturally Theo will be going with him."

"What?" Theo demands. "You didn't even finish stitching me up and you're sending me out again?!"

"I thought your arm was 'good enough'?" Addie retorts.

"Don't worry," Andrea says. "Now that everyone's

back and accounted for I'll grab some of the others and go get it. So where will we be going?"

After she has the location Andrea pulls her hood back up and leaves, saying she'll be back before midnight. Ryan stares after her with a slight frown. I think I see him try to get up, but Cassie gently coaxes him back down and continues treating his wound.

Theo finishes handing out the clothes to the boys before looking at Kyle and me and saying, "You guys are gonna need hoods like Andrea's if you decide you want to brave the labyrinth."

"Why?" Kyle asks, picking at the hem of his new tunic, which is made out of the same tan cloth as my dress.

"Your hair," Addie explains. "Blondes and redheads shouldn't go into the labyrinth without covering their hair. It's too bright and attracts the attention of predators, especially those with wings. You'll also be the first ones they'll go for when in a group."

Kyle seems to catch himself running a hand through his hair. I realize I'm doing the same, twisting one of my pale braids around my finger.

"What if I shave it?" Kyle asks.

"Your skin's too fair," Addie says. "The result will be the same, unless you shave your head and then paint it, although I'd advise against that. The closest thing we have to paint is mud and that tends to crack and fall off at unwelcome times. The hood is the safest route, barring staying inside Fates indefinitely."

Kyle doesn't say anything after that. He stares unhappily at his empty bowl of porridge.

"You guys must be tired," Theo says, to break the odd mood that's settling. "Why don't we find you somewhere to sleep? Addie – a hand?"

Addie sighs but ultimately pushes to her feet. I realize she's awfully short with thin, bony shoulders. She leaves the bat hide and bloodied arrow, heading straight for the door. The rest of us new Icarii collect our clothing and follow Theo back down the hall. In the main room, Gus smiles and nods at us. I see he's finished with the horse's head and is working on its mane.

Theo leads us down the other hall, where there's a door at the end and another hall to the left. Addie continues to the left and Theo motions for me to follow her.

"Sleep well," he says to me. "See you tomorrow."

I hesitate a moment, watching the boys as they follow Theo into the next room. Felix offers me a quick smile before ducking in after Kyle. I follow Addie. She's standing in front of a door near the end of the hall.

"The girls' room," Addie says before opening the door. The room is full of people, all female, sleeping on either side in a mess of blankets. There are no beds. Addie gestures to an empty pile of blankets near the left corner of the room, between two other sleeping girls. She drops her voice as she says, "You'll sleep there. Leave your old clothes at the foot of the bed."

With that, Addie heads back down the hall. Hesitantly, I step inside and close the door behind me. There's dull light coming from a small lantern that hangs in the centre of the room. Carefully I shuffle through the mass of blanket beds to my spot. To my left is a little girl who must be ten or eleven, while to my right is a girl who might be my age or older. I can't tell for sure because I can't see her face, which is mostly obscured by her tangle of dark curls. I stand there for a moment before I start to change. That's when I realize I'm still wearing Theo's jacket. I fold it neatly and lay it at the foot of my bed, leaving a space between it and my old, dirty dress. I change into the new dress, which feels too fresh for my grimy, bruised body. Then I carefully ease myself down, flinching as I try to find a position that agrees with my sore muscles. Finally I settle enough to pull the blankets tight around me.

I'm surprised by how comfortable this blanket bed actually is. A sense of familiarity washes over me which prompts a tidal wave of exhaustion. Just before I sink into a deep, heavy sleep, I realize the blankets are so familiar because I've been wearing this exact same material all day.

They're made out of Icarii robes.

Despite my exhaustion, nightmares quickly rouse me from my sleep.

I wake in a cold sweat, my heart racing. I look around the sombre grey walls of my room only to find wood and blankets and dim candlelight. And a girl's face. I'm shocked mute. She's the most beautiful girl I've ever seen. Her skin is dark and her hair is pitch black, curling over her forehead. Her eyelashes are long and thick and frame her mesmerizing stormy grey eyes. I think she must be one of the angels we all seek to become: a true Icarii.

I realize the girl is leaning over me, a hand on my shoulder. Her slim black brows are creased in worry. "Are you alright now?"

I try to nod but instead I end up shaking my head. Tears are sliding down either side of my face, pooling in my ears.

"It was a nightmare, wasn't it?" she whispers.

I flash back to the blood and screams and black feathers. I bite my lip and nod.

"They don't stay forever," she says, "and you're safe here. Nothing can get us inside Fates. We're safe and we have each other, so even if you're scared when you're sleeping, remember that as soon as you wake up."

"I don't know if I can," I whisper.

The girl brushes my hair back from my brow. Her touch is soft and gentle. "Then you have to make the dreams better. You can't spend all your time in worlds that terrify you. Make the world inside your head a happy place."

"How?"

"I don't know what will work for you." The girl smiles, and even though it's only a small smile it seems to make her entire face all the more beautiful. "What works for me are pillows."

"Pillows?" I whisper.

"We don't have any here," the girl gestures around us, "so I dream about pillows. All sorts of pillows. Velvet pillows and silk pillows and huge pillows stuffed with cotton with little tassels on the ends. I never had a pillow with tassels. Did you?"

I shake my head.

"Hmm." The girl props her head up with her hand, elbow digging into her blankets. "What do you think they feel like, then? I used to see them in the store, but they were too expensive for me so I'd never go near them. I always wanted to so I could try running my fingers through the tassels, but I was afraid that would be too much fun and then I'd know what I was missing. How do you think they feel?"

"Nice...?"

"I think they feel nice too." The girl falls flat on her bed, head tilted towards me. She grins. "But why dream about nice when you can dream about amazing?"

"Can I?" I whisper.

"Of course you can." I feel the girl take my hand, twining our fingers together. Her palm feels calloused, like Theo's, though not quite as much. Something about her touch is still soft. "Have amazingly wonderful dreams, OK?"

"OK," I whisper. The girl closes her eyes, still smiling. Gradually, I close my eyes too.

We're still holding hands when I fall asleep.

I wake up to find the girls' room nearly empty and all the blanket beds neatly folded. The only girl remaining is the one from last night, sitting on her bed next to mine. She's leaning against the wall while sewing a patch of cloth over a hole in a long brown tunic.

"Morning, Clara," the girl says. "How do you feel? You didn't wake up again, did you?"

I'm about to answer her question when I freeze. My lips tremble as I whisper, "Clara?"

"That's your name, right? Last night when you had your nightmare and I was trying to wake you up I asked you what your name was. I find it's easier to calm down others after you know their name. Anyway, you kept saying 'Clara'. Was I wrong?"

I feel cold all over. I'm shaking.

"Aren't you Clara?" she asks.

The way she says Clara's name is so lovely and I realize it's good to hear. It's almost normal. Back home, someone was always calling out to Clara. She knew everyone and claimed to be friends with almost all of them. Her name was everywhere, and she wasn't far behind, causing lots of trouble and even more fun. Clara's name meant something wonderful was coming.

"Are you alright?" the girl asks.

I mean to say "I'm fine" but instead I say, "I'm Clara."

The girl smiles. "I'm Elle."

Elle lays aside the tunic. I realize her job on the patch is actually rather atrocious. The stitches zig-zag everywhere and there are large gaps where there should be stitches. Even the ball of thread resting beside her is a tangled mess.

"Breakfast?" Elle asks, pushing herself up. Before I can answer she helps me to my feet, her hands as soft and warm as last night.

"The other Icarii are already out eating," Elle says as we head to the door. "Did you come with anyone?"

I nod, then mumble, "But, um, I didn't know them before..."

"Oh..." Elle says, then immediately perks up. "I'll show you around, then. If you don't mind. How old are you? I don't guess any more. I always end up insulting someone."

I tell Elle my age as we enter the hall. There's noise coming from the main room. I can hear children's voices.

"I'm seventeen," Elle says. "Since I'm a year older, I'll definitely have to look after you."

The main room is much busier than it was last night. Cassie is at the table with another girl, chatting while sorting through various folded cloths. Children are helping with the supplies at the table or playing with wooden toys on the floor. Gus is by the door again, this time working on a humanoid wooden figure. A very young girl is in front of him, playing with the horse from yesterday. She doesn't look like she could be anywhere close to ten, although I know she can't be any younger. Children below ten aren't sent into the labyrinth.

Elle leads me down the other hall, saying over her shoulder, "I'll introduce you to my brother if he's awake. He probably won't be; he usually sleeps through breakfast. His name's Prosper."

I'm shocked. Elle must see my surprise because she says, "We became Icarii together, two years ago. We haven't been apart since. Except when he's sleeping, or out on supply runs. He's a scavenger. I don't have the stamina for it myself, but I wouldn't want to be one anyway."

The room with the single hearth is as full as the other room. I see more familiar faces here. Addie is in the same spot as yesterday and even has Ryan's bloody arrow in front of her. Next to it is a clay bowl full of water emitting steam and one of water without steam. There's also a flat, oval object on the table in front of her. It shines green where it catches the light but is otherwise black.

Andrea's at the table as well, with a group of what must be other scavengers, judging by their clothing and the weapons they carry. Farther down the table are Kyle and Felix. Felix is chatting with one of the scavengers, but Kyle is making no effort to communicate with them. Kyle's frown deepens when he sees me, but when he sees Elle his eyes widen and his lips part a little. Then his face reddens and he looks away. Felix has likewise spotted Elle and has a similar reaction, although his staring isn't as obvious as Kyle's was.

If Elle notices the attention, she doesn't let on. She grabs a clay bowl from the table for each of us.

"Morning, Elle," says a scavenger with chin-length brown hair tied in a low ponytail. He looks to be a year older than me. "Who's the new Icarii?"

"That's Ryan's Icarii from last night," Andrea says. She grins at me. "How'd you sleep?"

"Ryan's finally gotten his own Icarii?" the scavenger asks. "Never thought I'd see the day."

"She's ours, if you want to be specific," Andrea says. Then to me, "We found your robes!"

"Those were hers?" the scavenger asks. "You didn't tell me they were a girl's robes."

"What difference does it make that they're a girl's? All the robes are made the same."

Elle, meanwhile, has filled both our bowls. She hands one to me and I find myself faced with the same grey porridge as last night. It tastes blander this morning, but I eat it all the same. I'm still hungry from going so long yesterday without food.

"Besides, Jay," Andrea continues, talking to the scavenger boy, "you're wrong; I totally told you the robes belonged to a girl. I told you the whole story of our Icarii pick-up."

"I don't remember that," Jay says.

"That's 'cause you never listen."

"Whatever." Jay turns to Elle and me. Elle doesn't even look his way, totally uninterested in the conversation, but it turns out Elle isn't the one Jay wants to speak to. "You had a rough time getting here, right?" Jay says to me. "Too bad my team didn't pick you up."

"Don't make it sound like you're the team leader," Andrea says to Jay, then to me, "You were lucky you got picked up by the A team. Jay's group is the B team."

"Why are we the B team?" Jay demands.

"Uh, because my team brought back more Icarii?"

"That was just by chance. If we'd taken that sector we would have picked up these guys. And we wouldn't have had to do a midnight run for a robe."

Addie speaks now, her voice ringing clear through the room: "I can't believe the importance of collecting such rare material has escaped the mind of a member of Fates, so I won't list the extensive number of uses for Icarii robes. I might, however, feel the need to recite said list should I begin to believe the importance of said robes has been forgotten."

Jay rolls his eyes while Addie dips Ryan's bloody arrowhead into the bowl of steaming water. She presses it to the strange oval object and peers at it for a long moment.

"Anyway," Andrea continues, "you guys are also the B team because my team has to be the A team – my name starts with A."

"Half the girls here have names that start with A," Jay argues.

"Want to go eat somewhere quieter?" Elle whispers, her breath tickling my cheek. I turn to look at her and she grins. She inclines her head towards the noisy table. "They won't be quieting down any time soon. We could eat back in our room?"

I nod quickly and Elle's smile broadens. She grabs

a flask of water from the table and nudges me gently towards the door.

"Look at that," Jay says to Andrea. "Thanks to you, the pretty girls are leaving."

"Want that porridge in your face?!"

The door opens when Elle and I are steps away. Theo comes in, Ryan right behind him.

"Morning," Theo says to us, then smiles at Elle. "I see you've met one of the Icarii we brought back."

"We're bed-neighbours." Elle clings to my arm. "I really like her. Ryan, can I have her? I heard you're the one who brought her back."

"Don't be ridiculous," Ryan mutters.

"Hear that, Clara?" Elle grins at me. "You're all mine. Is that OK?"

Hesitantly, I nod. I know I only met Elle last night, but I feel so comfortable around her. She acts sort of like how Tanner's older sister used to act with him, when they were younger. Their relationship grew strained when Tanner got older. Clara used to tell me how she'd hear them arguing from the floor above. Tanner's older sister always loved Clara, though. Maybe that's more what Elle seems to act like: Tanner's older sister towards Clara.

"Clara?" Theo repeats, startling me. "That's your name?"

"You didn't tell them?" Elle asks. Embarrassed, I shake my head. Elle slowly starts to smile. "Am I the first one you told?"

When I nod, Elle breaks into a full-blown smile. Ryan heads to the table without a word. Theo stays. He looks me over and nods to himself. "You look like a Clara."

That makes me blush. I've always envied Clara's name. It's so much prettier than the name my parents gave me. So much more unique. Three other girls in my grade had the same name as me. Clara loves her name too. She's the only person I know who's perfectly happy with her own name.

Knew. She's the only person I knew.

Suddenly the guilt is overwhelming. I can't do it. As nice as it is to hear her name, I can't steal it like this, not when this time yesterday her mother was still calling her by this name. Her mother probably still *is* calling her by this name. She's probably telling the neighbours all about her beautiful daughter Clara who's gone to join her brother in Alyssia.

My mouth is dry again. There's a lump in my throat. I have to fight it. I have to tell them Clara isn't my name.

"I'll trust you to look after her today," Theo says to Elle. He turns to me. "I've got to go out with the others for a quick run, but I'll be back later. Until then just ask one of the caretakers if you need anything."

"She'll ask me," Elle says, "and when you get back she'll be too busy with me to notice."

Theo grins. "We'll see about that."

Andrea comes over then. Ryan's right behind her, twisting the top on a flask of water. Andrea punches Theo in the upper arm. "Is the A team ready to move out or what?"

Theo rubs his arm. "Sort of got sliced by a bat here last night?"

"Stop being a baby. It healed up last night, didn't it? Besides, I bet getting it hurt more than this."

"*This* sure isn't helping."

"Ignore his whining," Andrea says to us.

"I always do," Elle says happily.

"C'mon, then," Andrea says, swatting Theo's arm again before heading down the hall. Ryan follows without a glance at us.

"I guess I better go," Theo sighs.

"Please do," Elle says, still smiling.

"You guys really make me feel wanted, y'know?" Theo shakes his head to himself, then grins at me. "Good luck today, Clara."

He squeezes my shoulder like he did multiple times last night. This time it's not the shoulder with the bruise. I find myself smiling a little. The smile fades after Theo's gone and I realize I didn't tell them the truth about my name.

"Clara?"

I look at Elle. She nods towards the door. "Shall we?"

Back in the girls' room, we settle on our blanket beds. Mine is still messy but when I start to fix it Elle says to worry about that later and just eat. The porridge has cooled off, but it's still a little warm and still fills my belly.

Elle stirs her porridge with her spoon for a moment, frowning at it. Then she blinks up at me with her amazingly pale eyes. "Sorry if it feels like we're treating you like an object. It's all jokes. You've got to joke about it, the whole Icarii business, otherwise it becomes something too painful to ever talk about. Maybe we joke too much. I don't know. I don't usually talk to the new Icarii."

"Why?" I ask, voice scratchy.

"Here." Elle uncaps the flask of water she took and hands it to me. "It's for us to share."

I take it with a mumbled thanks and sip from it, wondering if it really will help my feeble voice.

"I don't usually talk to the new Icarii because they don't usually sleep next to me," Elle says. She gestures to the blankets I'm sitting on. "The girl that used to sleep there helped me through my first night in the labyrinth. I told myself that the first Icarii to sleep there after her would be the one I'd help."

I try to ask, but all I get out is: "The girl...?"

Elle understands. "She died. People die in the labyrinth. Sometimes they get sick but mostly they get killed." Elle picks at the hem of her top blanket, unravelling a long string. She still hasn't touched her porridge. "She got killed. She was a scavenger. She'd been here a year before me. She made it a year and a half total. I've been here two years now with Prosper. That's the average life span of an Icarii: one year, two years. They didn't tell you, did they?"

It takes me a moment to reply. Instead of shaking my head, I make myself say: "No."

"They never do, the scavengers. They leave it to us, the homemakers, to break all the bad news. They figure if they get the Icarii back safe, that's their job done. We do the rest. We do the hard part. It's not the hard part to them. Fighting the monsters: that's hard. That's dangerous." Elle snaps a stray thread from her blanket. She quickly winds it around her forefinger, so tightly it starts cutting off the circulation and turns the tip of her finger white. She lets out a breath.

"I'm sorry," Elle says. "I should have waited to say all that. The day after isn't the right time. When you never leave Fates, time runs together so time doesn't seem like anything, let alone something right. But that's the price of survival, isn't it?" Elle starts unwinding the string from her finger. "Don't become a scavenger, Clara. Stay here, inside Fates. Most Icarii who become scavengers die. Most Icarii become scavengers because they get bored. If you get too bored you become deluded, thinking you can do things you can't." Suddenly, Elle takes the flask from me. She lays it down and grabs both of my hands in her own. "Together we won't get bored, OK? I'll do my best, Clara, to keep you from getting bored, so you do your best too. Don't become a scavenger. Promise you won't?"

"Promise," I say and, despite the water, my voice is hoarser than before; I can barely speak at all.

Elle smiles at me, shoulders sagging in relief. She drops my hands and takes her porridge spoon and bowl. She gestures to my own bowl with her spoon. "What are you waiting for? Eat up!"

I know how to sew. I used to sew with my mother, even though she wasn't very good at it herself. She'd sew the shirts Father would rip at work. He'd catch a frayed end on a cabinet or counter corner and cause a tear. Mother would try to fix the tear, but it would look untidy, and eventually she'd just give it to me. She'd sit with me while I sewed. I never knew if it was to spend time with me or so she felt like she was contributing to the repair effort. She would put the radio on or read a book from the library. Sometimes Mother would comment on something from the radio. I never replied. I think she was just talking to herself. I don't know if she realized I was listening. Mother and Father and Auntie and the neighbours would always comment about how I was "off in my own little world", but that was never the case. I had no little world of my own like they thought I did. Sometimes I felt like I barely had any world at all.

It was different when I was with Clara. Clara had a hundred worlds and, although she didn't share them all with me, she only ever had to share one. That was enough to make me happy.

Elle teaches me how to sew. I let her. She's patient with me and gives me plenty of simple practice, walking me through every step. She fills the silence while I practise by listing every ingredient she'd like to add to her gruel. They call it gruel here, not porridge. I find it more fitting.

"The first thing I wanted was chocolate," Elle says. "I've gotten more creative since, but I always come back to chocolate. I think about it a lot. I wouldn't recommend that. It makes you hungrier and if you're thinking about it right before supper it makes the gruel taste even more like sand. I always liked dark chocolate best. Something about the bitter taste. But everything's so bitter here I think I'd rather have white chocolate now. It's just pure sugar anyhow."

Despite advising against thinking about chocolate, Elle continues to talk about it. She asks me my favourite kind and I tell her I always liked milk. Clara and I used to buy milk chocolate chip muffins from the bakery on Fridays, during our break between classes. It used to be just the two of us, when we first entered tertiary, but gradually other girls started accompanying us. I always enjoyed the muffin, but I came to enjoy the trip less and less.

I learn quickly and by the end of the day I'm helping Elle repair some old dresses. Elle says this is what I'll do as a caretaker – although she keeps calling it "homemaker". I'll stitch up clothes and wounded scavengers. I'll help make food and clean and look after the younger Icarii.

"We're also supposed to make things," Elle says. "New clothing and bowls and cutlery and arrows, for the archers. And sometimes we're expected to do weapon maintenance, but usually the scavengers like taking care of their own weapons. They're very particular."

When Elle and I go for supper, we find the scavengers haven't yet returned. Elle says it's typical for them to be gone this long. We take our portions and Elle leads me back to the girls' room, saying the other homemakers will look after feeding the kids and cleaning up today. After eating we return to stitching the dresses.

There's a knock at the door. Elle tenses. A male voice calls out for her. I think it's her brother, but she doesn't relax as she lays aside her needle and thread. She opens the door only a crack, blocking the room with her body. From this angle I can't see the person to whom she speaks.

"The new Icarii's with you, isn't she?" the boy asks. His voice is deep, making him sound surprisingly old. "I need to see her."

"You can't come into the girls' room," Elle says. I might be imagining it, but I think she closes the door a bit more.

"Please, Elle. It's important. Call her over or send her out here. At least let me see her."

Curious despite myself, I lay aside my sewing and creep closer to Elle. From here I can see the boy. He has cropped golden hair and light blue eyes that widen as soon as he spots me.

"Clara?" he whispers. Elle, alerted to my presence, glances back at me. The boy pushes the door wide while she's distracted and walks right up to me. The next thing I know, he's scooped me up into a tight hug. Over his shoulder I can see Elle's mouth drop in open astonishment, but then the boy is spinning me around and I lose sight of her. He sets me down, back to Elle and catches one of my braids. "You still wear your hair like this."

I scramble for something to say but find nothing. I don't understand who this boy is and I don't know why he's looking at me so affectionately.

"The ribbon I gave you," he says, running a thumb over the bow in my hair. "I wanted to see you so much, Clara. I can't believe you're here. It's really you, isn't it? The hair, the ribbon – it's got to be you. Please say it is."

I continue to stare at him, mute, and he starts to frown.

"Don't you remember me, Clara?" he asks. "It's your brother, Collin."

I don't remember Collin very well. I doubt he'd remember me at all. I was just Clara's tiny, shy friend. Clara and I played more at my house anyway. But I remember the Fallen Day that he was chosen, although his name didn't mean anything to me when it was first called. I didn't realize what had happened until afterwards, when everyone was mingling after the service and Clara started crying and screaming. Her mother had to bring her home because she wouldn't quiet. I remember watching them leave, thoroughly confused as the lift doors closed behind a teary-eyed Clara.

"Really, even a child should understand what an honour this is," Auntie said to Mother and Father. "Her mother must be skipping their prayers if the little one is that confused. Your daughter, she would understand."

I think Father agreed with Auntie and put a hand on my shoulder. He was always putting a hand on my shoulder when someone was talking about me. When I was little, it used to hurt because he'd squeeze too tightly. I got used to it and it stopped hurting.

I never saw Collin again after he got on the lift with his mother and Clara that day. I hardly remember what Collin looked like at all. He certainly bears no resemblance to the giant boy in front of me, aside from his colouring.

He's changed entirely.

"Do you remember?" Collin asks again. Chilled, I nod. Collin hugs me again, whispering Clara's name into my hair. He's trembling.

"I wanted to see you," he says again. "I missed you so much, but I wish you weren't here. Now you're trapped too. I promise I'll take care of you. I won't let anything happen to you, Clara. Nothing's going to take us away from each other again."

I feel empty as he hugs me. Silent tears are running down both our faces for entirely different reasons. This is what he wanted. This is what Clara wanted.

"Clara," he says. "*Clara.*"

I don't say anything.

Collin takes me through Fates, introducing me to all the members and telling everyone that I'm his little sister. He keeps his arm around my shoulders the entire time, while Elle sulks behind us.

Elle returns to the girls' room when Collin leads me into the room with the single hearth. Even though I've been here three times now, Collin acts as if he's giving me a tour. As he opens the door he says, "...and this is the mess hall. Not much of a hall, but there's usually some kind of mess."

He grins back at me when I don't react. "C'mon, you used to give me a hard time for my bad jokes. I haven't changed that much, you know. At least, not in that way."

I try for a weak smile. It's good enough for Collin because he leads me into the mess hall, where the scavenging teams are eating. Addie remains where she was earlier, with the same bowls of water in front of her. The only thing different is that the oval object is gone, replaced by the bat hide.

"Hey guys, listen up," Collin says. "I've got something to say."

To my surprise, the scavenging teams cease their chattering to focus on Collin.

"I'd like to introduce you to someone." Collin steps behind me and I feel his hands gripping my shoulders. I try not to flinch even when he touches the bruise. "This is my little sister, Clara."

"What?!" Andrea exclaims. Theo starts choking on his food and immediately goes for his flask. Ryan stares at me openly, shocked. Even Addie turns around. She scans us both so intently I feel as if I'm some kind of exhibit on display. I hate everyone staring at us like this. All I want to do is go back into the girls' room and hide. Clara would like this. She'd love the attention. She wouldn't even care about the attention, because she'd be back with her brother.

"When you say that," Jay says, "is it for real or did you just decide when you saw her she'd be your little sister?"

Collin's hold on my shoulder tightens. "She's my sister, understand?"

Jay pales, averting his gaze. "Yep. Got it. Your sister."

"This is crazy," Theo says, lowering his flask. "I saved her, so you know, Collin. I saved your sister."

"*We* saved your sister," Andrea corrects. "It was a team effort."

"What did *you* do?" Theo demands. "I – specifically *me* – got that digger."

"Baby digger – and how many times do I have to say it? You only got it because Ryan distracted it."

"Ryan, not you–"

"Alright," Collin breaks in, silencing the argument. "Thanks to all of you for bringing my sister back safely. I mean it."

"In that case," Theo says, "I was wondering about taking a week off?"

"Sure," Collin says, "talk to Addie about caretaking shifts."

Theo's clearly disappointed by this response, but Collin ignores him. Collin walks around to face me and blocks the table. Right before he blocks my view I realize Ryan and Addie are both still staring at us.

Collin asks if I've eaten yet. When I nod he tells me he's just going to get something and then we'll talk all night. I force a smile. Whether it's convincing or not, Collin heads over to the hearth.

Theo pushes himself up and comes over to me while Collin's busy. "You should've told us you were the boss's little sister."

Collin's in charge?

"Maybe you could put in a good word for me?" Theo asks. "I don't need a week off, really. I guess four days or so would do."

I start to frown and Theo laughs, squeezing my arm. "I'm only kidding, Clara. I'm glad you've found someone in–"

"Theo." Collin's voice is ice-cold. "Are you done eating?"

"Er, not quite."

"Then maybe you should go finish." Collin is staring at where Theo is still touching my arm. Theo immediately lets go. "You're up early again tomorrow, aren't you?"

"Am I?"

"You are." Collin gives him an incredibly pleasant and incredibly fake smile. "Sleep well."

Collin leads me back through the main room. We head in the same direction as the girls' room, but instead Collin turns to the door across the hall, which leads to a smaller room. Inside he lights a lamp on a desk. Beside it are piles of wooden crates and sacks. One of the crates is open and I see it's full of arrows.

"Scavenger storage," Collin explains as he pulls an extra chair from by the wall. "Also food storage. We have another storage room, but this is where we keep immediate supplies."

Collin pulls out the chair at the desk for me and I sit down. He takes the chair that he brought over, which seems considerably older. He sits there for a moment, just looking at me. I can't help averting my gaze.

"Sorry," Collin says. "I just... I feel like if I stop looking at you, you'll disappear. You look so different, Clara. Then again, you are grown up. We're both grown up, I guess. Do I look different?"

I nod, still staring at my lap.

"You haven't said anything to me," Collin says. "Is it the shock? Is that why you're so quiet?"

Again, I nod.

"This is part of why I didn't want you here." Collin's hands ball into fists. He makes a visible effort to relax them. "Mum... how is she? After I left, how did... how did she cope?"

A sweat breaks out at the back of my neck. What do I say? How do I answer this?

"Sorry. I'm an idiot, aren't I? I shouldn't push all this on you after what's happened. I heard you and Andrea's group had difficulty getting back. Bats, right? Nasty things. Don't worry, Clara, you won't have to see them again. You won't have to see any of the monsters again. I'll make sure you're taken care of here. I'm one of the people in charge of Fates, along with Addie. We've been here the longest. Five years for Addie, six for me. I can't believe it myself sometimes, that I've been here six years. It feels so much longer."

Collin is quiet after that, thinking. Eventually he picks up his bowl and starts eating. After a moment he offers it to me and I shake my head.

"I don't blame you," he says. "It's only been two days, but are you sick of it yet?"

I shake my head, even though the gruel lost its taste for me a meal and a half ago.

"We have better meals, sometimes," Collin says. "It's going to be harvest season soon for some of the plants that grow in the labyrinth. Meals get a bit more colourful then, but you'll have to get used to the taste. Do you still dislike vegetables?"

I remember how Clara would push around her carrots on her plate whenever she came over. I shake my head.

"I guess it was just a kid thing," Collin says, half smiling to himself. "I wasn't much help with that. Remember how Mum wouldn't let you have anything sweet until you ate your vegetables, but I'd sneak you sweets anyway? I shouldn't have done that, but I didn't like vegetables either and I liked the idea of us always liking and disliking the same stuff. I still hated vegetables when I came here, but by the time harvest came up I was willing to eat anything that wasn't gruel."

Collin's silent again after that. I don't know if he's lost in thought or trying to think of something to say.

"Sometimes we have meat," he finally says. "Hunting in the labyrinth is difficult. Fighting monsters long enough to kill them is dangerous and there aren't that many that are edible. Sometimes we come across a boar or deer, but lately they've been straying deeper into the labyrinth than our teams go. We're looking at expanding our search area, but when we get into certain territories we have competition… anyway, we have a successful hunt every so often. Twice a month, usually. Just wait. We'll eat better. I'll bring back something good for us, I promise."

My mouth waters at the thought of cooked meat. I flash back to my last meal with Mother and Father and Auntie, the night before I entered the labyrinth. We had chicken. At the time I thought it tasted kind of bland, because Mother used her herb sauce that she claimed was meant for 'adult taste'. I'd love to have chicken with herb sauce now.

I remember what Elle said about chocolate: that thinking about it isn't a good thing because we'll never have it again. Will I ever have chicken again? It seems like a silly thought compared to everything else that's happened. What's even sillier is the thought makes me start to panic a little.

"Are there chickens?" I ask quietly.

Collin freezes, spoon inches from his mouth. He lays down his bowl and stares at me, dazed. He blinks. "Chickens? Um, no. We haven't found any chickens. That sort of animal would get picked off right away in the labyrinth."

There aren't any chickens. It's stupid but my eyes start to sting and then I'm crying.

"Clara?" Collin's instantly concerned. He collects me in a hug so that I'm half in his lap. A sob climbs my throat and this time I let it out. I cry into his shoulder as my body wracks with sobs. Collin holds me tighter, arms like a protective barrier from the outside world, from the labyrinth which doesn't have any chocolate or chickens.

"I want to go home," I wail. "I want to go *home!*"

Collin starts rocking me gently, despite our awkward position. He keeps rocking me and hugging me and I keep crying until my vicious sobs descend to sniffles and hiccups. I fall asleep in Collin's arms and the last thing I hear is: "I'll protect you, Clara."

I wake up in the girls' room. Elle, again, is the only one here. She's sewing another large tunic, almost identical to the one from yesterday.

"You slept later today." Elle offers me a bowl of gruel. "I got one for you. It's cold now. Maybe you'll like it better. If you have one bowl of cold gruel a day and one bowl of hot gruel, it's almost like two different meals."

I mumble my thanks and begin eating. Elle is right that it tastes different cold. It almost doesn't taste like food at all this way.

"Collin brought you in here last night," Elle says. "Boys aren't allowed in the girls' room, like girls aren't allowed in the boys' room, but he came in twice yesterday. I know he's your brother, but Prosper's my brother and he doesn't come in here."

Elle doesn't say anything else, stitching quietly and messily. I'm not sure how I'm supposed to reply, if at all. I keep eating.

"Collin's gone for the day," Elle says, "since he's a scavenger. Prosper's with him. They look out for each other so they'll be back later. Can you and I look after each other while they're gone?"

I realize she wants a response. Hesitantly, I nod. Elle breaks into a relieved smile.

"I was afraid now that you've found Collin you wouldn't want to work together any more. It was silly of me, really, since Collin's out most of the time and you'd be alone anyway. This is perfect, isn't it? I have my brother and you have your brother and while they're gone they'll have each other and we'll have each other... Oh! I have a great idea!"

Elle casts away her sewing and scrambles over to kneel in front of me. Our knees bump. "Let's be sisters! Collin and Prosper act like brothers anyway, so it only makes sense, doesn't it? Do you want to be my sister, Clara?"

The question makes me immediately uncomfortable, because it's a question, deep down, I've always wanted to ask. Word for word.

Elle holds up her right hand. Her fingers are all curled into her palm except for her pinky. "We'll make it this sort of promise, like back in primary. OK, Clara?"

Hesitantly, I hold up my own hand. Elle instantly locks our pinkies together. She beams. "Our hands are almost the same size, aren't they? Maybe we really are sisters."

Elle laughs. I realize that despite her beauty, her laugh is cutting.

I fall into a pattern at Fates. Every morning Elle is waiting for me when I wake up. As I get back to more normal sleeping habits, we start waking up around the same time. If I'm up first, I wait for her. We go to breakfast together. It's always gruel. I don't think of it as food any more. I heard Andrea refer to it as 'gruel fuel' on my third day here, so since then that's how I've been thinking of it: fuel.

Since the scavengers are out all day, I don't see much of the group that rescued me. Andrea always smiles and greets me when our paths cross, but she's usually in the middle of talking to other scavengers when I see her, so we don't speak beyond that. Theo seeks me out several times to ask how I'm doing, if I'm adjusting to Fates. It always seems like he wants to talk longer but someone, either Elle or Collin, interrupts him to pull me away. The few times I've seen Ryan, either with his group or with Cassie, he's ignored me completely.

Cassie, for her part, has been very sweet to me. I found out she's the one who took care of my old clothes and I thanked her for that, as well as the extra clothes she left for me. She's the one who always brings and collects my sewing projects, and as she always asks me how my day is going, I do my best to show the same interest. And I am interested; I just don't know how to express it as genuinely as Cassie does. For someone who seems like she should be incredibly easy to talk to, I find myself losing my voice even more than usual around Cassie. It doesn't help that whenever I try to talk to her, Elle is hovering, impatient for her to leave. I catch Cassie giving Elle a few annoyed looks when this happens, although the annoyance doesn't seem to fit on Cassie's usually smiling face.

I haven't seen much of Kyle or Felix either, but I have spotted both of them in the main room, making arrows and cleaning weapons. One night I see Felix helping Cassie with dinner. Perhaps he'll really become a caretaker. A part of me hopes he does, because although Kyle always gives me dirty looks, Felix always smiles when he sees me. Perhaps we could become friends.

Elle and I spend every day sewing in the girls' room. When other girls come in to collect something from their beds, Elle always falls quiet. If a girl comes in to lie down for a while, Elle brings our sewing into the main room, where we sit in one of the far corners, away from Gus and the hearths and the table. The younger Icarii don't come over to us, though they cast curious looks our way, mostly at Elle.

When the scavenger groups return to Fates, Collin comes to see me right away. He'll hug me and reassure me that he's fine. Then he goes to meet with Addie and the other scavengers. Elle says it's to exchange reports on how the day's gone and make decisions on the running of Fates. The meetings usually don't last long and then Collin brings me with him to the storage room like he did before. Elle always wants supper early, so I eat with her and just watch Collin eat later. He talks to me between bites of his supper, but the conversation's usually awkward and short. He'll ask me about home and then retract the question. He'll start telling me about how scavenging's going, only to skip over parts of his day. He's trying to shield me – to shield Clara – from anything that might hurt to hear or remember. I know this is what he's doing and I'm glad he's doing it. It makes it easier to pretend I'm not in the labyrinth.

Collin usually talks about things he and Clara used to do together, or how Clara used to act as a child. He'll say: "Remember when…" or "Remember how…" and I'll always get excited to hear another story about Clara's childhood. The excitement is immediately followed by guilt as I nod along with Collin's stories, pretending I remember a past that was never mine.

One day, I bring up Prosper, adding, "Elle keeps saying she'll introduce me to him, but she hasn't. She said you two are close, so I was wondering…"

Wondering what? Why Elle's pretending she wants me to meet her brother, when clearly she'd rather put it off? Or is it that Prosper himself doesn't want to meet me? I'm not sure how to confess my worries to Collin. I'm afraid he'll think they're silly.

But the look on Collin's face is nothing close to dismissive: it's stricken.

After a moment, he says, "If Prosper were here, I'd introduce you to him myself, Clara."

Confused, I wait for Collin to continue. He's staring into the distance, and his hands are clenched over his kneecaps, white-knuckled. "What Elle told you – that Prosper and I were close – that much is true. He was like a brother to me. We could conquer anything in the labyrinth, if we were together. We could conquer the labyrinth itself, I thought, one day. But then a supply run went wrong and Prosper was killed."

I go cold. "But Elle, she... she..."

"Acts like he's alive? I know. There's nothing we can do about that. We tried to tell her, but she wouldn't believe us, and if we pressed she'd have fits. Now we just play along when we have to. With someone like Elle, it's easier that way."

"When did Prosper...?"

"Three years ago."

"Elle said she's only been here two years."

"She and Prosper were here two years when he died. Elle herself has been here five years now. Something else she refuses to acknowledge. Look, I know I don't need to tell you this, but be careful what you say around Elle when she's talking about Prosper. Don't let on that you know."

"I won't," I murmur. "I'm sorry about your friend."

Collin gives me a sad smile and squeezes my shoulder. "I just hope you never have to go through that, Clara."

I want to tell him I already have. I want to tell him that I lost someone as important to me as Prosper was to him. But I can't. Collin's lost too much to lose his sister too.

I've been at Fates over a week. I know almost everyone's name now, even though I hardly speak to anyone but Elle. I know there are twenty-six Icarii in Fates, total. I know when Collin joined there was almost twice that number. He let it slip a couple of days ago before changing the topic.

Elle and I are out in the main room because Cassie's in the girls' room catching a quick nap. Elle's been shifting uncomfortably for a while now so I'm not surprised when she gets up to go to the washroom. She says she'll be back in a minute before heading down the hall that leads to the girls' and boys' rooms. There are two more rooms down that hall: smaller rooms, containing crude, foul-smelling bathrooms. My first few times using them were horrendous. They're still horrible, but I'm getting used to it, slowly.

At least I'm used to the general smell of Fates. Bathing doesn't happen very often around here since water is so scarce. Luckily there's a rain-made lake not too far from Fates, where scavengers and sometimes caretakers venture out for water, when the area's confirmed clear of monsters. This means the extent of washing is usually just rinsing ourselves with wet rags every few days. I wish

I could wash my hair. It hasn't been clean since I first arrived and it's a shade darker now due to the grease. I hate when I accidentally touch it or when it brushes against my face. At least my braids make its texture a little less noticeable.

I'm still worrying over my personal hygiene when a shadow falls over me, obscuring the next stitch I was about to make in a pair of tattered britches. I glance up, thinking it's Elle. It's Felix.

"Hi," he says. "Clara, right? Mind if I sit?"

I scoot over a little. Felix sits next to me. Seeing the sewing in my lap, he pulls a face. "They've got you doing that too."

"I don't mind," I whisper.

Felix is startled to hear my voice. Then he smiles. "I guess it's not so bad compared to what we could be doing. Still, I'm not really good at it, even though they're trying to teach me. Kyle's surprisingly good, but don't tell him I said that."

Felix shifts his legs to a more comfortable position. "We haven't really talked much since we got here. I know we didn't actually talk before getting here, but since we lived through that first day together, I feel like... I dunno, it's like some kind of connection, maybe. Is that a weird thing to say?"

I shake my head.

"Thanks. Um, so I think I've decided something. I think I might try to become a scavenger. Andrea told me they train anyone who wants to become a scavenger and take us out for test runs and stuff. Do you think I'm being stupid? Kyle's going to become a scavenger too, and I think he can do it, but I know he and I are nothing alike. We never even got along, back home. We just knew each other. So… do you think I have a chance?"

I can tell Felix wants something from me, but I can't tell what answer he's hoping I'll give. I don't want to think about it. This question makes me uncomfortable because it means recognizing the labyrinth's still out there, just beyond the walls of Fates.

Elle returns before I can answer. She glares at Felix openly before he sees her, then she plasters on a fake smile. Collin's fake smiles are very obvious. Elle's aren't. If I hadn't seen her glare seconds before, I'd think this smile was real.

"I was just asking Clara if she thought I'd make a good scavenger," Felix says to Elle as she gathers up her sewing.

"It's worth a try, isn't it?" Elle says. "We always need more scavengers. Besides, if you're brave enough, you might even enjoy it. Being inside Fates all the time is boring, isn't it?"

"It's OK," Felix says. "I don't think I'm much help around here, though."

"Then you might be loads of help out there." Elle smiles at him, then turns to me. "Shall we go back, Clara? The room's free."

Elle's heading back to the girls' room before I've finished picking up my sewing.

"Thank you," I mumble to Felix, before pushing to my feet.

"What for?"

"Not letting Kyle kick me out of the shelter." I hurry after Elle without looking back at Felix. My face is burning and my chest feels funny. I realize that, as embarrassed as I am, I'm happy I finally thanked him.

Back in the girls' room, Cassie is just leaving. She casts Elle a surprisingly dirty look before noticing me and turning sheepish. She mumbles a greeting and disappears into the hall.

"She shouldn't nap," Elle says, after Cassie's gone. "She's always grumpy afterwards. Besides, she still has the new caretakers to train. The old head caretaker had Cassie herself properly trained by this time after her Fallen Day."

"When was her Fallen Day?" I ask.

"Last year," Elle says, and I wonder if that's on her timeline or real time. "Ryan found her. That was back when the groups were different. Prosper and Collin found a boy. Andrea was with them and saved the boy from a screecher. After that he wouldn't leave her alone. I liked that boy. He never noticed when I entered the room because he was always so focused on Andrea. That's why he decided to become a scavenger, so he could join her group. Andrea wasn't able to save him from a screecher a second time."

Elle's finished stitching in the patch on what she says is one of Prosper's tunics. She bites off the end of the thread. "Nobody talks about that boy. It's because we don't like talking about dead Icarii, but also because we've forgotten him. I don't even remember his face. He was only here for three weeks, after all. I don't even know what his name was, that's how well I remember him. I'll always remember your name, Clara. Not that I'll have to worry about remembering it because you'll always be right here. You have to stay right here."

"What about Felix?"

Elle pauses in winding up her thread. "Who?"

"Felix." My voice is strained and I'm starting to shake. "You told him he should try. You said... you told him to be a scavenger."

"That's what he wants, isn't it?" Elle asks. Her brows knit in confusion. "Sorry, Clara, but I don't see what this has to do with what we were talking about. Felix is just another Icarii, after all."

My voice breaks. "I'm an Icarii!"

"Oh, no, Clara." Elle smiles. She takes my hands and speaks to me like I'm a child. "You're my sister, remember?"

For almost two weeks now I've been sitting with Collin while he eats his supper and thinks of things to say to me. This is why I know his silence tonight is strange. It's longer than usual.

Finally, Collin says, "You've been spending a lot of time with Elle."

He uses the same tone Mother and Father would use before a lecture of some sort. I wasn't lectured very often, but the few times I was has led to my fear and sensitivity of the tone.

"She's been through a lot," Collin says. "Has she told you that she and Prosper survived in the labyrinth for a week before we found them? No Icarii lasts that long on their own, but Prosper managed to get them through it. Elle... I don't know what she was like before the labyrinth, but this place changes everyone who enters it, Clara, and it didn't change Elle for the better. It broke her, faster than most, but it broke her in a different way than it breaks most people. And then, after Prosper died... I know you two are friends and I'm not saying that should stop. I want to look after Elle for Prosper, like I know he'd have looked after you. It's just... maybe you should try getting to know some of the other people here at Fates, or doing some different activities. You must be bored with sewing every day. I asked Addie and she said, if you ever feel like it, she could find something else for you to do. You might find Addie's work interesting. Just go talk to her some time, please."

I don't say anything after that and neither does Collin, for a while. Then he gives me a now familiar half-smile and says: "Remember when..."

The next day on my way to get breakfast, I see Kyle and Felix in the main room talking to Gus. Instead of his usual half-constructed toys, Gus is holding a bow. He seems to be showing Felix and Kyle how it works.

I have breakfast with Elle and then we go back to the girls' room to sew. When it's time for supper Elle and I go to collect our gruel. Before we leave the mess hall I say, "Can we eat here?"

Elle stares at me like I'm crazy. "Why would you want to?"

Normally I wouldn't want to. Normally there would be too many people in too small a space and I'd clam up. But I'm clammed up anyway, all the time now, and I think I'd be more comfortable here than in the girls' room with Elle. At first I thought maybe Elle could be like the Clara I always wanted – one who was happy to just spend time with me, who didn't need to be surrounded by ogling crowds – but Elle isn't Clara. Just like I'm not Clara.

I'm also not strong enough to stand up to Elle's imploring gaze. I mumble something a cross between "never mind" and a breath and I follow Elle back to the girls' room.

I don't think Collin realizes how hard it is to follow through on his advice. I can't find a way to escape Elle.

On the third day after he spoke to me about her, when we go for breakfast, Addie stops me. "When you're done, come back here. I need your help with something."

"Can't one of the others help you?" Elle asks.

"Doesn't Prosper have another shirt for you to fix?" Addie asks crisply. Elle bristles. To me, Addie says, "When you're done."

I nod and Elle and I return to the girls' room. I find myself eating faster than usual, although Elle eats much slower. When she's finally finished I collect her bowl and flask, saying I'll drop off the dishes.

"You don't have to go just because she told you to," Elle says.

"It's OK," I mumble.

"If you're sure." Elle smiles so suddenly I'm not sure if it's a mask breaking or sliding into place. "Come back soon, OK?"

I nod and quickly carry the dishes out of the room. After the door closes behind me I feel surprisingly relieved. My feet seem lighter as I go down the hall. I pass Cassie in the main room. She smiles and says, "Finally free of her?"

Surprised by Cassie's seeming dislike of Elle, I mumble something about going to see Addie and hurry down the hall. The mess hall is empty of everyone but Addie.

"Close the door," she says, without turning around. I do as she asks before going over to the table. Like usual she's sitting on the very end of the bench and the spot next to her is taken up by a basket of odd materials. I sit across from her. She has various different-shaped blades laid out to her left. In front of her is the hide of some kind of monster, spread flat.

Addie doesn't look up when she says, "Did you bring your sewing?"

I shake my head.

"Use your words." Addie's attention is on the blades. "It's enough that you have my ears when I'm trying to concentrate; I'm not going to look at you too."

"I don't have my sewing," I choke out.

"Then what do you plan on doing? You're not just going to sit there, are you?"

"You said..." I can't get out any more than that. My tongue ties and I warm with embarrassment. Why can't I talk to anyone normally, when I manage to talk to them at all?

"What I said was an escape route," Addie says. "A favour for Collin, since you don't seem able to separate yourself from Elle on your own. Do you even want to be free from her or is that only what Collin wants for you?"

I don't know what to say. It feels horrible to even think about admitting I want to be away from Elle after she's been so kind to me.

Addie picks up a chipped arrowhead and holds it to the lantern in between us. She turns it around, inspecting every angle. "If you want to go back to Elle, feel free to do so. I certainly never needed your help with my studies."

I'm silent as I watch Addie slide the tip of the arrowhead down the hide. The hide doesn't cut. It doesn't even tear a little.

"What studies?"

Addie peeks up, slightly surprised I've asked, then her attention's back on her work. "If we have any hope of defeating the monsters in the labyrinth, we have to understand them. Naturally that requires certain levels of observation, but it also requires levels of experimentation. The scavengers observe and retrieve and I experiment on what they retrieve."

"What are you doing?" As I ask it my voice gets quieter and quieter, but at least I get the question out before going silent entirely.

"Trying to figure out if anything can pierce *orinthes areii* flesh. I've been exposing it to different temperatures and chemicals in hopes of eliciting some reaction." Addie picks up a small knife from the pile of blades. "So far no reaction has been elicited."

"Orinta... Orintee..."

"Orin. Tes. Ah. Ray. *Orinthes areii*. The scavengers call them bronze beaks. A suitable nickname, considering their physical attributes, but their real name suits just as well. It means 'birds of war' in Ancient Daedalic. They're very large, with feathers made of a metal-like material. Somehow they can still fly, yet their flight is slowed.

Their torsos have no feathers to speak of but are, instead, covered in this flesh." Addie gestures to the hide in front of her. "Theo collected it for me. He cut out this section by starting at the neck, where the flesh is softer and can be cut. They killed the bird itself because they were lucky enough to find one while it was distracted feeding. They managed to bash its skull in before it pecked their heads off. I'm trying to find a material that can pierce the underbelly so we can shoot them down if need be. *Orinthes areii* aren't often found in our scavenging grounds but should they suddenly choose to migrate, it's better to know."

Addie tries the blade against the skin. Her tool breaks and I wince. Addie frowns and lays the broken blade aside. "There's no need for you to concern yourself with the monsters of the labyrinth. You'll never encounter an *orinthes areii*. You'll likely never encounter anything other than Icarii and dead monsters. Now that Collin has you back, he'll never let you farther than the lake, if he ever does let you that far. You should hope that he does, if you ever want to wash your hair again."

I grab my braids, self-conscious. If Addie's noticed how dirty my hair is, doubtlessly the others have too. Then again, most everyone here seems to be dirty. The scavengers don't seem as bad as those of us stuck in Fates, but that's probably just because I don't see them enough to notice things like greasy hair.

I focus on this issue, the issue of hygiene, because I know if I think about being trapped in here for the rest of my life I'll panic.

Will I really be stuck here forever?

"Is there an end?" I whisper.

"To life? Quite certainly. There's an immediate end for people like you right beyond our front door. However," – Addie looks up at me from under her short eyelashes – "that's not what you meant, is it? You want to know if there's an end to the labyrinth. A way out."

I nod.

"None of us know," Addie says. "We don't venture farther into the labyrinth than needed for scavenging. We're content with keeping ourselves alive and Fates up and running. Aren't you content, being alive?"

Unsure of what else to do, I nod. Of course I'm happy to be alive. I just can't imagine spending forever inside here, sewing and eating gruel and waiting for a brother who isn't mine.

"You'll get used to it," Addie says, as if reading my thoughts. "People like you always get used to it. You'll probably end up thriving here, so don't worry, because your brother wouldn't want you to." Addie smiles at me, and it's empty of any genuine feelings or effort. "You'll be content with this simplistic life soon enough."

That night I find out that Collin's been asking Addie to spy on me.

"Addie said you spent some time with her today, but that you spent the rest of the afternoon with Elle. Don't you like Addie?"

I don't like her at all, even if she knows interesting things. She makes me feel horrible and stupid and pointless.

"I like her," I say.

This pleases Collin, like I knew it would. "Do you want to spend more time with her?"

"If she doesn't mind."

"Of course she won't mind," Collin says. "Addie may act like she wants to be on her own, but I've lived with her for five years. It's all a front. She loves company."

The next day, at breakfast, Addie requests my help again. Elle reacts the same way, if not more irritated. After we're finished eating I go to Addie.

"Let's make something perfectly clear," Addie says when I sit down. "I'm helping you out for Collin. You're a nuisance and you're distracting me from my work. If we're going to continue this charade, start bringing your sewing or something else with which to amuse yourself."

I do start bringing my sewing after that, but I never actually do any work. I just watch Addie experiment on different monster hides. On the fourth day of sitting with her I see a hide that I realize is familiar.

"Digger," I say, staring at it.

"You sound like a toddler. And that's another scavenger name. They're called *chtons* – chia tons – from Ancient Daedalic for 'of the earth'. One almost had your face for a snack, didn't it?"

I flash back to the digger coming at me, as I'm sure she intended me to do. I say: "Theo hit its head."

"Yes, so I heard. And, so I heard, Ryan distracted it first. Not that it's particularly difficult to distract *chtons*. They're blind and their hearing is disastrous, but they have impeccable tremor sense. As long as they're on the ground and you're on the ground, they'll know where you are. Since this one was a baby, its senses would still be confused, assaulting, even. As they get older they seem more capable of interpreting their senses and focusing on a target. Still, arrows and air-borne projectiles tend to confuse them. They can't perceive anything not related to the ground. To them it doesn't exist until it hits them in the head. You, at that instant, throwing a rock at it would have had the same effect as Ryan's arrow, and given Theo the same chance to get close."

"Can you only kill it by hitting its head?"

"That's the most effective way. Arrows are too weak to penetrate its flesh, even if they make a good distraction. Any heavy weapon aimed at its head does the trick. Of course, if it were pulled apart or submerged in water, it wouldn't survive, but those aren't exactly tasks we small and weak Icarii can accomplish."

My next question, if I even had one, instantly disappears. Addie's words echo in my head. *Pulled apart.*

I return to Elle early today.

Collin has been suggesting I stop having supper early and eat with him and the others when he gets back. He says we can still have our private chats after supper. Since I spent a lot of time with Elle today, I decide tonight I'll eat with Collin.

I accompany Elle to the mess hall. When she picks up two bowls I tell her I'm not very hungry and that I'll eat later.

Elle puts back her bowl. "Then I'll eat later too."

"With Collin and the others?" I ask.

"Oh." Elle's lips form a thin line. "That's what you meant."

We return to sewing in the girls' room. Elle is quieter than usual. When the scavengers get back, Collin comes to collect me. Elle doesn't follow when I get up to go to the mess hall.

"I'm not very hungry," she says, staring at her stitching instead of me. "I'll eat later."

I realize it's the exact same thing I said earlier. I hesitate, an odd discomfort overcoming me. Have I hurt Elle? Is she mad at me? She must be, because when I whisper "bye" she doesn't say anything back. Then again, maybe she didn't hear me. Sometimes she doesn't hear me when I say something and keeps on speaking herself. When I leave, though, she still doesn't look up.

Seeing Collin waiting for me in the hall with a smile makes me feel better. He asks if I've eaten, like he always does. Tonight I shake my head. His smile broadens.

All the scavengers are back. They're sitting in their usual places at the mess hall table. Jay and Theo on Addie's side, Andrea and Ryan across from them. Now that everyone's back in Fates, Gus doesn't need to stay by the back exit, and is sitting next to Addie. Cassie's taking her supper late too, as she always does, and is sitting with Ryan, talking to him quietly. He never seems to be paying much attention to her but, then again, he never seems to be paying much attention to anything within Fates. I haven't spoken to him since my first day in the labyrinth and, even though he saved us from the bat, I can't see myself wanting to speak to him ever again if I can help it.

Collin serves up food for both of us. I don't sit in my typical daytime spot across from Addie, because that's where Cassie's sitting. Instead I end up squeezed in between Addie and Collin, across from Ryan. I can't say I'm particularly happy with this seating arrangement, considering I'm across from the boy I was just thinking about never wanting to speak with again, and next to the girl who's constantly belittling me and dragging up my worst memories.

Collin starts telling me about how he and his group found a good scavenge site today. Apparently it was a tiny room, barred up with wood that they brought back for the fire. Inside were old crates, which will be used for weapon materials and more firewood.

"Why are there crates here?" My voice peters out at the end, as it usually does with Addie. I can speak a bit more steadily to Collin, usually, so I'm not surprised when he doesn't hear me correctly. He must think I asked about what they'll use the crates for, because he repeats they'll be for firewood.

While Collin keeps talking, I notice two familiar faces behind him, who I'm not yet used to seeing with the scavengers. Felix and Kyle are sitting at the other end of the table, across from each other. Kyle's next to Andrea, which is in keeping with the teams to which they've been assigned. They completed preliminary training a couple of days ago and have since been out for short runs in the afternoon, or so Collin tells me. Although they haven't been out doing any real scavenging yet and certainly haven't encountered any monsters, Collin says the other scavengers report they're holding up well. I was surprised at how relieved I was to hear that both of them are doing OK.

"Hey, Clara," Andrea calls down the table, immediately halting conversation and drawing most everyone's attention to me. I try not to squirm. "Kyle was telling us something strange today, and I wonder if you could set it straight, 'cause quite frankly we're not sure we believe him."

Kyle scowls at that, a blush spreading across his face. Felix tries to whisper something to him, but Kyle just shakes his head.

Andrea continues, "He said the day we found you guys you two saw a woman, gathering Icarii robes."

Jay and some of the other scavengers laugh. Collin does too. He has a deep, throaty laugh that almost reminds me of what Father's laugh used to sound like before it started getting wheezy.

"Don't be ridiculous," Collin says. "Clara didn't see anything like that – did you?"

Suddenly Collin's gaze is on me. Despite his jovial tone there's something about his expression that's the same as his fake smiles.

"I know she didn't," Andrea says, "but we gotta cross-check everything, don't we? So Clara, did you see a woman?"

Collin's still looking at me. His blue eyes don't seem as light as usual. Everyone's looking at me now. Even Addie and Ryan seem interested in my response. Kyle's glaring at me.

"Does it take that long to remember?" Jay mutters.

Collin's jaw clenches and his eyes dart to where Jay's sitting. By the way Jay tenses, he knows he's in trouble. I tug Collin's sleeve under the table, drawing his attention back to me.

"I don't remember," I mumble.

"Are you kidding?" Kyle snaps. Everyone looks at him. He's half out of his seat. Reddening, he clamps his mouth shut and sits down again.

Addie's voice, clear and cool, carries through the room. "The first day in the labyrinth is, by nature, extremely stressful. Quite often those who survive can't recall details about the experience. Likewise, they find themselves imagining details."

"I can vouch for that," Theo says. "My first day, I thought I saw a pink screecher."

"A pink screecher?" Jay demands.

The left end of the table devolves into teasing and hallucination stories. Collin relaxes, then pats my knee and says in a low voice, "Don't think about that day, Clara. What's important is that you're here now."

I nod and return to my meal. A few minutes later the mess hall door opens. The little girl I've seen around Fates scrambles in. She ignores the table full of scavengers and goes straight to Felix. She tugs on the back of his shirt until he faces her, at which point she says something to him I can't hear. Felix shakes his head.

"What is it?" Andrea asks Felix, but then I realize she's speaking to the girl. "Gina, do you want something?"

The little girl nods shyly to Andrea. The table's fallen silent again. The girl peeks around at us, then mumbles: "Lullaby."

"Want me to sing for you, Gina?" Cassie asks, starting to slide off the bench. The little girl shakes her head so that her matted brown hair whips against her cheeks.

"Felix," the girl says, tugging at his shirt again.

"Is Felix that good at singing, Gene?" Theo asks, grinning at the girl in a way that makes her start to grin back. "Should we get him to sing for us here, in front of everyone?"

"Yes!" Gina pipes, while Felix goes beetroot red. "Yes, yes, yes!"

"That's decided, then." Theo grins at Felix while Andrea claps, egging him on. "Pick a good one. Something upbeat."

Gina leaves a very flustered Felix and goes over to Gus, who immediately helps her up into his lap as if he's done it a hundred times before. Once she's seated with Gus's arm around her, Gina turns her attention expectantly to Felix.

"Go on, then," Jay says to him. "If you can't sing one song for a little girl, what makes you think you can face a flock of screechers with a piece of scrap metal?"

Jay's goading works. Still red-faced, Felix starts to sing. At first his voice comes out scratchy, like mine so often does, then, also like my voice, his grows very quiet.

"Not like that!" Gina orders. "Can't hear you!"

Felix clears his throat and starts again. In the beginning it's quiet, like before, but slowly his voice gets steadier and louder and when it does I find myself awestruck. Everyone at the table seems shocked, except for Gina, who smiles contentedly and leans her head against Gus's chest. I'm so stunned by Felix's voice that he's reached the second verse before I realize what he's singing. It's the Daedalum anthem, but not the version they play over the radio or in the lift. It's the version they sing in the Icarus Temple Choir. The way Felix sings it makes it sound like a lament.

When Felix finishes everyone is stunned silent. He averts his eyes sheepishly and reaches for a flask. Theo is the first to speak.

"I've never much liked that song," he says, "but coming out of you, I think it just became my favourite."

"I've never heard it sung like that before," Andrea muses.

"It was fitting," Addie says. Everyone seems surprised that she's spoken. She continues, "You sing it like a requiem, and that's what it is. The words are Ancient Daedalic and depict the fall and subsequent death of Icarus from the perspective of his mother."

"That can't be what it means," Jay cuts in. "Icarus didn't die. Were you so busy reading snuck-in library books during service that you missed the entire story?"

"I know the story better than you, I'm sure," Addie says. Before Jay can say anything she gets up, collecting her basket of materials from the floor. "That really was excellent, Felix. You've got a marvellous talent. Goodnight, everyone."

There's a chorus of "Goodnight, Addie" as she leaves. Even though her spot is free now, I don't move down to the end of the table. It doesn't feel right to take her spot, even if she's only gone to bed.

"Sing us something else," Theo says. "Something upbeat this time. I think you missed out on that part of my request."

"Shh," Gus says, carefully rising from the bench with a sleeping Gina in his arms. "Keep the party for after she's in bed."

After Gus leaves with Gina, Theo and Andrea start listing multiple songs and rhymes and ask Felix if he knows any of them. They're talking too quickly for Felix to possibly keep up, but he's smiling now, even if he still looks slightly embarrassed. I'm happy for him until

I remember what Addie said about the true meaning behind the anthem, and my spirits drop. It can't be that the song I've been hearing and singing all my life, that I thought told of the coming rise of Icarus and his Icarii, really cloaks such tragedy.

Then again, it's not as if the labyrinth was as I'd been told, so why should the tale of Icarus be any different?

Felix sings two more songs for us before Collin and I leave. Andrea and Jay are arguing over the next song as we close the door on the mess hall. In the storage room the chairs are where we always leave them: by the desk.

Collin starts telling me about transporting the firewood back through the labyrinth, as apparently his group had some difficulty. I let him continue for a while but ultimately find myself unable to keep from blurting, "Would it be so strange?"

Collin's clearly confused, with good reason. I knot my hands in my skirts, fingering a tear I've sewn three times since being given this dress. It's quickly become a habit, pulling the holes in my dress farther apart, but I can't seem to stop.

"Seeing a woman," I say. "Is that strange?"

"More than strange," Collin says. "It's impossible. There aren't any adults in the labyrinth; none. No Icarii has ever made it to twenty, let alone past that. Don't worry, Clara. We'll be the first generation of Icarii to make it past that, way past. But you just need to understand it hasn't happened before."

Collin squeezes my knee like he did in the mess hall, when he told me not to think about my first day in the labyrinth. I'm surprised when I'm able to say, "I heard your age is almost a record here. How old was the person with the record?"

"Who told you about that?" Collin asks. I don't say anything, hoping he'll just answer the question, since I don't want to rat out Theo and admit I was thinking about my first day all in one. Finally, Collin sighs. "There was someone who reached nineteen, just barely. She's been dead for years now. She was the leader of Fates before me. She... she was a good leader for a long time. That's what anyone who knew her will tell you, but there's not many of us that knew her left. It'd be true, though; she was a good leader."

I'm sure there's something Collin's not telling me, but he doesn't elaborate. Instead he asks me what I thought of Felix's singing. When I say I really enjoyed it, he says we should get Felix to sing for everyone every few nights.

"It'd keep everyone's spirits up," Collin says. "Gina would certainly like it."

"How old is Gina?" It's a question I've been meaning to ask, but I wasn't comfortable enough with anyone to say it until now.

"We're not sure," Collin says. "We think she's around eight."

"But that's too young to be an Icarii."

"Gina isn't an Icarii," Collin says. "She was a toddler when I first joined Fates. Apparently over a year before that they found her in the extra storage room, bound in Icarii robes. That's why we don't know if we should think of her as an Icarii or not."

"How did she get there?"

"The old Fates members weren't sure. They used the extra storage room like us, not just for storage but also as an emergency exit and entrance. They think, maybe, someone snuck Gina in. That's why we're so concerned with that route being breached. It's why we have Gus by the door until all scavengers get home, so that he can let us in with the secret knock."

"Secret knock?"

"Yeah. Ryan did it when he brought you through that way, didn't he?" Collin starts to frown.

I realize if I say Ryan made me plug my ears, he'll get in trouble. Despite the fact I'm not a big fan of Ryan, he did get me back to Fates. To Collin's question I offer a nod and, before he can ask more about that night or change the subject, ask, "There are Icarii outside Fates?"

"There used to be." Collin smiles. "There aren't any more. Nothing for you to worry about, Clara."

It doesn't seem like there's ever anything for me to worry about where Collin's concerned, yet I know I have everything to worry about. Still, I can't see how other Icarii outside of Fates should be cause for concern. Wouldn't that just mean more people to fight the monsters?

I don't get an answer to my thoughts, because Collin changes the subject. He starts talking about songs we used to sing with our mother, who apparently was quite adamant that he joined the Temple Choir, even though he could never carry a tune.

I smile and let Collin tell his stories, because I don't have anything to worry about.

The next day, when I slide in across from Addie, I'm speaking before I've fully sat down. "Are there adults in the labyrinth?"

Addie sighs. She lays down the knife she was about to pierce through a feathery hide. "No, there aren't *adults* in the labyrinth. There's one, singular, and there's no proof she exists. Unless you count what you and Kyle supposedly saw."

"Who is she?"

"A woman who wanders the labyrinth alone. Some say she's an Icarii who's survived decades in the labyrinth, at the cost of her sanity. All we really have of her are tales passed down by late members of Fates, such as the time a group of scavengers was being chased by a stray *leo nemeum*. The woman appeared and wrestled the beast into submission with her bare hands. In another, she shoots down a flock of *harpyiae* before one of our scavengers can so much as notch their first arrow. Naturally, these tales have been exaggerated over time, though I doubt any version happened at all. There is, however, another story, much more widely believed."

Addie pauses. She takes a sip of water from the flask by her side. As she recaps it, she starts again: "It happened on Fallen Day. A group of scavengers were scouting their quadrant, searching for new Icarii, but the labyrinth was empty. Then they came upon a clearing. Every inch of the ground was covered by Icarii bodies, their robes stained through with red. And standing in the midst of them, axe and armour splattered with blood, was the woman. This story is how she earned her name: the Executioner."

Addie picks up the knife she held when I came in. She turns it so that its blade catches the lantern light, reflecting in my eyes. "Of course, this is all just legend. Rumour. All bred from the ridiculous pastime of sitting around the fire telling stories."

Addie moves the blade. I can see again, and I see that she's looking right at me. "After all, there aren't any adults in the labyrinth. That's what Collin told you, isn't it?"

I nod.

"Then just listen to him." Addie's voice goes snide. "He's your brother, isn't he?"

Could she possibly know? Why else would she ask something like that, in that tone?

Addie continues and I realize it wasn't really a question. "The word of your own brother should mean more to you than what I have to say."

"It does," I say, so quick to defend my fake relation to Collin I don't realize how rude I'm being. Shocked with myself I physically cover my mouth.

"Charming." Addie slides her blade down the hide. The feathers bend with the movement but nothing is cut. Addie holds up the blade again. This time she doesn't use it to reflect the lantern light into my eyes; she just looks at it.

Or maybe it's me she's looking at. It's hard to tell.

"Useless," Addie declares, "just like the rest. I'm not surprised."

I wanted to ask Addie about the 'X' in the Executioner's mouth, but now I'm not sure I want to know the answer. I'm still debating whether or not to ask when Andrea bursts in. It surprises me, because the scavengers aren't due back for another few hours. Andrea comes over, out of breath and panicked. Seeing her expression makes me begin to panic. Has a monster somehow gotten into Fates?

All Andrea says to Addie is: "Stinger" and Addie's up from the table and following her to the main room. I get up to follow, but by the time I reach the door it's filled by younger Icarii being herded inside by one of the caretakers.

"What's happening?" I manage to ask.

"One of the scavengers got hurt. The kids don't need to see him being treated."

I hurry into the main room. What if it's Theo that's been hurt, or Kyle? Kyle was with them and he's new to scavenging. After we made it through the first day I'd hate to see something happen to him now. I don't even want Ryan to be hurt. I don't want any of them to be hurt.

Supplies that usually litter the main table have been shoved to the ground. Theo and Andrea are fighting to keep a thrashing Ryan on the table. Cassie is standing beside them, paler than I've ever seen her. Kyle is nowhere to be found. Did he make it back at all?

I don't know what to do with myself so I just stand there, watching. There's gauze wrapped tightly around

Ryan's right thigh. It's bleeding through, but the blood looks darker than it should.

Suddenly Addie and Gus appear from the emergency exit. Gus is carrying a small, open crate and Addie is uncorking a bottle with murky green liquid inside.

"Is the water ready?" Addie demands. Cassie snaps out of her stupor to retrieve a pot from the hearth. Addie turns her attention to Theo and Andrea. "Would you take off that bandage already? He needs to bleed."

Andrea seems hesitant but Theo isn't; he rips off the gauze, which he then drops in the boiling water. Cassie, meanwhile, has brought over another pot of water from the other hearth. Addie directs Theo to rip open Ryan's pants leg, which he does, revealing the full wound. The blood coming from the gash is mixed with black streaks. The flesh around his wound has bubbled and the bubbles are gradually turning black.

Addie dips a dagger into the second bowl of hot water while passing the bottle of green liquid to Cassie. Gus shoves a balled-up rag into Ryan's mouth while Theo makes room for Addie. He braces Ryan's upper body while Andrea reaches to brace his lower legs. Addie brandishes her dagger.

"No," Cassie squeaks.

"Leave if you don't want to see it," Addie says as she starts cutting Ryan's wound wider. Ryan struggles against the hold of his team. The rag mutes his scream, but some sound still gets through. Addie continues regardless. Blood gushes out of Ryan, streaked with the same tendrils of black. When Addie's content with the size of the wound she starts cutting open the blackened bubbles. These ooze black liquid more than blood.

Addie keeps cutting into Ryan and Ryan keeps screaming and groaning into the rag while the others hold him down. Addie only pulls back when all the bubbles are popped and the only liquid pouring from Ryan is bright scarlet.

Gus takes another rag from the box and rinses it in the second pot. He hands it to Addie and she starts cleaning off the blackened blood before dumping the soiled rag in the first pot. This process continues through a few rags, until all the black blood is gone from Ryan's leg. By now, Ryan has started to calm down a bit, but then Addie presses the next rag to his open wound. He bites down hard on the cloth in his mouth, squeezing his eyes shut.

After Addie's done cleaning the wounds on his leg, she takes the bottle from Cassie and starts pouring the green salve onto Ryan's leg. It must sting because Ryan winces again, and continues to do so while Addie rubs the salve in with a rag. When she's finished she dumps this rag into the first pot, then goes to the second pot to rinse her hands. She sighs, tensed shoulders relaxing. "Bandage him up. I think I got it."

"You think?!" Andrea demands at the same moment Cassie exclaims in a shrill, panicked voice: "But all the black came out!"

"I've told you the venom isn't that simple. Still, he has a good chance. He would have had a better chance had you done this immediately after he was poisoned."

"As if we could have done this outside!" Andrea yells.

"It's OK," Theo says as he wraps fresh gauze around Ryan's leg. I realize Ryan's passed out. "Andrea, he'll be OK. We got him back quickly."

"Quickly enough, I hope," Addie says as she dries her hands and turns to Gus. "Help me put away the supplies."

Gus nods and collects the box from before. The two head back to the emergency exit. Meanwhile, those who remain crowd around Ryan. Feeling out of place, I turn to leave. I don't get the chance to decide whether I'll return to Elle and the girls' room or go help with the younger Icarii, because Elle is right behind me. I have no idea how long she's been there. She's staring past me, at Ryan.

"That's going to be a bother," she says.

"What?" I ask, my voice extremely small.

"His britches," Elle says. "They've ripped them down the side. You know, whether he lives or dies, we'll still have to stitch them up."

I don't know what to say to that. Elle doesn't seem to care. She just smiles at me and says, "I guess this means you're done with Addie today, doesn't it?"

I follow her to the girls' room, at a loss for what else to do. When we turn down the hall I see Kyle in front of the boys' bathroom, leaning against the door and staring at the ground. His lips are parted and his face is ashen.

"You're alright," I say before I can stop myself. Kyle's eyes snap to mine and he seems to break from his daze, if only a little.

"Yeah," he says. "Yeah, I'm really alright. I killed it."

I stop walking even though Elle is trying to tug me to the girls' room. "What?"

"It was really big," Kyle continues, making vague hand gestures. "It was huge. And I killed it – the monster. I killed it."

I get the full story at supper. While scavenging, Ryan
went scouting ahead like he usually does, but this time
he took Kyle with him as a lesson. They were attacked by
a stinger: a monster that hardly ever frequents this part
of the labyrinth. Apparently the last time one was seen,
let alone fought, was well over two years ago. Andrea
describes a stinger for my and Felix's benefit. Essentially,
she says, they're giant scorpions with a poisonous tail and
pincers. Theo adds that they're "crazy fast".

When the stinger showed up, it went after Ryan. His
arrows were useless and, while he was distracted firing,
the stinger managed to corner him, at which point it
attacked with its pincers and got him in the leg. He was
wounded and trapped.

Kyle took the opportunity to attack with the spear
Theo had given him. It didn't do any damage, but it
pulled the stinger's attention from Ryan. Just when the
stinger was about to attack, Kyle ran at it head-on, so
he was right in front of the stinger where the pincers
couldn't reach him. He then rammed his spear through
the stinger's mouth before it could attack with its tail. He
jumped over the pincers and out of the way before the
stinger started thrashing. It died shortly after that and

Kyle ran back for Andrea and Theo, who had heard the stinger dying and were already on the way.

When the story's done, Theo claps Kyle on the shoulder. Kyle's sitting between Andrea and Theo today, who seem like two impossibly proud parents. They started telling the story, but Kyle quickly picked up the tale. He seems a hundred times more comfortable at the table than he did last night.

Everyone praises him and congratulates him, telling him he's truly meant to be a scavenger. Theo admits that in all his time in the labyrinth he's never taken down a stinger and Kyle says next time he runs into one he'll show Theo how it's done. Most everyone laughs at that and Theo tells him it's a deal.

Addie's quiet through the whole story. I watch her expression as the others talk. She's frowning, her eyebrows actively twitching and lowering depending on what someone says.

It's easy to watch Addie tonight, since I'm sitting across from her like I do during the day. Cassie isn't here. She's in the boys' room with Ryan. Usually they don't allow the genders to mingle in their rooms, but since Ryan's injured they're letting Cassie look after him, at least while the others are at supper. I can't say their presence seems missed around the table, considering Ryan never talks to anybody and Cassie only ever talks to Ryan.

After supper Collin tells me to head to bed. He apologizes and says we'll catch up tomorrow, because he has to talk to the others about what happened today.

I nod and get up to leave at the same time that Theo says to Kyle, "You must be exhausted after today. Why not go on ahead of us. Heroes need to keep up their energy!"

I think it's the fact Theo calls him a hero that gets Kyle to leave. I'm surprised when he holds the door open for me. He lingers for a moment to call back a thank you to the others who, by the sounds of it, are still praising him for today. Then, to my further surprise, Kyle catches up with me.

"I still can't believe today happened," he says, as if he and I are close and talk all the time. "I never imagined I'd be able to go out in the labyrinth again after that first day, let alone kill a monster out there. Isn't it crazy, how much things have changed?"

I nod, but Kyle doesn't notice. He keeps talking, not looking at me. "For the first week here I kept trying to forget where I was. All I wanted was to go home but, when I think about it, home was really boring. What would I have done there anyway? My father ran a news-stand on one of the shopping floors. I used to work there part-time and I hated it. I can't imagine running the place, and I know he wanted me to take over for him. Maybe this – becoming an Icarii – was really what I was meant to do. Icarus really did choose me for a reason."

It's starting to get annoying listening to Kyle. At first I was amazed that he could kill such a horrible monster. Then I was impressed and even happy for him. But the more everyone talked about it, and the way he's talking now, the more frustrated I feel. Maybe because it's making me a little jealous.

I'm not jealous that he goes into the labyrinth. The thought of it still terrifies me. I'm jealous he's found something to live for here.

But it's not that I have nothing. I have Collin, the kind, caring, doting sibling I never had. And, strange as she may be, I have Elle. Then there's Addie with her interesting stories and experiments, and Theo and Andrea and Felix are always friendly to me. I'll surely get to know them better if I stay here. So of course I have something to live for too.

Of course.

We reach the boys' room and Kyle doesn't even say goodbye when he slips into the room. I wonder if, later, he'll remember it was me he was speaking to, or if he'll just remember having spoken to someone.

I'm right in front of the girls' room when I remember my needle and thread. I left it in the mess hall earlier, when Andrea's group returned early. I meant to look for it at supper but Kyle's story distracted me.

Retracing my steps to the mess hall door, I find Kyle didn't close it completely. I can hear voices from within and it makes me hesitate. Maybe I should just try and find the needle and thread at breakfast. I don't want to interrupt an important meeting.

I'm about to leave when I hear Collin's voice say above the others: "The fact is, we're running out of scavenge spots."

This is met by a chorus of angry voices. I pick out Andrea's, but the loudest of all is Theo's.

"It's too dangerous," he says. "If there's a stinger this

close to Fates, there's no telling what we'll run into if we go deeper. Sybil was against this for a reason!"

"Sybil lived in a different time," Collin says.

"It was three years ago!" Theo yells.

"Three years is like three decades in the labyrinth," Addie says. "Three centuries, even. We all know how quickly things can change and today's just another reminder. Things *have* changed and if we want to keep Fates running as it is now we need to push farther."

"You'd like that, wouldn't you?" Andrea says, her voice colder than I've ever heard it. "You don't care how many of us fall, as long as one of us comes back with information for you, so you can add another corridor to your little map."

"Andrea," Collin says coolly, "it's thanks to Addie's work that we understand as much of the labyrinth as we do. If not for her, do you really think Ryan would have survived what happened to him today?"

"Ryan has nothing to do with this!" Andrea snaps. "No matter how much work Addie does, it's not like she's the one out with her neck on the line!"

"Somebody needs to keep track," Addie says. "We don't have as much material for documentation as we used to."

"So you stay holed up in here to protect the information in your brain?" Andrea demands, disgusted. "Isn't that just an easy way of saying our brains aren't as important? We all know you think the rest of us are stupid, but that doesn't make our lives any less significant."

"I think we all have our uses," Addie says. "I also think we should know our uses and react accordingly."

Andrea starts to snap something else but Theo cuts in, "I feel like you're forgetting something, Addie, but that can't be, because you remember everything, don't you? You can't possibly forget that you know everything you know because *Sybil* taught you, and Sybil was out fighting and scavenging every single day. I'm not going to think for one moment that you've forgotten the person who saved us on our Fallen Day."

"I haven't forgotten," Addie says crisply. "I just don't factor into our situation variables that are no longer in play."

"You can't keep bringing her up every time we make a decision you don't like," Collin says – to Theo, I think. "Sybil was a great leader, but the labyrinth was different back when she led Fates. That labyrinth is gone now, just like her."

"So the decision's made, is it?" Andrea demands. "No vote?"

"What's there to vote on?" Collin asks. "We push farther or we start rationing. Do you all really want that kind of vote?"

The room is dead silent.

Collin starts speaking again. "If you're concerned about being the first group to try uncharted routes, don't be. My team will go first. You guys just focus on training the new scavengers and bleeding out our current scavenge points. We'll get a feel for the new territory before sending in anyone else."

"What if you run into the others?" Andrea asks.

"There's no proof any of them are still alive," Addie says. "The boys haven't been spotted for almost two years. If they did attempt a mass scale relocation it likely ended in a massacre on their end."

"You mean to say," Andrea cuts in, "the unknown parts of the labyrinth killed them?"

"Would you shut up already?" Jay says. "Collin and Addie are right. Stop arguing about it when you should be paying more attention to keeping your team in one piece."

There's a crash from within the room. I flinch. Several voices drift out, telling Andrea to calm down.

"Watch it, Jay," Theo says.

"What? I'm just saying what everyone else was thinking."

"We're all on edge after what happened today," Collin says, when Andrea starts shouting at Jay again. "I think it's best we all get some rest now. We'll meet again before heading out tomorrow, when we're more clear-headed."

I realize this is the end of the meeting and I have to move if I don't want to be caught eavesdropping. I hurry back to the girls' room, slipping into my blankets as quietly as possible. Seconds after I've settled, Andrea and a few other female scavengers come in, but Addie isn't among them. Is she still back talking to Collin, or is she putting away her experiments?

It doesn't really matter where Addie is right now. What matters is what Andrea said Addie possesses – a map of the labyrinth.

The next morning I concede that Andrea might have meant Addie has a mental map. But even for someone as smart as Addie, wouldn't it be impossible to remember all the twists and turns of a labyrinth through which she never journeys?

I don't know what I'd do if I knew for sure Addie had a map. Part of me just wants to see it, even if it's an incomplete map. It's not that I plan to leave Fates. I know I could never face the monsters like the scavengers do. But I've never even been through Fates' front door. I'd like to see what it looks like in the form of ink traced on parchment.

When I sit with Addie after breakfast I don't ask her about the map. I know I can't because she'd figure out I was eavesdropping. Instead I ask her about the creatures she mentioned yesterday, during her story of the Executioner.

"*Harpyiae* means 'snatchers' in Ancient Daedalic, since there isn't a word for 'screechers'. *Leo nemeum* means 'lion of the temple' because they're known to make their dens in fallen temples. They're very large cats with black pelts impervious to metal."

"There are temples in the labyrinth?"

"Destroyed temples. Some think they used to be resting places for Icarii travelling through the labyrinth

– checkpoints, if you will. Now they're fairly useless, often dangerous ruins. There aren't any near Fates, although there are two on our various scavenge routes. The scavengers avoid them, naturally, although none of them are inhabited by *leo nemeum* any more. One was, many years ago, but the *leo nemeum* were killed when the temple roof caved in while they slept. A planned assault, naturally."

Today, Addie has two bowls next to her, along with her regular assortment of blades and hide. She picks up an arrowhead. "I'm surprised you remembered the Executioner's tale well enough to ask about it today, after all the commotion yesterday. I assumed, if anything, you'd ask about the *skorpios*."

"Scorpion?" I ask.

"Yes. A simple Daedalic name. The beasts themselves are far more interesting." Addie dips the arrowhead in the bowl that isn't steaming as she says this. It comes away covered in dark red. "Ryan's lucky he was stung by the pincers. The poison there isn't as concentrated as in the tail. If he'd been struck by the tail, he would have died before reaching Fates. Even before Kyle slew the beast, most likely."

The door opens then and Ryan himself comes in, supported by Cassie. I figured Ryan wouldn't be scavenging today, but I wasn't sure until now. He's limping and I'm sure his leg is still bandaged under his britches.

Addie makes a shooing motion at me with her hand. "If you're going to stay, shift down, unless you expect a temporary cripple to climb over the bench just so you don't have to move."

I blush, quickly scooting down the bench. I didn't realize Ryan would be coming to sit with Addie, otherwise I would have moved right away. If I'd known, I likely wouldn't have come to speak with Addie at all.

"Not a cripple," Ryan says, as Cassie helps him slide onto the bench.

"*Temporary* cripple," Addie stresses.

"Do you want me to stay?" Cassie asks Ryan.

"I'm sure you have work to do," Addie says, "as do we. If you're needed I'll send her to fetch you." Addie indicates me when she says this.

Cassie still hesitates a moment before leaving. I don't continue asking Addie about the labyrinth, even after Cassie's gone. Now that Ryan's here, I'm far less willing to speak. The regular chalky quality is returning to my mouth just by sitting next to him. Although there's already a good distance between us, I have the urge to shift farther down the bench.

"May I remind you again," Addie says to me, "you don't need to be here. I need to speak with Ryan now and won't have time for your mindless curiosity so, unless you plan to make some headway with your sewing for once, there's no reason for you to stay."

I can't tell if Addie genuinely wants to speak to Ryan alone or if she's just being mean. I only nod in reply, turning my attention to the blanket I'm stitching together. A few days ago, Cassie gave me some pieces of cloth to sew together into a new blanket. As soon as she handed them to me I knew they were from an Icarii robe. Maybe they're even from my old robe.

I start on the blanket in earnest because I don't want to return to Elle so soon. I only just came to Addie a few minutes ago and, after Elle's comments about Ryan last night, I'm even less comfortable with Elle than usual.

Addie begins moving her supplies to the side. Once she's cleared a spot in front of her, she pulls a sheet of rolled-up parchment from her supply basket. An ink jar and a quill made from a black feather follow. "We'll begin with the usual. Details and observations, no matter how small. Whatever you can remember."

Ryan doesn't speak right away. He's staring at the bowls Addie has moved farther down the table. "Is that my blood?"

"Yes," Addie says, dipping her quill in the ink jar. "Please begin."

Ryan starts describing the stinger. His tone is as impassive as always despite the fact he's talking about a monster that almost killed him. Apparently its skin was shiny and like armour. It was dark but not quite black, reflecting a rusted, reddish colour in the sunlight. Its eyes were tiny and black and well protected. Its mouth was its most obvious weak point but in order to get to it one had to get past its pincers, which – due to its speed – would be nearly impossible.

"Kyle managed it," Addie says.

Ryan doesn't say anything.

"He told us in extensive, redundant and poor detail how he defeated the *skorpios* in a stroke of heroism and saved you."

"Is that supposed to be a question?" Ryan asks.

"Tell me what happened in the fight with the *skorpios*. In actual detail, if you wouldn't mind."

"Kyle already told you."

"In actual detail," Addie repeats crisply. "A new scavenger can hardly be expected to give a proper – if at all accurate – account of a fight with a monster."

"He ran right into it," Ryan says, anger seeping into his voice. "I told him not to go ahead. He did. Ran right into it around a corner. I barely managed to shoot at it in time to keep it off him. Right between the eyes. Arrow didn't pierce, but distracted it, made it change targets. I yelled at him to run, but he didn't. I tried to pull him up. The stinger came at us. I shoved him out of the way and tripped. The stinger got me in the leg. It switched targets. It surrounded Kyle with its pincers. It was going to hit him with its tail. I screamed at him to use the spear, put it through the stinger's mouth. He listened at the last moment. After that he managed to roll away before the stinger could crush him. While it died he got up and ran. A minute later he came back with Andrea and Theo."

"Hm." Addie has been making notes on the scroll. Her writing is a tiny chicken scrawl that I doubt I could read even right side up. "Why did it switch targets?"

"Kyle's hood fell back. He didn't have it attached right. Again. That might have been it."

"Hm." Addie adds another note. "Why didn't you leave him before you were attacked?"

Ryan's jaw clenches.

"Normally," Addie says, "you'd leave him and be right in doing so. If your partner freezes, you flee. Isn't that the rule?"

"The spear Theo gave him," Ryan says. "Sybil made that. He wouldn't let it go. If he'd let it go, I would have taken it and left."

"Sentimentality? Strange, for you. Still, quite easily understandable in this instance. And – in this instance – advantageous to us. That's one *skorpios* less in the labyrinth and one giant ego boost for a fledgling scavenger. A pity you didn't bring back any collectibles for me. I'll just have to hope Theo and Andrea harvest something good today, if the corpse isn't already ravaged. Typically you have more presence of mind to bring something for me. What happened?"

I expect Ryan to say that he was poisoned or attacked, since under the circumstances Addie's request is ridiculous. Instead he says: "I was pissed."

"Anger clouding your judgement? Perhaps you're more like yesterday's foe than we give you credit for." Addie suddenly looks at me. "*Skorpios* are easily enraged. If a particular target has enraged them, they'll focus solely on that target until it's poisoned, ripped apart and half in the *skorpios'* stomach. Although, I suppose, after yesterday's findings, they must have the same reaction to bright colours as other labyrinth creatures." Addie turns back to Ryan, waving in my general direction as she does so. "She likes monster stories while I baby-sit her."

I blush and drop my gaze, surprised that I have to fight the urge to glare at Addie. Typically I take her mean comments in stride, preferring her aloof dislike of me to Elle's bizarre clingy behaviour, but for her to insult me in front of someone else is too much, even if it's someone who doesn't like me anyway.

Ryan glances at me when Addie says this, but only for a moment before he turns back to Addie. She starts asking him about the feel of the stinger's venom, from the initial puncture to his journey back to Fates to the medical procedure. She questions him aggressively so that he must be reliving it four times over. If I were being questioned like this about something so painful I'm sure I'd cry and clam up. Ryan answers with as much indifference as if he's describing the taste of gruel, even when he describes how he could feel the venom coursing through his veins and burning him from the inside.

"It must have actually burned you a little, considering all the blisters." Addie makes an adjustment to one of her earlier notes. "Any other relevant observations?"

Ryan shakes his head. Addie dips her quill back in the ink jar. "Alright. Now, let's go through it all again, in case we missed something."

An hour later Addie's scroll is filled with notes and scribbles on both sides and Ryan has gone through a full flask of water. She finally dismisses Ryan, directing me to go fetch Cassie for him.

"Don't bother her," Ryan says, meaning Cassie. Then, speaking to Addie but looking at me, he says, "She can take me back, since she's not doing anything."

I look at the basically untouched blanket pieces in my hands, instantly sheepish.

"Brilliant idea," Addie says, with no enthusiasm. She says to me: "Please don't come back when you're done dropping him off. I need to sort through this and it's bad enough knowing you'll be back to disturb me tomorrow."

My face heats in embarrassment and anger. The last thing I need is Ryan and Addie joining forces to belittle me. I push myself up and scramble to get over the bench, wanting to be away from them as soon as possible. My dress snags on the bench and I grab the nearest thing to balance myself, which ends up being Ryan's shoulder.

"Perhaps we *should* disturb Cassie," Addie says. "If this one needs the help of a temporary cripple to stand upright, I doubt she'll be able to help you back to your room."

Ryan reaches to flick my hand off his shoulder, but I've already yanked my hand back. On my feet properly now, I go over to Ryan's side and stand there. For a moment, I'm unsure of what to do. Then I move to slip my arm under his shoulders.

"Are you an idiot?" Ryan demands, shoving me away from him. "I can get up on my own."

Which he does, albeit with some difficulty. Once he's up, he leans on me, an arm around my shoulders. I have to bite back from commenting that this is the exact position I tried to get us in before. I know he'll just snap at me if I say that, which will probably prompt something snide from Addie.

I support Ryan to the main room. Cassie sees us and immediately drops her medical supplies to come over.

"Thanks Clara," she says. "I'll take him from here."

"Don't worry about it," Ryan says. Cassie still tries to support him. Instead of shoving her back like he did me moments before, he stops her with a light touch to her arm. "Cassie, go back to work."

Cassie doesn't seem to want to, but eventually she listens. I know she watches us until we disappear down the next hall. At the door to the boys' room, Ryan says: "Come in and help me down."

I haven't been in the boys' room before. I've never even seen inside. I'm a bit disappointed to find it's identical to the girls' room, but I suppose that's only fair. As Ryan directs me to a bed to the right, near the door, I realize there's no one else in the room.

"What are you going to do now?" Ryan asks as I help him ease down to his blankets. "Sewing?"

A snide note has entered his voice. Despite that, I nod, since it's true I'll go back to sewing with Elle after this. I may even go back for the blanket and finally get a serious start on it. I just have to get away from Ryan first.

I'm relieved when he's finally down, quickly pulling my hands back and planning to make my retreat just as quick. Before I've so much as straightened up, Ryan grabs my hands again. He yanks me down so suddenly I trip and fall on top of him. He flips me over in an instant so that my back presses into the blankets and he's looming above me. I gasp for breath as much as in surprise and he covers my mouth.

"Scream if you want," Ryan says, "but no one will hear you. Have you noticed that aspect of Fates? I bet you haven't. You're not exactly sharp. The walls are soundproofed – all of them. It's why nothing has discovered our base, because nothing can hear us. No one can hear you now, except me. Not that I expect you'd say anything if anyone *could* hear you." Ryan removes his hand, glaring down at me. "You're a mute little mouse, aren't you? Mice don't survive in the labyrinth, even when their older brother's a warrior."

I want to scream. I try to scream, even if Ryan's telling the truth about the walls. My lips don't move. The sound doesn't even lodge in my throat. There's no sound at all.

"I thought maybe I was wrong about you," Ryan says, "on that first day, when you made it over the wall. Of course I was right in the end. You're just another useless coward who can't get over your first day in the labyrinth – except you're worse than most. You have your brother to hide behind. It made me wonder how you'd act without your brother around to coddle you. So?" Ryan's pupils have grown wide, making his eyes seem impossibly dark. "What are you going to do, *Clara?*"

It's the first time Ryan's said my name. I hate it, the way he says it. I never wanted to hear anyone say that name in such a horrible voice.

"Nothing?" Ryan scoffs. "Of course. Just like your first day, in front of that digger, and again with the bat. Addie said she tells you a lot of stories. Did she tell you what bats do? When they hunt, they each have their own role in their groups of three." Ryan suddenly brushes the back of his left hand down my bare arm, making me tense and my hairs stand on end. "One of the bats goes for the target's arms." Ryan's hand moves down to my left thigh, where my dress rode up in the tussle. My breath catches as his fingers trace my bare skin. "Another goes for the legs. And the last one..." Ryan reaches up to my face, to cup my cheek, "it goes for the head. Between the three of them, they pull the target clean apart. They share the torso, when they're done feasting on the other parts. The way the bat that came after us attacked me, I'd say we got the head. You were right to be terrified of them. You reacted like any normal little mouse would. And if I hadn't had to kill it to get it off me..." Ryan suddenly grips my chin, making me look right at him, "I would have let that bat rip your head clean from your body and bloody these cute little braids."

"Stop it." My voice trembles so much I can barely get the words out. I'm seeing it again. Clara's braids. Clara's blood.

"Stop what?" Ryan asks. "Making you think about reality? You've got to wake up at some point. Collin won't be around forever and when he's gone, terrible things are going to happen to you. You'll be in this situation again, but it's going to be with someone a lot worse than me. You might not like me – I might scare you – but I can promise you the people that seem friendliest are the ones fastest to slit your throat. Unless..." Ryan's hand is still gripping my chin as his thumb grazes my lower lip, "you give them a reason not to."

I whimper before I can stop myself. Ryan's instantly repulsed, moving his hand to splay beside my head like his right one is. "I'm not going to do anything. Don't be an idiot. I don't touch mice. They disgust me."

"Then let me go," I whisper, barely able to get the words past my lips.

"What was that?" Ryan asks. "Speak up, Clara."

My eyes start stinging and I feel a tear slip down my cheek. I want Collin or Andrea or Theo. Anyone who would make Ryan go away.

"I can't believe you can still cry. Haven't you used up all your tears by now? I bet that first day of yours wasn't even so bad. I bet you heard a screecher in the distance. Or maybe your slippers tore and your feet blistered. Is that why you kept crying for hours and hours while we tried to get the three of you idiots back to Fates alive?"

I reach to brush away one of my tears, but Ryan catches my wrist. He squeezes so tightly I flinch in pain.

"Want to know what happened on my first day?" Ryan asks. "A group from Fates found me after a flock of screechers slaughtered my entire group of Icarii. Before we got halfway back to Fates, my saviours suddenly split up. One of them took me with them, but wouldn't tell me what was happening. We were the lucky ones: all three bats went after us. They attacked my saviour, ripped him into six parts in front of me. They slunk off in three corners and feasted on his head and arms and legs.

"I couldn't escape without passing them. His torso was still there, in the middle, his sheathed sword still attached. So I went to his torso and pulled out the sword. The handle was bloody. He'd been reaching for it when the bats descended on him. I took the sword and I crept up to the closest bat and I sliced off its head. That's how I found out they have surprisingly weak bones, easy to crack and cut. The second one heard me before I could attack it. It pounced on me and would have torn off my arms, but someone from Fates arrived and shot it. Sybil saw her friend's dead body, and she still held it together enough to save me. It was my first day in the labyrinth and I held it together enough to try and fight the bats – I'd just turned eleven and I could still do more than you did, and you hadn't even seen anyone killed."

"I saw her killed!" I scream at him, tears streaming down my face.

Ryan seems surprised, but only for a second. "So you saw a fellow Icarii get killed, huh? You'd already seen death and you still did nothing to try and stop it. You just cried. Someone like you is never going to make it here. You might as well just step outside hoodless – save some rations."

I slap him. Ryan's eyes spark and he grabs onto my arms, but before he gets my right one, I slap him again, harder. It feels good, hitting him, and I like the red mark it leaves on his face.

"You think a screecher would let you go if you slapped it?" Ryan snaps. "They'd bite out your throat before–"

I scream at him and pound on his chest. Startled, Ryan backs up from me a little. It's enough for me to try and slide out from under him. He grabs me by the waist, keeping me from completely getting free. But I'm half up now and I see something. He's wearing his weapons belt and he has a dagger sheathed in back. I reach over him and pull out the dagger. I get a hold on its hilt seconds before Ryan slams me back onto the blankets.

He's furious as he looms over me, but then he sees the dagger I'm holding between us, tip pointed at him. He sneers. "As if you would–"

I jab the dagger into his wounded thigh. Ryan gasps in pain as blood pulses out. I dig the dagger in deeper and he buckles over, his head right in the crook of my neck. I can feel his ragged breath down the front of my shirt. Something about how it gets quick when I twist the dagger excites me. He's terrified me and treated me so cruelly and all it takes is me doing one thing to make him this weak.

The excitement gives way to a numbing cold when I realize what I've done. I shove Ryan off me and scramble to my feet. The dagger's still in his leg, now soaked in blood. His britches are soaking through too and his chest is heaving in quick breaths. His eyes are glazed, but as I stare at him they start to rapidly regain focus.

In seconds I'm in the hall and shutting the door to the boys' room tight behind me. I hurry to the girls' room where Elle is on her bed, making patterns in 'Prosper's' ripped shirt instead of stitching it. When she sees me she smiles.

The next thing I know I'm throwing myself at her. She drops the shirt as I cling to her and sob into her shoulder.

"What's wrong, Clara?" she asks, hugging me back instantly. Even though there's tendrils of concern in her voice, she mostly sounds excited.

"I'm horrible," I sob. "I don't know what's happening to me, but I'm becoming horrible."

"It's alright." Elle smooths my hair. "You're with me again now. I forgive you."

When supper comes I tell Elle I want to stay in the girls' room. Elle asks if I mean to eat supper with Collin again, but I tell her I don't want to do that tonight. She's so happy she goes to get food for both of us.

For the whole day I've been waiting for someone to come retrieve me, and that worry doesn't lift as the evening passes. I'm sure any moment someone will call me out to speak to me about what happened. What if they kick me out of Fates for hurting Ryan? Collin surely wouldn't let them do that, not after I explain what happened. But even if Ryan was bullying me so terribly, does it excuse the fact I stabbed him?

Elle doesn't notice anything's wrong. She chatters happily, seeming in a better mood than she has been since I started spending time with Addie. She even fetches the blanket pieces for me so I can get to work. I'd like to finish this, at least, before I'm dragged out to answer for my crime.

When I first reached Fates, I thought it was a haven from the monsters in the labyrinth. Then I thought the girls' room was a haven from the bustle of my fellow Icarii, and after that the mess hall was a haven from Elle's suffocating presence. But even there, Addie was rude to me and I was never comfortable. I was never comfortable in any of my supposed havens. None of them are substitutes for my flat, back in the tower. I was always comfortable there. Even when we had company, I could retreat to my room. I didn't even mind when Mother came in to wake me up when I slept in five minutes past my alarm or to put away laundry while I was studying. I would always end up helping her with the laundry. I loved the smell of the fresh clothes, but not as much as I loved Mother's fleeting thanks.

If Mother and Father were here, they'd make sure I didn't get in trouble for what happened with Ryan. They'd want him in trouble. Father would bring him to the priest, and Mother would speak to his parents, and one or both of them would tell Auntie, and she would spread nasty rumours about Ryan and his whole family. They would each protect me, in their own way, even if I asked them to let it lie. Even if all I wanted from them was a hug.

But Mother and Father aren't here. The closest thing I have is Collin, and Ryan may have already turned him against me. I don't know what I'll do if that happens.

When Collin comes to ask me to supper Elle happily tells him I've already eaten with her. Collin is surprised and a little worried, but ultimately leaves me be. I'm sure it's the last time he'll be worried about me, after somebody at supper tells him what happened.

After supper, Collin comes to collect me for our nightly chat. Elle is reluctant as always to let me go and, tonight, I'm even more reluctant than her. Still, this might be my only chance to explain to Collin what really happened –

who knows what Ryan's told him? – so I steal what little courage I have and leave the girls' room.

To my surprise, Collin is as sweet and caring as usual. Our talk goes as it usually does. Gradually, I begin to relax. He must not know yet.

It's late when Collin falls into a silent mood. Then he says in a serious voice, "There's something we have to talk about."

I start picking the tear in my dress apart so quickly I scratch my leg underneath.

"My team's going to be gone longer tomorrow," Collin says. "For the next week, we'll be out late. Some days it might be really late. As much as I want to talk to you every day, I don't want you losing sleep. If I'm not back by suppertime, eat with the others and get to bed when you're tired. After this week we'll go back to talking like usual. I promise."

I'm so relieved he didn't mention Ryan I almost forget what he's telling me would worry his sister. And it worries me. The thought of not seeing Collin for a week, coupled with the idea of something happening to him in those long hours he'll be gone, is unbearable. I remember what Ryan said would happen to me when Collin's gone. Surely he was just saying that to be cruel. I'll be fine, and so will Collin, and in a week we'll spend time together like this again.

"Be safe?" I say to him, and it comes out more of a question than a statement.

"Of course." Collin squeezes my knee. "Don't worry, Clara. In a week everything will be back to normal, I promise."

It's hard not to worry when I find out Ryan's spending another day in Fates instead of returning to scavenging. I hear it when Elle and I go for breakfast, when one of the new Icarii is complaining about having to look after the kids while Cassie looks after Ryan.

Instead of going to sit with Addie, I stay with Elle after breakfast. Elle doesn't ask if I'm leaving, but when I stay she's visibly pleased. She grows steadily happier as the morning progresses. Until Cassie comes in, that is.

"Clara," Cassie says, seeming confused even though she's the one addressing me, "Ryan wants you. He said yesterday you agreed to do something for him."

The needle I'm holding falls out of my hand.

"Should I tell him you're busy?" Cassie asks.

Elle's nodding at me, but I know I can't do that. I don't know what it is Ryan wants with me, but if he sent Cassie – with a request worded like that – he might mean he'll tell the others what I did if I don't comply.

Trying to keep my hands from shaking, I lay aside my sewing and push to my feet. Elle scowls as I leave, but at the last moment calls out for me to come back the second I'm done.

Ryan's sitting in the main room, at the end of the table

closest to Fates' entrance. It's the same end they cleared to treat him two days ago.

"We're doing lessons now," Cassie says to Ryan, "but just wave to me if you need anything. Gus or one of the others can take over."

Ryan thanks her and Cassie goes to start herding the younger Icarii together. They gather in a semi-circle in the empty space of the main room near Gus's door. The kids sit and watch as Cassie starts drawing something in the dirt with an old, rusted short sword. She and the other older Icarii give the kids daily lessons five times a week, something like school back in Daedalum. They're doing maths right now, by the looks of it. Gina, the only child too young for these advanced lessons, is sitting with Gus as usual. She's talking as she makes her wooden horse and soldier butt heads, but I don't know if she's speaking to Gus or to herself.

Not looking directly at Ryan, I start to slide in across from him.

"No," Ryan says. He motions to the spot next to him. I hesitate a moment before rounding the table and climbing over the bench. I try to keep a wide distance between us but, below the table, Ryan grabs my arm and tugs me closer. I'm not right next to him, but close enough for him to whisper without alerting the others. I wait for a threat of some sort.

"You haven't bothered to learn how to make arrows, have you?" Ryan says, in his normal tone of voice. He's taken a stick from the pile in front of him. I realize there's also a pile of feathers and arrowheads, and a bowl of some kind of grey cream.

"It's simple," Ryan says, pulling out a dagger from his belt, "so even you should be able to manage it."

My gaze is riveted on the blade as he starts cutting curls of wood from the length of the stick. "Cut off all the bumps so that it's smooth and aerodynamic – so that it can fly through the air." He finishes smoothing off the stick and starts cutting an indent in the top. "You have to make a nook at the top, where the arrowhead can rest when you attach it." Ryan lays the dagger down between us and reaches for an arrowhead. He sticks the oval end of it in the grey cream and then sticks that end into the nook of the arrow's shaft. "Make sure the pointy part is out straight, alright? That's sort of the key to arrows being effective. Then you leave it to dry and – after the arrowhead's fixed in place – you attach the feathers."

Ryan leaves that arrow to dry and picks up another that's already dried. He sticks the blunted end of the stick in the cream and picks up a feather. He presses the feather to the end, so that it sticks in the cream. "Three feathers, like this, at this angle. Make sure they're dried at the right angle before adding the others, which would go here and here." He points to the spots. "Like a triangle, see? You did do shapes in school, didn't you?"

I glare at him, which he ignores. Ryan carefully sets down the stick against another, so that it doesn't roll the drying feather/cream mash on its side. Then he picks up the dagger and holds it up to me. At the last moment he spins it so the hilt's facing me. "Here. Get started."

Hesitantly, I wrap my hand around the hilt. I realize it's the dagger from last night.

"Don't stab anyone with it."

My gaze snaps to Ryan. He's already turned back to the pile of arrows. He hands me an untouched stick. "Hurry up. I lost more arrows than I planned to the other day."

"I don't want to make arrows for you," I murmur.

"And I didn't want my wound reopened." Ryan picks up a half-finished arrow and a feather. "Unfortunately – and mysteriously – it started bleeding again yesterday. Cassie saw to it. If it had been Addie, I'm sure she would have questioned the strange shape in which the wound reopened. I might show it to her later, see what she thinks."

With a jerk of my wrist I shave off a kernel of wood.

"Besides," Ryan adds, "you're making them for everyone. I'm not the only archer."

I keep working on the arrow. I hate that the idea of making arrows for the others makes me feel better, since the idea came from Ryan.

Suddenly, Ryan catches my right wrist, stopping me from moving the blade.

"You're holding it like you're cutting carrots," Ryan says. He forces my thumb higher and moves my forefinger, then clenches his hand over mine to make my hold tighten. "There."

"Am I cutting wood now?" I mutter.

"You're cutting bone."

I glance sharply at Ryan, but he's entirely focused on the arrow and feather in his hand. Hesitantly, I turn back to smoothing down the wood. Ryan and I don't talk after that and I'm glad. I just focus on preparing the arrow shaft and attaching the arrowheads while he affixes the feathers. If I ever fall behind and he has nothing to do he just sits there. I always feel like he's watching me, but when I risk a look at him, he's watching Cassie teach the kids.

After lessons are done and the kids are led into the mess hall, Cassie comes over to help Ryan to supper. Before she reaches us Ryan says to me, under his breath, "Finish a dozen in full before you even think about eating."

As Cassie helps Ryan up, she says I should join them for supper. I mumble that I'd like to keep working and she leaves it at that. I find myself watching Ryan as he limps to the mess hall. His limp isn't nearly as bad as yesterday. I hope that means he'll be healed soon and return to scavenging.

"Mind if we sit with you?"

I glance up to find Gus and Gina. I shake my head and Gus sits across from me. Gina climbs onto the bench beside him, where she kneels so as to better access the pile of sticks. She seems to be using them as a forest for her horse and soldier.

Gus must see me peeking at the emergency exit because he says, "I'll hear it, if someone comes in that way. The only one who knocks quiet enough that I'd have to be right next to it is Ryan. The others hammer like their hands are about to fall off."

"You can hear them?" I ask quietly. "Aren't the walls soundproofed?"

"Only the outer walls," Gus says. "Inner walls and doors aren't a problem, otherwise our secret knock would have a few flaws."

"Let me in," Gina squeaks as she wiggles the horse around. "Let me in, let me in!"

Gina moves the soldier through the sticks with her other hand, saying, "This is my castle! Go away!"

Gus chuckles and ruffles Gina's hair. She's so absorbed in her game, she doesn't so much as look at him.

"Sick of sewing, huh?" Gus says, gesturing to the arrow material. "Did Collin ask Ryan to teach you?"

I'm about to shake my head, but on second thought I shrug. Maybe Collin did ask Ryan to teach me this, last night or this morning before he left. Collin seems set on finding things to keep me distracted and away from Elle.

"You're lucky you've got your brother here," Gus tells me as he watches Gina play with her toys. "I always envied Icarii siblings chosen together, but for you two to find each other after so long, that's even luckier. It must be down to the Fey."

"The Fey?" I repeat.

"The spirits our group was named after." Gus waves his hand around, indicating the safe haven. "Addie says it's an old word for Fates. She also says the stories about them are silly and fake, made up by desperate Icarii trying to come to terms with the labyrinth. I think there's more to it than that, though. Not that I believe in the Fey, but I think they mean something important."

"What are the stories?"

"Oh, nothing much. Old stories, anyway. Supposedly there used to be three spirits that knew the fate of every Icarii to enter the labyrinth. The first one would lead the Icarii destined to become angels to the exit, while the second would lead astray those destined to fail. But it's said the third one liked to meddle with Fate. Sometimes she'd lead Icarii previously meant to become angels astray; other times, she'd lead those doomed to fail out of the labyrinth. The idea was, if a Fey appeared before you, then you had to find out which one it was and, if it was the third, why she was there. It's said there was one Icarii whose fate the Fey couldn't see. This frustrated the third one because she couldn't play her trick, so instead of leading the Icarii out or astray, she decided to play a game. There were seven other Icarii travelling with the fateless Icarii, all destined to make it out of the labyrinth. The third Fey stole the fates of these seven, turning them into prizes that she dispersed throughout the labyrinth. She promised the fateless Icarii that if she uncovered one of these prizes, the fate would become hers and lead her to Alyssia, where she would become an angel."

When Gus finishes, he's stroking Gina's hair again. Gina's stopped playing to listen to his story, toys forgotten in the mass of sticks.

"What happened to Fateless?" Gina asks.

"Nobody knows," Gus says. "It's said not even the Fey knew. Not being able to see what happened to her drove all three insane and the Fey themselves did what they were forbidden to do – they looked into their own futures to see if they'd ever know the fate of the fateless girl."

"And?" Gina breaths.

"And what the Fey saw made them disappear." Gus waves his hand through the air in front of him.

"Gone forever into mist that wafts through the labyrinth, seeking the fates to which they are now forever blind, and searching for the one fate they could never see."

Gina stares at Gus, open-mouthed. Then she claps her hands excitedly and requests another story. Gus ruffles her hair again. "Later, kiddo. How about Clara takes you for supper? You're hungry, aren't you?"

"I don't want her to take me." Gina tugs on Gus's sleeve. "You!"

"I can't, Gene. I've got to watch the door. You know that."

"I can watch it," I hear myself say. "I want to finish these anyway."

"You'd do that?" Gus asks.

"Of course." My mouth is getting dry, but I make myself keep talking, "What's the secret knock again? It's been a while since I've heard it."

"Oh, right." Gus knocks four times on the table, pauses, knocks twice, then knocks four times again, pauses, and knocks three times. "Got it?"

I nod, unable to use my voice any more. Gus thanks me again and takes a very hyper Gina into the mess hall. I realize too late that Gina's forgotten her toys. I collect them to give to her later, so they don't get lost with the arrow wood. As I get back to work I think about Gus's story. There's one thing I don't understand. If the Fey knew how to get out of the labyrinth, what made them stay? Did they enjoy toying with the Icarii so much or did the gods curse them to never leave the labyrinth? Why wouldn't they escape?

The question nags at me and I shake my head, as if that will get rid of it. My greasy braids whip against my shoulder before settling. I shouldn't dwell on the Fey. Gus admitted that not even he thinks they exist.

It's only a silly story, anyway.

As Collin expected, he didn't get back until very late. It's only when I wake up the next day that I find out from Cassie that he got back at all. And now they're gone again.

At the same time Cassie tells me the arrow supplies are out when I'm ready. I take it that means Ryan wants me to make more arrows. Sure enough, when I finally break free from Elle, Ryan's sitting where he was yesterday. He doesn't speak to me except to say I'm not smoothing the shafts very well and I'll have to go back over the ones from yesterday. He also says I'll have to reattach the arrowhead and feathers of several arrows and, in the process, will probably destroy the shaft and have to start all over. After he's had his fill of criticizing me, we return to the same silence as yesterday. I want to ask if Collin requested he do this, but, like with so many things, the words can't climb their way up my throat. So I make the arrows in silence until Cassie comes to collect Ryan again. Even though he hasn't told me to work through supper I do anyway, in case those orders carry over from yesterday.

The next day, before I go to make arrows, Elle says something strange to me. Rather, she says something stranger than usual, and even more out of the blue.

"Ryan saved Cassie on her first day." Elle waits until

I look at her to continue. "She's stuck by him ever since. She's the first homemaker he's ever gotten along with. It's not very surprising. She's rather pretty and very helpful around Fates and they're the same age. Don't you think they look cute together?"

I quickly realize Elle has misunderstood my situation with Ryan. I agree with her that Ryan and Cassie are very cute together, hoping this will sate her. It seems to work, but a few minutes later she starts talking about how sweet it is that Cassie's looking after Ryan while he's sick. She tells me that whenever Ryan's injured, Cassie always looks after him and is the most concerned. Later, when I get back from making arrows, Elle starts talking about them again.

Two days later, when Ryan returns to scavenging, Elle stops talking about him and Cassie entirely. She's extremely content the first morning Ryan's gone, until I leave to make arrows on my own. I suggest she come out and help me, but she refuses, saying I should bring the materials in here. I tell her I can't because that would be too messy. She scowls after that and makes some kind of comment about Fates having "a mountain of arrows by now" while I leave.

Making arrows alone is the most content I've been in a long time. I can focus on the task and if I start to think about something that makes me unhappy, I just have to watch the younger Icarii playing for a while to feel better. Soon I find myself listening to Cassie's lessons. I wonder if, one day, I might be able to help teach. I wasn't at the top of my class but I did alright in school. Well enough to tutor Clara sometimes.

I shut the memory down instantly, locking my gaze on the younger Icarii while they play. This is my world now. These children and these wooden walls and this dirt floor.

The only Clara here is me.

Someone shakes me awake. When I see it's Addie and that everyone else is still sleeping I panic. I went to bed so excited for the week to be up and Collin to come back, but what if Addie's here to tell me something's happened to him?

"It's Collin," Addie whispers, realizing my fears.

I shove myself up so quickly, I almost tangle in the blankets. When I find my feet I follow Addie quickly but quietly out of the girls' room. She leads me to the main room where a figure is waiting. Collin. Uninjured. My heart leaps in relief.

As we draw closer, I notice the expression on Collin's face. It's hard, removed. He waves a hand and Addie silently disappears down the hall to the bedrooms. I glance after her, then turn my attention back to Collin, confused.

"What's going on?" I ask, unnerved by the way he's looking at me.

"My team was exploring new routes," Collin says coolly. "We found a screecher's nest."

My voice shakes. "Are you OK?"

Collin speaks over me. "Did you know screechers collect trophies from their prey? That's why they're also called snatchers. They collect colourful parts of their prey – clothes, weapons, accessories – anything that attracts and keeps their attention. They also like hair. Brightly coloured hair that catches the light. Red hair. Blonde hair." Collin takes my braid in his hand, the one with the ribbon. "They have this habit of, when they feast on prey with such hair, keeping the head as a prize."

"That's horrible." My voice catches before I've finished.

"Not as horrible as being the prey." Collin's hand clenches around my braid. Then he lets me go, digging his hand inside his jacket as he turns from me, walking away. He pulls something out but I can't see what it is. "I found something in the nest. Want to see it?"

I shake my head. He glances over my shoulder and notices the action. "Oh, you want to see it alright."

Collin walks over to me and I look away, not willing to see what's in his hands. He holds it up to my face, right by my left cheek. The scent of rotting flesh is so powerful it makes my stomach heave. It's all I can do not to throw up.

"I think you lost this," Collin says. "Look at it. I want to be sure."

I squeeze my eyes shut.

"Look at it!"

Collin physically jerks my head to face the object, which swats against my cheek. It sticks there a moment, as if covered by some kind of sticky gel. My eyes fly open as I gag, and then I gag again when I see what's in front of me. A mangy, bloody, blonde braid. Tied at the bottom with a dirty ribbon.

A ribbon just like the one in my hair.

"I should have seen it earlier," Collin says. "I did, but I ignored it. I ignored the instincts that have kept me alive all this time. Your face, your voice, the way you carry yourself and the way you act and your dull helplessness – even the shade of your eyes – I knew it was all wrong. But I believed it anyway, because I wanted it so badly. I wanted you to be her. But you aren't. You never were."

Collin starts walking away from me again. I try to say his name, but it's all too much. The smell and the braid and what he's saying. I feel like I'm going to explode.

Collin explodes. He screams: *"You're not Clara!"*

For a moment I think he's going to throw the braid at me, but he doesn't. He clutches it tightly in one hand, as if to protect it, then he marches back to me. I try to back up, but I hit one of the supports. Collin slams his free hand into the pillar, inches from my head. I flinch.

"Why did you do it?" he growls. His voice rises instantly. "Why did you pretend to be her? Did you rip this ribbon from her body? Was she still alive when you took it?!"

Collin physically tears the ribbon from my hair and I squeal. He holds it inches from my eyes. "You knew I was in charge, didn't you, and then when I mistook you for my sister I bet you thought it was your big chance to survive this nightmare! Pretend to be the boss's little sister so that he'll protect you and look after you and do everything he can to keep you safe and happy! Nice set-up, was it?" Collin's voice rises to a scream. "Was it?!"

I try to say, "It wasn't like that," but all that comes out are whimpers. I see Collin's hand squeeze into a fist around the ribbon. The next thing I know, pain explodes in the side of my face. My legs buckle under me, but before I can fall, Collin punches me in the stomach. I gasp.

"You think this is bad?" he hisses. "How do you think it felt to leave my sister safe and sleeping, only to find her rotting *head* in a screecher's nest?"

I slide to the ground, fingers shaking as I touch my stomach, my face, as if I can brush away the pain like I brush away my tears.

Spit lands on my arm. "You're just like all the monsters in this graveyard. You're worse than the monsters, because they can't help being disgusting and vicious and cruel. You chose to do this. You sullied my sister's name and memory."

"No," I wheeze. "I'd never do that! Clara was–"

"Don't you dare say her name!" Collin yells. "It doesn't belong to you! You're not Clara!"

He keeps screaming it over and over: *"You're not Clara!"*

His face is red and his breathing is ragged, but he keeps screaming at me and then he starts to cry. But he keeps screaming. Just like the screams I heard on my first day except, if possible, there's even more pain behind the anger.

Then there's just anger as his foot connects with my stomach.

In the morning I'm sore all over. My head hurts and my body hurts and my heart hurts. I dreamed about Clara dying again, except this time I was out there too and instead of ripping me apart the screechers kept bashing me into the ground of the labyrinth. Clara's head landed in front of me and I realized she was wearing both her ribbons and then when I looked back at her face, it was my face. That was when I realized I was actually Clara and the one who was dead was me.

Then I woke up and remembered my reality is even worse than that nightmare.

Elle is sitting beside me, the only other girl in the room, as usual. She smiles at me. "Good morning! I already went for breakfast. I only had a bit, since they wouldn't let me bring it back here today. Addie told me not to bother to bring you to the mess hall since you're skipping breakfast today. You're not missing out on much. The gruel's as papery as ever."

Collin's not letting me eat? After how he reacted last night I'm not surprised, but a cold horror is creeping over me. What if he never lets me eat again? Will I starve in here?

As I push myself up, Elle crawls over. She touches my cheek, gently, but it still stings. "I heard the other girls talking about it," she says. "Everyone probably knows by now. They'll definitely know before the day's over. They won't be happy. They'll think you pretended to be Collin's sister to get special treatment."

"But that's not true," I whisper. "I don't get special treatment."

When I think about it, though, Cassie has been working tirelessly ever since the day I reached Fates. She's always doing something or helping someone or teaching. I was mostly left to my own devices with Elle. If I was given work, it was as a distraction from boredom. Collin organized my sit-ins with Addie, who kept me entertained in her own, curt way. Collin himself said he never sent me out on water runs for a reason.

Realizing how easy I had it compared to the others, I feel horrible. But it didn't feel easy to me. It felt surreal, like a nightmare from which I couldn't wake up. Aside from some times with Collin, Addie and Elle, I was constantly reliving memories from my first day. That or trying to forget about them and my life back home. I never could.

Elle strokes my bruise again, making me wince. "You should have told me sooner that Collin wasn't your brother. You don't need such a bossy brother anyway. You have me. Right, Clara?"

I don't leave the room all day. I barely do any sewing and when I do, I prick my finger. Part of me thinks I do it on purpose. Compared to the pain still throbbing through my body, the needle prick is nothing.

Even if I'm not allowed to eat, I'm at least allowed to drink. Elle shares a flask of water with me. Today her favourite topic is how sisters are better than brothers, unless the brother is Prosper. I hardly listen at all, but I still always hear her. I can't ignore anything that reminds me of what happened last night and what's going to happen from now on.

The only time I leave the room all day is to use the washroom. I'm terrified to leave the room alone, and ask Elle to go with me. She agrees instantly, waiting right outside the door until I'm finished, then links arms with me and skips back to the girls' room.

I don't go for supper so Elle doesn't either. My stomach growls the rest of the night. The gruel isn't much to go on even when I have it twice a day. Skipping one of those meagre meals leaves me light-headed. Or maybe I have a concussion. I'm not sure how hurt I really am, let alone in what way. I don't want to check what's under my dress because I'm afraid my body will be more purple than pale.

I go to sleep early. Although no girls come into the room all day, I'm worried they'll start coming in for bed soon. Elle lies down when I do, staring at me with wide, joyous eyes. She's not tired and she makes that plain by continuously talking. When the door opens she finally falls silent. I take this chance to pretend I'm sleeping. I pretend I'm sleeping while the room fills up. I hear girls whispering and I'm sure they're talking about me.

To these whispers, I fall asleep.

The next day is exactly the same and Elle is as happy as she was when we first met. My stomach growls twice an hour. The water isn't helping and there isn't as much of it today. I'm not sure if Elle took a half-full flask at breakfast by accident or if it was handed to her on purpose.

Elle's right: everyone must know by now. Collin probably told them last night, if not sooner. I wonder what Andrea and Gus and Felix and Cassie think of me. I wonder what Theo thinks. He was always especially kind, even though I could never work up the nerve to talk to him properly. Will he think that all this time I've been hiding how horrible I really am?

I'm sure Addie isn't surprised. She always seemed suspicious. Ryan might be surprised, though, but only because he probably doesn't think I have the backbone to do what I did.

But it wasn't a matter of backbone. What it was, I don't know. Not something justifiable, I'm sure. Maybe I deserve what Collin's doing.

When supper approaches, the door opens. I freeze, worried the girl who comes in might say something to me.

Then Elle shrieks, "Boys aren't allowed in the girls' room!"

I start shaking when Collin's voice says: "Aren't you going to greet me? You were my precious little sister for a month and a half, after all."

I can't get up. I try, but I can't. Collin reaches down and yanks me roughly to my feet, spinning me to face him even as Elle snaps at him to get out.

"Remember how I was telling you I'd hunt something nice for you to eat?" Collin asks. "Well, my team struck gold today. A nice, juicy boar. You're going to come join us for a celebratory feast. Aren't you excited? Elle, you can come too, if you want."

"Clara and I are staying here!"

Collin's hold on my arm tightens so hard I know he's left another bruise. I'm worried he may break my bones. "That isn't her name, Elle, not any more. She doesn't have a name. She's nameless. Nameless. How do you like the sound of that?"

Collin is looking at me now, gaze impossibly cold. I start shaking harder, looking away. He grabs my chin and makes me look at him. "You like it, don't you? Or should we call you Screecher? It would be ironic, considering how little noise you make, but at the same time it's very fitting. After all, what you did to her was as bad as what they did, wasn't it?"

"No–"

Collin speaks clean over me. "I have a few presents for you, and you have to wear them to the feast. It's the sisterly thing to do. Here. A new dress." Collin drops the bundle under his arm at my feet. Then he draws something out of his pocket. "And new ribbons."

He holds up two long, thin strips. Although they're the same length as the ribbons, I know they're not made out of cloth. I realize what they are made out of when the smell hits me.

Collin grabs my hand, forcing it palm up even as I try to pull back. He drops the soft, squishy strips into my hand. "Ribbons of Icarus, just like the last ones. I found them in the nest, near the one you lost. Be sure to wear them and your dress to dinner. Now hurry up and change, so you don't miss the meal."

I shake my head, slowly at first, then violently. Collin forces my hand to close around the ribbons and squeezes so hard I think he'll break my fingers. "You're going to wear my wonderful gifts, Nameless, otherwise I'm going to dress you myself and – let me be honest – I'm a little clumsy when it comes to dressing other people. So you'll wear your gifts, won't you?"

Tears sting my eyes as Collin crushes my hand. I fight to make my lips work, but when I do speak my voice comes out brittle. "I didn't mean to trick you. I didn't want to, but you were so kind, and I was so scared, and I didn't know what to do. And then it was too late and I couldn't find a way to tell you the truth, because I... I didn't want to think about her being dead, and I knew if I told you it would hurt you even more than it was hurting me. She was my friend. My best friend. Pretending to be her, it was almost like it kept her alive, and I know that's no excuse, but I just wasn't ready to face it."

My voice trickles out at the end, as if I've used it all up, even though I want to say more. I haven't even apologized yet.

Collin doesn't speak for a long minute. Then he goes to the door. Over his shoulder, he says, "Be sure to tie the ribbons tightly. You don't want to lose one again."

And just like that, he's gone.

Realizing I'm still holding the ribbons, I throw them as far away from me as possible. Then I fall to my knees with a sob. Elle kneels behind me and I feel her arms wind across my chest and waist. She hugs me to her, whispering, "Do you see what a bad brother he is now? I bet you're glad we have each other. Sisters are so much more reliable than brothers. So don't worry, Clara. You'll always have me."

*Don't worry, Clara.*

I sob harder and harder.

I know I have to go to the dinner. If I don't Collin really will come back and beat me up again. After I've cried out all the tears in me and swallowed my sobs, I reach to rub my eyes. Immediately I recoil from my own hands. They smell like the ribbons.

This makes me want to cry again, but instead I pick up the dress. I realize it's my grey Icarii dress. Holding it up I see the tears haven't been fixed. There are little holes over the stomach and there's a slit in the side. The area over the chest has been half ripped open. I can't remember if it was that ripped before or not. I'm sure I would have noticed if it was.

"You can't wear that," Elle says to me, echoing my thoughts. "It's hardly even clothing any more. It's going to be like wearing a few rags to supper. Collin really has a skewed sense of evening wear. Another reason he's such a horrible brother."

Swallowing, I start stripping out of my dress. Of the two "gifts", wearing this one will be the easy part. Maybe the embarrassment of wearing something so tattered and revealing will distract me from what I'm going to put in my hair.

After changing I realize just how much of me shows through the dress. My face heats just thinking about wearing this in front of the others. It's definitely more ripped than it was before.

"It looks horrible," Elle tells me. "Maybe the ribbons will make it look better. Oh! Can I tie them for you?"

"No!" I grab Elle's arm when she starts to run to where I've thrown the ribbons. No matter how odd Elle may be, she's my only ally here now, and I do care about her. It's bad enough that I've touched those ribbons; I can't let her sully her hands too.

Elle seems hurt. I say: "I want you to tie ribbons in my hair when I have ribbons to tie in your hair."

Elle beams, thoroughly pleased. I leave her and retrieve the ribbons. My legs feel weak as I walk towards them. Tears sting at my eyes again as I stand over them. I can't do it. Even if Collin beats me up I can't touch them again.

A violent knock on the door makes me jump. Collin's voice booms: "Almost done? The boar's getting cold!"

I fall to my knees in front of the ribbons. My eyes blur from the tears as I reach for them. I close my eyes completely. If I don't look at them and don't breathe through my nose maybe I can pretend they really are ribbons. My hands shake so much I drop the first ribbon on my bare knee. I let out a shuddering sound, a cross between a gasp and a sob, before peeling it off my knee.

I get it knotted in my hair, but I pull the bow through too hard and it rips, slapping against my cheek. My stomach heaves. I'm going to throw up before I've even put anything in my stomach. I'll dry heave all over the ribbons.

Yanking the ripped ribbon from my hair, I start with the other one. I'm gentler this time. I keep telling myself it's a regular Icarus ribbon. It's like the ribbons Mother and Father always wanted me to use to tie back my hair. That's what this is. I pull the bow through carefully. It doesn't tear this time.

Collin comes in before I pick myself to my feet. He looks me over and scowls when he sees the ripped ribbon at my feet. "You broke it."

"It fell apart," I whisper.

I'm sure Collin's going to hit me, but instead he gives me a considering look. "It's fitting," he finally says. "You came here with one and now you have one again."

The relief I feel at not being hit in this instant is nothing compared to my overall terror and disgust. Collin hauls me to my feet again before I can find my feet on my own. He drags me to the door, where he pauses and says, "Are you coming, Elle? Prosper will save you some boar if you don't. Being an older brother, I know that he wants to do everything he can for his little sister."

"I'll go," Elle says, surprising me, "but only if I can sit by Clara."

"I guess you won't be coming, then," Collin says, "since there's no one with that name here."

Collin pulls me into the hall after him, slamming the door shut. Elle doesn't come out. Part of me wishes she would, since she's probably the only one who can help me get through whatever Collin has planned, but another part of me doesn't want her to witness my embarrassment. Maybe what Collin's planning might make even Elle hate me.

Collin drags me through the main room, where the young Icarii are seated at the long table, finishing their servings of boar.

"They'll go to bed when they're done," Collin says. "They won't be joining us for the actual feast. Only older Icarii have that honour. Aren't you glad you're old enough for the feast, Nameless? Or are you? I have no idea how old you actually are. Oh, well. Let's pretend you're old enough for tonight."

My blood runs cold. I dig my heels in when we reach the door to the mess hall. Collin squeezes my wrist so tightly I have to bite my lip to keep from squealing. "You're not shy, are you, Nameless? Weren't you getting used to having dinner with everyone before I left? You'll get used to it again, fast enough. It's just like swimming. You get used to it faster if someone just shoves you in the deep end." Collin opens the door, smiling a smile far worse than his fake one. This smile is entirely genuine and entirely cruel. "Can you swim, Nameless?"

I can smell the boar before I even enter the room. I could smell it in the main room, from the younger Icarii's plates, but nothing is as tempting as the scent that envelops me when I step into the mess hall. My mouth waters instantly at the scent of roasted meat. On reflex I brush the drool from my mouth. In doing so, I bring my hand close to my nose, and another scent mingles with that of cooked boar.

I go cold as my stomach heaves. It doesn't matter how delicious the boar smells or tastes; I know I won't be able to eat anything tonight. Not when every time my hand gets so much as halfway to my face I smell it. If I breathe through my nose at all I can smell it from my braid. Its scent is mixing into my hair now and the thought sickens me further. What if I can never get this smell out of my hair, out of my flesh? What if it's stuck with me forever?

That's probably what Collin wants. He's branded me with bruises and now he'll brand me with the scent of rot.

When Collin enters the room all he has to do is clear his throat to quieten the festivities. Even though it was Collin who called their attention, they all stare at me. Everyone's here: all the scavengers and Cassie and Addie. Only Gus is missing. A few of the girls are looking at me in disgust, others in pity. I see Cassie flinch at my bruises. Andrea's expression is so furious I can't bear to look at her. What if that fury is directed at me, for lying to everyone and getting special treatment?

Everyone else seems to be looking at the state of my dress. I keep the front closed as best as I can with my free hand, but there's nothing I can do about the frayed and tattered ends, nor the slits in the sides and the holes that show my stomach.

Some of the guys are looking me over in a strange way that makes me want to flee the room even more. Kyle, who's usually short with me, is staring openly. Ryan isn't looking, but he was. He was almost as obvious about it as Kyle a moment ago, but now he's scowling at his lap, red-faced. I can't bring myself to look at Theo, afraid of his reaction. But then I see Felix. He's clearly very upset and that gives me some hope. He mustn't hate me for what I did, not if he's worried about me.

Collin pulls me over to the table. He seats me next to Jay, across from Theo. Then he sits beside me, with Addie on his other side. The change in seating arrangement doesn't escape me. Is it somehow part of his plan to humiliate me?

The roasted boar is at the centre of the table, already half-carved to pieces. Collin serves himself and then me. Even with the pink, sizzling meat in front of me and a growling stomach I can't bring myself to eat it.

Conversation starts up at the table again, but the atmosphere is entirely different than before. Everyone keeps peeking at me, while others stare outright. Kyle is the worst for it. Although Jay is right next to me and I can't see where he's looking as easily, I know his eyes are on me. I lean my head forward, trying to hide myself in my loose hair like I'd always do at temple service.

"Something wrong?" Collin asks. "I went searching for this boar just for you. Won't you at least try it? Here."

I peek up at Collin. He's holding my knife out to me. "Cut off a piece. Go on."

Hesitantly, I reach to take the knife. He keeps the hilt entirely covered so I have to take it by the blade. Even though I'm careful about it, as soon as my hand is close enough Collin digs the blade into my palm. I grit my teeth at the pain.

"On second thought," he says, pulling the knife back and slicing my skin, "I'll cut it for you."

Collin leans across me, cutting into the slice of boar. My blood on the knife mingles with the meat. Collin wipes both sides of the knife off on the piece of boar he's cut and says to me, "You don't want to miss out on any of the juices, even the ones that stick to the knife. It's that good. And who knows when you'll get to taste boar again? This might be the last time."

Collin stabs the piece of boar with my fork and holds it up to me. My own blood is smeared across its surface, along its edges. "Take it. I've cut your food for you. You don't expect me to feed you as well, do you?"

I reach carefully for the fork. I half expect him to stab it at my face but he doesn't. He drops it when my fingers are inches away, so that it clatters on the dirt floor, away from the bench.

"Oops," Collin says, "I guess you didn't have a very good hold on it. Better go get it."

I start shivering.

"Go on." Collin juts his chin towards the fork. "Then you can get on with your meal. Aren't you hungry?"

Hesitating a moment longer, I grab onto the table with one hand and turn to reach for the fork with the other. It's just out of reach. I strain for it, not wanting to get up from the bench, worried that's somehow part of Collin's plan.

It turns out I play into his hands. I feel sharp pain in my wrist as he grips it and yanks my hand from the table. I topple off the bench, onto the ground. Everyone stops talking and those close enough to see look at me. I quickly yank down my dress from where it rode up over my thigh.

"A little clumsy there, aren't you?" Collin says. "You're fine, though. Not even a scratch, I bet."

Trembling, I push myself up.

"Don't forget the fork."

I grab it and return to the bench. I have the sudden urge to jab the fork into Collin's shoulder. But if I do something like that, everyone in this room will turn on me and most of them are trained fighters. Collin wouldn't let them have me, though. He'd want to beat me himself.

I sit down again and start scraping the dirty, bloody meat off onto my plate.

"Now, now," Collin says, taking my fork from me and stabbing the piece of meat back onto it. "You don't want to waste even a morsel of such a rare delicacy, do you? My team and I put our lives on the line to bring this back for everyone. I want you to enjoy it all."

He offers the fork to me and I take it. I stare at the meat on the end, full of dirt and bits of dust that stick to the thin layer of my blood. I shut my eyes and put the full piece in my mouth. I chew it only enough to force it down my throat. The taste seems to fill every corner of my mouth and I hate that under the metallic flavour and bits of dirt, it's delicious.

"Eat up," Collin says, gesturing to the other pieces he cut. As I lean in to get another piece with my fork he adds, "Careful not to get the ends of your new ribbon in your food. You don't want to stain it."

I drop my fork. It clatters off my plate, falling into my lap instead of on the floor. My appetite is gone in an instant and the tiny bit of meat working its way into my stomach suddenly threatens to climb right back up.

"I'm glad you like it so much," Collin says. Then, as if he's just noticed something, adds, "Don't cover your dress. It's perfect for you. Don't you want everyone to see it?"

Everyone started talking again when I sat down but I know, even now, they're listening. They haven't commented up till now so I'm surprised when Andrea shoves to her feet. "I can't do this any more. It's disgusting. How can the rest of you stand it?"

Andrea's glare circles the table, but no one will meet her eyes; no one but Collin.

"You're not enjoying the boar?" Collin asks coolly.

Andrea grits her teeth and marches from the room. I'm surprised when Ryan hops to his feet and follows her, his expression open for once, and very panicked. Cassie looks after Ryan, concerned and confused. I think she'll follow him but ultimately she settles back down.

I don't know how to feel after Andrea and Ryan are gone. I could cry, because Andrea doesn't hate me. She tried to help. But when her first attempt failed, she left me here. Alone.

"Your hand," Collin prompts me, as if Andrea never spoke. "Show off your dress."

My hand trembles as I let go of my dress front. The hole falls open again, showing off more of my chest than anything I've worn before. I work my hands into my lap, pressing them between my legs so hard I think I'll cut off circulation. I almost hope I do. That would take my mind off what's happening.

I know some of the boys are looking at me again. Theo is. I hate this. He was always so sweet and gentle with me before. No boy was ever as kind to me as he was, and if they were, it was usually to impress Clara. Now Collin's taken that from me too.

"What do you think of her dress?" Collin asks, speaking over me to Jay. "Doesn't it suit her?"

"It really does," Jay readily agrees. I peek at him through my hair and he grins at me in a way that makes my stomach roll. I want to run away from this. I want to be back in the girls' room, alone with Elle. I want to be back in my apartment or in the lift listening to the Daedalum anthem on my way to school. I want to be home.

"Why are you doing this?" someone asks, in a wobbly, desperate voice.

The table goes silent and all eyes land on Felix. Kyle tries to shush his friend but shuts up when he notices everyone looking at them. Felix himself has gone ashen and his fork is shaking in his hand, but he doesn't look away from Collin.

"Why not have a feast?" Collin asks. "After everything we've been through to survive, we Icarii deserve to celebrate."

"That's not what I mean." Now Felix's voice is definitely shaking. "It's cruel. Clara doesn't deserve–"

Collin slams his fists on the table. I jump, as do most of the others. A vein bulges in Collin's neck and his face has gone red with rage. Looking at him side-on is terrifying enough; I can't imagine what it's like for Felix, being the focus of that wrath.

Except I can imagine it, because I felt his wrath two days ago.

Collin rises to his feet and half the table shrinks back. His gaze is set on Felix, who looks as petrified as he did on our first day in the labyrinth.

Before I can really think it through, I grab hold of Collin's sleeve. It's not a sharp action, but it's enough to catch Collin's attention. His wrath returns to me and my heart hammers. I'm sure he'll hit me again. Or worse. I try not to glance at the blade. Can I reach it before he can? Would it matter, when Collin's so much bigger than me, and has all of Fates behind him?

But then Collin's cruel smile returns and he sinks back into his seat. He sends his smile down the table and says, "Kyle, why don't you and Felix go find Gus? He must be finished putting Gina to bed by now. He'll miss all the food at this rate."

Kyle swallows and then he scrambles to his feet. It takes several tries for him to get Felix up. When it looks like Felix is about to protest, gaze set on me now, Kyle whispers something in his ear. Felix stills, then mouths, "I'm sorry" at me and follows Kyle.

As they leave Collin starts talking to Addie, whose responses are as clipped as always, but that doesn't seem to bother him. I wait for him to say something about me or to me or do something. He doesn't, for a long while. Andrea and Ryan don't return. Neither do Felix and Kyle, and there's no sign of Gus. I don't do anything as I sit there. I just stare at my plate of boar meat until the pieces blur together into one indistinguishable pink blob.

"Are you tired?" Collin asks me after twenty minutes of frayed nerves. "I think you're tired. I'm not quite done here, but I could still walk you back to your room, unless someone else wants to take you?"

I see Theo open his mouth, possibly to offer, but Jay speaks first. "I'll take her."

"I appreciate it." Collin gives Jay a fake smile, then squeezes my knee so hard I think my kneecap cracks. "Sleep well."

I know what's coming, but I'm not as scared as I thought I'd be. Maybe it's that I'm so scared I've grown numb to it. Or maybe this is resolve. Since I'm not familiar with that feeling, I can't be sure.

I've just started following Jay to the door when Collin calls: "We'll talk more tomorrow, don't worry."

Jay holds the door open for me with a grin. If he notices my tears he doesn't say anything. There's no way he doesn't notice my tears. I follow him to the bedrooms. When I move towards the girls' door he blocks my way. "Before you go to bed there's something Collin wants me to give you. A third gift, he called it." Jay gestures to the storage room across the hall. "In there."

I go into the room because I know I don't have any other choice. Jay shuts the door behind him.

I'm staring at the chairs where Collin and I had so many conversations about his and Clara's past when Jay comes up behind me. His arms wrap around my waist, tugging me to him. I'm sickened, but unsurprised.

Jay's breath is on my neck and I feel his hands snake their way up my stomach to my chest and the hole in my dress. I reach behind me as carefully as possible. My fingers aren't shaking. I thought they'd be shaking. I wrap them around the hilt of the dagger I saw on his belt earlier. I'll have to be quick.

"Let go," I say, my voice hiding the sound of the dagger sliding free. "I don't like this."

Jay ignores me. I reach back with my right hand, brushing his side lightly so that he won't feel it, but so that I know where to hit. I jab the dagger in.

Jay shrieks and lets me go. I don't have time to pull the dagger out so I run for the door. Like every other door in Fates, there isn't a lock. I'm in the hall before Jay's recovered, then I'm running into the girls' room and slamming the door behind me. I get halfway through the room when I fall to my knees. Elle starts to smile and say something about being glad I'm back when I scream. I scream and I scream and I don't stop. I rip the disgusting bow from my hair as tears streak down my face and then I vomit. I stare at the little bit of greyish-red sludge and then I start dry heaving over it. I feel filthy inside and out and I don't know how to erase the feeling. It only seems to grow.

Elle crouches in front of me. In between my dry heaves and shuddering I hear her say, "Don't worry, Clara. Look: I fixed it."

I look up and see Elle's tied the two ends of the broken ribbon back together. She beams at me so openly and so innocently it breaks everything in me that was left unbroken.

Nobody comes for me in the night. I wake up as I went to sleep, wrapped in Elle's arms. For once I wake up before her. I stay there, staring at her peaceful sleeping face with its tiny smile. Is she dreaming of pillows?

Elle still hasn't woken up when Cassie comes to get me. I didn't expect them to send her. I see the same concern in her eyes I saw last night when she takes in my bruises. She's apologetic as she struggles to say whatever it is Collin told her to say. I start easing myself up, so she doesn't have to say it. I know how hard it is to get out certain words. Most words, in my case.

I hesitate a moment, then I lean in and kiss Elle's forehead. I've finally realized that, even though she's a year older me, she's the one that needs an older sister to look after her. And now I have to go.

"I'm so sorry," Cassie whispers as she leads me down the hall. "I wish I... that there were something..."

"Thank you," I say, "for being nice to me all this time."

Cassie's face crumbles. She starts to say something else when we reach the main room, where Collin is waiting for me. Abruptly clamping her mouth shut, Cassie immediately heads towards the mess hall. I don't miss the last, anxious glance she sends me over her shoulder before she disappears.

"My team didn't go scavenging today," Collin says to me. "We decided to take a day off, considering that prize we hauled in last night. You had a fun night, didn't you?"

I realize Gus isn't in his usual spot by the door. Collin and I are alone. He pulls a dagger from his jacket as he walks up to me. I don't move as he presses the blade against my side, in the exact same spot I wounded Jay last night. He presses just enough for me to feel it, not quite enough to break skin.

"Jay didn't enjoy his night so much," Collin says. "You wouldn't happen to know anything about that, would you?"

I refuse to respond and I don't meet Collin's eyes. If I show any defiance he'll definitely cut me. Maybe he won't let anyone bandage my wound either.

Someone comes out of the mess hall. It's Addie. She doesn't seem surprised by our situation. Ignoring me completely in favour of speaking to Collin, she says, "Can we do this quickly? I have to get back to work."

Collin stares down at me a moment longer. He presses the blade just enough to draw a thin, stinging line of blood, then pulls it back. I force myself not to reach for the pain at my side. Collin grabs my arm in another bruising hold and pulls me over to the spot where the young Icarii usually have lessons. Addie has picked up Cassie's drawing sword and goes to the softened patch of dirt. She starts tracing what seem to be random lines and shapes. When she's done, she marks one of the squares with an F.

"This is Fates," she says, tapping the square. She draws a continuous line between the other lines she's drawn and my stomach twists when I realize this is a map. "You'll follow this exact path to reach the watering hole. Study it until you have it memorized. Don't deviate unless you want to get lost and subsequently eaten. Although deviation is ultimately up to you. This path has been scouted and pronounced clear of threat. Get to the watering hole, fill your buckets, and get back."

Addie taps the Fates box again, then lays the sword where she found it and says to Collin, "I'm going back to work now. Don't bother me again, if you can help it."

"Thanks, Addie," Collin says, then hauls me over to the table. He leaves me there as he grabs two empty wooden buckets from beside the hearth. "Both of them full to the brim, understand?"

I'm shaking all over. This is worse than I imagined. He's not just going to kill me. He's going to let the monsters do it.

"What's the matter?" Collin asks. "You don't want to do this most basic task? Everyone does it. Even the kids go to collect water. The only reason you've gotten out of it until now was... well, I think you know. Speaking of the kids, we have a companion for you, so you don't get lonely on the trip."

Collin leaves the room, telling me to have the map memorized by the time he gets back. A seed of hope is blossoming within me. If he's sending one of the other Icarii with me, he can't possibly mean for me to die out there. As much as he hates me, he loves the other Icarii and does all he can to protect them.

I'm in front of the map when someone comes out of the mess hall. I know it's not Collin because he went down the hall to the bedrooms. Suddenly, Gina is beside me, peering at the map. Gus is right behind her, drinking from a flask. When he spots me his eyes fill with pity.

Gina blinks from the map to me to the rest of the room. She spots the buckets and her face brightens. "Water run!" She turns to me. "You're going for a water run! I wanna come!"

"You can't, Gina," Gus says. "C'mon, I've almost finished your new toy. Let's go play over there."

"No!" Gina stomps her foot on the ground, blurring a corner of the map. "No, no, no! I wanna go on the water run!"

Gus tries to quieten her, but before he can, Collin returns with Felix. I'm surprised to see him. I'm even more surprised by his black eye. There's something desperate in his gaze as he stares at me, something cornered, but he doesn't say a word.

"What's going on?" Collin asks.

"I wanna go on the water run!" Gina wails. "I wanna go outside!"

"It's OK, Collin." Gus catches her shoulder and starts pulling her back, towards his chair. "I've got her. She'll calm down soon."

"No!" Gina shakes him off. "I wanna go, I wanna go, I wanna go!"

Collin crouches in front of her, smiling. "You really

want to go, Gene? There are scary monsters out there, y'know. You're really little, so little they could just snatch you up."

Gina's shaking her head viciously. "You're lying! No monsters! They never attacked me before!"

"She's got a point," Collin says to Gus, who's gone ashen. "Alright, Gene, you can go if you really want to."

Gina claps her hands excitedly. Gus's voice comes out choked. "Collin..."

"The girl wants to go." Collin ruffles her hair as he gets up, fake smile plastered on his face. "She can go. It's decided."

Despite Gina's enthusiasm Gus keeps pleading with her to stay inside. He promises new toys and treats at lunch and says he'll play with her all day, but Gina won't waver. Gus looks close to tears when Collin brings over the buckets. He hands one to Felix and shoves the other roughly at me. Then he goes to the front door and waves for us to follow. I almost trip over my own feet on my way to him.

Gina is still with Gus, who's kneeling in front of her. He whispers something to her in a strained voice, then hugs her. Gina seems confused, but when Collin calls out, asking if she's still going on the water run, her face lights up and she scampers over.

Collin digs out something from his jacket and offers it to me. At first I think it's just a pile of cloth, but then I realize it's an old hood, like Andrea's. "Just in case. We both know how much screechers like those blonde braids of yours, don't we?"

I try to keep my hands from shaking as I put on the hood. Meanwhile, Collin pulls up the bar to the front door and opens it, revealing a small and very dark foyer. The door in the foyer has a bar across it. Collin shoves the bar up and opens the door. Sunlight streams into the foyer, so bright I'm blinded.

I hear Collin's voice right by my ear, "Don't worry, Nameless. It'll be over soon."

Then he shoves me into the blinding light. I still can't see anything but, behind me, I hear the door to Fates slam shut.

A noise reaches my ears. It's my own whimpering.

"I can't see anything," someone murmurs. It's Felix. His voice is shaking.

"It goes away," Gina chirps, too loud. "Gus says just wait thirty seconds or sing the alphabet song. I like the song better so I do that. Counting's boring. Don't sing the song out loud though. Gus says don't do that."

Gina hums to herself. I start to make out shapes in the brightness. Blinking rapidly makes the shapes take on definition more quickly. Before Gina's done humming I can see what's in front of me. It's still insanely bright. Looking anywhere close to the sky makes my head pound harder, but I can see.

"I'm good!" Gina declares, when she's done humming. "Let's go!"

Gina starts skipping ahead. I struggle to pull the map to my mind. We're in a passageway right now, but which way did Addie tell me to go first, left or right? Gina's going right.

"Gina," I call, but instead it comes out a whisper. She's too far away to hear me and I'm too terrified to yell in the labyrinth. I don't even know if I could yell. I hurry after Gina, catching up quickly since my legs are so much longer. I grab her shoulder and she tries to pull away. "No, Gina. Wrong way."

"Right way!" Gina snaps. "Gus and I always go this way for water runs!"

That makes me falter. Did Addie show me the wrong way? Or maybe she showed me the longer way. Still, I don't know the labyrinth at all and I can't leave our safety in the hands of an eight-year-old. What if she forgets or takes a wrong turn and gets confused? At least with the route Addie showed me, I'll know how to get us back to Fates if something happens.

I start pulling Gina back in the other direction. She protests and whines, but she stays relatively quiet. Gus really must have impressed on her the importance of silence in the labyrinth.

"We're going a new way," I finally manage to say. "More fun."

Gina immediately stops resisting me. She perks up. "Fun? OK!"

I'm surprised when Gina takes my hand of her own accord and dutifully follows down the left fork. Felix trails silently on my other side.

"What happened to you?" I whisper to Felix, but Gina presses her finger to her lips and tells me to "Shhh!"

I try to focus entirely on the map in my head. I should have gone looking for Addie's possible map earlier, in the supply room or extra supply room. It's not as if either were locked, and I could have looked through them while the others slept. Why didn't I think of that?

Because I thought I was safe in Fates. I didn't think I'd ever have to enter the labyrinth again. Yet here I am.

It's so silent out here. Almost peacefully silent. The air is fresh and smells wonderful, like the botany floor back home. Being outside for the first time in so long is actually a little energizing. I could almost be content, walking through here with Felix and Gina, like Clara and I used to stroll through the botany floor. Sometimes we'd play hide and seek and get yelled at by the gardeners when we stepped on produce.

This isn't like the botany floor. The whole labyrinth is a deadly game of hide and seek. Even if I forget that for a second, it always comes rushing back in. I can never relax out here.

Eventually Gina lets go of my hand and skips ahead. She always stays within sight. I watch her dance around and pick up rocks and bits of dirt from the labyrinth floor, examining them as if they're precious jewels.

"Collin hit me," Felix says.

I stare at him, shocked, although I should expect it from Collin by now.

"It happened last night, after dinner. He said it was punishment for standing up for you, and then he said the punishment would continue today."

I'm too horrified to speak. Felix, and Gina too, have been pulled into this because of me, even though I didn't go into Fates intending to be Clara. It was just one misunderstanding after another. I wasn't aiming to deceive Collin or to get special treatment. But I did like the thought of Collin being there to protect me and look after me and love me. I liked having an older brother. I liked being Clara.

*You're not Clara.*

I never should have let the lie continue this long. I shouldn't have lied in the first place. All I needed to do was tell Collin I wasn't his sister, even if I still said my name was Clara. When he first came in and hugged me and touched the ribbon in my hair I should have said those ribbons were popular in my building, that I was an only child. Anything would have worked. I just shouldn't have stayed silent.

But that's all I'm good for, isn't it?

"I'm sorry," I whisper to Felix.

He doesn't say anything, and when I look at him he won't meet my eyes. That makes it even worse. Although he stood up for me last night, he must blame me for what's happened to him now. He must think as badly of me as the others back at Fates. I only know that Elle, for sure, doesn't hate me.

Watching Gina, I realize I'm wrong. This demanding, trusting, innocent little girl doesn't know anything about what happened. To her, I'm just another older Icarii taking her outside.

We reach the watering hole, which isn't what I expected. It's in a roofed corridor. A set of steps goes down into the still, murky water that stretches into the darkness of the corridor. It's impossible to tell how deep the water is, let alone where these stairs might have otherwise led.

Gina runs ahead of me, scampering down the stairs to the step before the water. She splashes her face and laughs as water drips onto her dress. Then she sticks her head under the water's surface. I'm about to rush forward and pull her out when she surfaces and shakes her head like a wet dog. She lets out a long, satisfied sigh.

"I know you probably..." Felix whispers, then clears his throat and starts again. "I know you didn't mean for anyone to get hurt. You still shouldn't have done what you did, but what *they* did... it was just so awful. I thought only the gods could be that awful."

"I'm sorry Collin made you come out here with me."

"I don't want to be there any more, not if that's what Fates is really like. But even with my scavenger training... even with that..." Felix turns to me, with the same desperate expression he wore earlier. "I'm not ready to face the labyrinth."

For the first time in a while, I remember I'm older than Felix. I should support him and Gina. But how can I do that when I can barely support myself?

So instead of saying "We'll face the labyrinth together" I say, "I'm not ready to face it either."

Felix's expression crumbles and I know I've said the wrong thing. He goes over to join Gina, leaving his bucket at the top of the steps. He drinks and ducks his head under water. All the while his thin frame trembles. Gina, oblivious, splashes the water happily.

Why couldn't I just lie to Felix? He's out here because he supported me. The least I can do is support him in return.

I decide to try speaking to Felix again, but something keeps me from joining him and Gina. I don't like the darkness into which the water disappears. I don't like the silence here. The stillness of the water unnerves me.

Except the water isn't still, not any more. Felix surfaces for a gasp of breath and ducks his head in again. The movement sends ripples through the water, which join those made by Gina's splashing. The ripples disappear into the darkness. It creates an odd effect. It almost makes it look like the ripples are coming instead of going.

Suddenly Felix goes rigid and slumps into the water. Slowly, he starts to slide down the steps.

"Felix?" I whisper. He doesn't reply, but keeps going further into the water. My skin crawls as his upper body disappears. What's going on?

"Are you going swimming?" Gina asks him. Suddenly, Felix starts sliding faster into the water.

I just manage to grab his legs. I try to pull him out, but he's too heavy. No, that's not it. Something's pulling him from the other end.

I yank as hard as I can and Felix stops sliding. The water around him has darkened. Shaking all over, I pull him out of the water, only to realize I'm only pulling half of him out. I gasp and let go. His legs thud on the steps. There's a moment of silence, of nothing. Then the water ripples and what remains of Felix's body is slowly dragged below the surface.

"What's going on?" Gina asks, staring up at me. She's shaking too. I see the water behind her bubble. At the sound, Gina turns towards it.

I grab the back of Gina's dress and pull her up the steps just as a digger breaches the water's surface. But it's not a digger. It's the same serpentine shape but thinner and covered in dark blue scales. It snaps at the space where Gina was a moment ago, revealing rows of pearly-white, deadly sharp teeth. Gina screams.

Suddenly the water is teeming with serpents. They thrash through the water's surface and snap at us, emitting gurgling, hissing sounds. The water is getting very dark and bits of cloth and something else are floating to the frothy, foaming surface. There must be dozens of the serpents in there.

I drag Gina away from the steps, as far back from the corridor as we can go. I cover her mouth to mute her screaming and soon cover her eyes too. She shouldn't see this. No one should see this.

More and more of the serpents are surfacing to snap at us, even though they'll never reach us. They're in the water now, but what if they can come on land? I don't know anything about these creatures. I didn't even know there were aquatic monsters in the labyrinth. Addie never told me.

But that was the point, wasn't it? She never liked me and she never trusted me. She wouldn't warn me about something they might use against me later.

They planned this, to get rid of me, to get rid of Felix, my ally. And Collin was willing to sacrifice Gina to go through with it.

Gina's stopped screaming, even into my palm. She's shaking in my arms now. I grab her hand and shove to my feet, pulling her up as well, and then we're running back the way we came. I have to get her back to Fates. If she's with me, maybe they'll let me in, but even if they don't they have to let her in at least. Gus will take her in. I can't think about what I'll do after that.

Gina's crying as we run. Suddenly another cry joins hers, from overhead. I tell myself not to look and just keep running. There's a whoosh of wings and Gina screams as her hand's ripped from mine. A screecher has her in its talons. I look just in time to see another screecher dive at me. I manage to roll out of the way and the monster shrieks as it swoops back into the air. Gina's still screaming and thrashing in the screecher's hold. She's still alive.

The other screecher's going to dive at me at any moment. I don't have much time. I don't have any time. I see a rock on the ground and duck to grab it. A scream comes from overhead. Multiple screams. Gina's and the screechers. I hurl the rock as hard as I can at the screecher holding her. It misses. The screecher doesn't even look at me. It's going to rip Gina apart or bite off her head. She's only eight and she's going to die because she came out with me. Just like Felix.

"Hey!" I scream at the screecher. The other one dives at me again and I roll out of the way, scraping my arms and legs. Immediately I push back to my feet and wave my arms and jump to get its attention. I scream until my throat is raw, and tear back my hood.

The screecher notices me instantly. It drops Gina, who isn't screaming any more.

I run for Gina as both screechers dive for me. I throw myself on the ground under her seconds before she lands.

My back cracks against the stone and cracks again when Gina lands, knocking the wind out of me. There are long, fresh gashes across Gina's stomach where the screecher grabbed her in its talons. She's bleeding freely through her dress and onto mine, but she's still alive. She hasn't even passed out. She's whimpering while tears run down her cheeks and she stares at the screechers circling above us.

Despite the pain I wrap my arms around Gina and roll us over, covering her with my body. She whimpers more, but this is all I can do. We can't outrun them and there's nowhere to hide and even if there was, with her wounds, Gina wouldn't last that long. I can only cover her like this and protect her for a few seconds longer.

"I'm sorry," I whisper, and then I'm saying it over and over: "I'm sorry, I'm sorry, I'm sorry."

I know I'm not saying it to Gina any more. I'm not even saying it to me. I'm saying it to the most important person in my life, who I couldn't even protect for this long.

A screecher screams overhead and a split second later something thuds to the ground right next to us. I don't want to look because I know how this goes. The screecher will crouch beside us and it's going to bite off my head or my arms or maybe jump on me, piercing me through with its talons and getting Gina too. There's another thud behind me: the other screecher. With both of them here like this they'll tear me apart, like they should have on that first day.

I wait for it, squeezing my eyes shut against the fear and the coming pain, wishing that in these last moments –

at least – I wasn't crying. But the tears don't stop and the pain doesn't come. The labyrinth is silent.

I wait longer but no screeches fill the air and nothing grabs me. Hesitantly, I peek to my left, where I heard the first thud. The screecher is there, on its side, an arrow in its forehead. I hear footsteps in front of me.

My attention snaps to the person approaching us and my eyes meet hazel, then an X. My heart stops.

The Executioner.

# EXECUTIONER

The Executioner is not as tall as I remember. I don't believe she's any taller than Addie. But she must be very strong because she keeps a brisk pace even while carrying Gina on her back. Gina's sleeping now. I think she actually passed out, but I pretend she's sleeping.

I follow the Executioner because I don't know what else to do. She hasn't spoken to me. She hasn't even acknowledged my presence.

Aside from her bow and the quiver of arrows on her belt, she has a short sword sheathed to her left side and some kind of axe to her right. There's a seemingly empty black rucksack on her back, now covered by Gina. The bandages tied tight around Gina's torso are almost the same colour as the rucksack. It makes it impossible to tell if they've started bleeding through. If I get closer, I might be able to tell. I don't get closer.

The Executioner stops and cocks her head to the side. She lowers Gina to the ground and lays her down gently. Then she's on her feet and running silently around the corner ahead. I hesitate. Stay with Gina or follow? What if she's decided to ditch us after all?

I stand awkwardly by Gina, who's still asleep. A screech sounds in the distance and I freeze. Another screech. Another.

The Executioner returns a minute later, slinging her bow over her shoulder. She hoists Gina onto her back and starts walking again. When we round the corner I realize we've reached one of the bottlenecks with multiple exits. Scattered throughout the wider space are three screecher bodies. I stare at them as we pass.

This happens twice more as I follow the Executioner through the labyrinth. The third time, I see her wiping off an arrow as she returns. Her arrows aren't like the ones I made at Fates. They're entirely black and don't seem to be made of wood. But maybe they are. The way the black doesn't catch the light makes me think it's some kind of paint or covering.

Every time the Executioner goes to kill screechers she leaves Gina and me well behind, out of sight. She's clearing a path for us.

We walk all day, taking so many twists and turns I have no idea in what direction we're heading. Nothing is familiar yet everything looks the same. Gina wakes up eventually. She asks what's happening in a quiet voice. I don't know so I don't answer. The Executioner keeps going as if she hasn't spoken. Gina doesn't ask again. She clings silently to the Executioner, whimpering every few minutes. Her wound must still be hurting her. Or maybe she's just scared. I don't blame her. I'm scared too.

The sun is sinking when the Executioner stops in front of a wall. She presses her hand against one of the bricks and, to my surprise, the brick grinds inwards under her touch. As she pulls back a rectangular section of the wall slides apart, revealing a passageway. The Executioner ducks inside. After a split second of hesitation I follow. The wall seals shut seconds after I'm inside. I blink around, but I can't see anything in the darkness, not even the Executioner. I can't hear her footsteps.

A light appears, but I'm surprised to find it's below me. Then I realize ahead of me are a set of stairs, leading down. It's just like the stairs leading into the water. But there's no water here. There's the Executioner, with Gina, descending the steps. Soon they'll be out of sight and the light showing me the steps will be gone. I start down the stairs.

As I hurry to catch up to the Executioner, I notice alcoves in the wall, full of candles and matches. Some of them even have lanterns, just like the lanterns back in Fates.

By the time I reach the Executioner, the steps have evened out into a corridor with stone walls and ceiling. The Executioner goes to a door at the end of the hall, which seems to be made out of some sort of dark stone. This door has a keyhole.

The Executioner pulls a chain up from the baggy confines of her jacket. On the chain is a fairly large, silver key. Hanging next to it is a silver bell, like the ones on cat collars, except this one is much larger and – as the Executioner fits the key into the lock – the bell doesn't jingle. It's silent.

Suddenly, the Executioner fixes me with a glare so intense I catch my breath. She pulls out the key and stuffs the chain and bell back inside her jacket, out of sight. Only then does she look away from me to open the door.

The room beyond may be spacious, but it's too full to tell. There are crates and sacks, but more than that there are piles of stone and bone and feathers and cloth and wood. I see a pile of ripped Icarii robes, in between the rags and bones. There's not just one pile of bones. There are many, seemingly separated in a senseless fashion. Different sized bones are in piles together. I don't understand why she'd keep bones, let alone where she got them or why she's sorted them like this.

The piles of feathers make more sense. Her largest pile is of black feathers, but she also has a pile of golden brown feathers, and one of curious bronze feathers that catch the lantern light. Next to the pile of bronze feathers I see a pile of something that I realize are horns. Next to that are fangs. There are lots of fangs, all different shapes.

Gina has seen the strange piles and clearly doesn't like them, for she buries her face in the Executioner's back. The Executioner sets her down on a pile of bedding between two crates, then puts the candle in a lantern on one of the crates. She goes to a row of open crates and starts putting her weapons in them.

Unsure of what else to do, I go over to Gina. She cuddles into me before I even sit down, whispering, "I don't like this. I want to go home."

I stroke her hair, unable to do anything else. Even if I could find my voice, I wouldn't know what to say. Fates may be the only home Gina's ever known, but I have no idea how to get her back there and I don't think I'd want to anyway. If Collin was willing to put Gina in danger to get rid of someone else, there's no telling he won't do it again. As creepy as the Executioner may be, she's Gina's best chance right now. My best chance.

The Executioner closes and locks the door, then disappears behind a stack of crates to the right of the room. A few seconds later I hear a crackling and then light shines from where she disappeared. Does she have a hearth here too?

She must because when the Executioner returns she's holding a pot of boiled water. She sets it on the crates next to our bedding and disappears again. She returns with a sack over her shoulder and a small wooden box under one arm. These she sets down in front of us. Then she locks eyes with me and juts her chin in the direction of the supposed hearth. When I don't move she makes the same gesture, but more sharply. I scramble to my feet.

Gina clings to my leg. "No! Stay!"

I try to tell her it's OK but my words are utterly gone again. I gently pry her fingers off my leg and hurry past the Executioner. Gina calls out for me to come back, then starts whimpering as the Executioner moves towards her. I hide by the crates and watch as the Executioner unwinds Gina's bandages and pulls her dress further open, fully revealing the wound. Then she pulls a rag from the small crate and dips it in the boiled water. She starts cleaning Gina's wound. She doesn't stop even when Gina starts crying in pain. Then she takes a glass bottle of salve from the box and rubs that into the wound. After that Gina doesn't whimper as much. The Executioner produces another salve from the crate which she also adds to the wound before pulling out a fresh roll of gauze.

Relieved that she's taking care of Gina, I go around the stack of crates as the Executioner directed. As I thought I would, I find a flaming hearth. What I didn't think I'd find is a skinned animal leg roasting over the fire. Looking around I realize that, using the crates as counters, the Executioner has turned this area into a tiny kitchen. There are pots and wooden utensils and knives on the left crates, while to the right are small but bulging sacks that must contain some sort of food. There's a larger sack that's shaped vaguely like the leg of meat now over the fire, while an empty sack is beside it. There are also little, corked glass bottles filled with crushed herbs.

The Executioner comes up behind me, making me jump. She doesn't so much as look my way, instead going straight to the fire and turning the leg over on its makeshift spit. Still not looking from the fire, she grabs something from the left counter and holds it out to me. A flask, just like the ones they had at Fates, with water sloshing inside. She nods back the way we came and, carrying the flask, I return to Gina.

I'm surprised to find Gina not only bandaged but wearing a new dress. It's much nicer than anything any of us wore at Fates. It's a pretty peach colour with blue ribbons hemming the neck, skirt and sleeve cuffs. It's a little small on her but Gina is delighted with it, so much that she seems to have forgotten her wounds entirely. She takes the water when I hand it to her.

"Isn't it pretty?" she asks, playing with her skirt. "I can't wait to show Gus!"

I sit with Gina, unsure of what to do. After what

feels like an hour, but is more likely ten minutes, the Executioner returns. She's holding two clay bowls with steam winding up from them around wooden spoons. She hands one to me and one to Gina. I see that there's broth full of little green herbs in the bowls.

Gina sniffs the broth, which prompts me to do the same. It smells delicious. My stomach growls and I'm reminded of how little I've had to eat over the past two and a half days. By the time I pick up my spoon Gina's already slurping her meal. The broth is as delicious as it smells. It's surprisingly salty and tastes of some sort of meat. Although it's not quite the same, it reminds me of chicken broth.

That reminds me of what I said to Collin when I first met him, right before I broke down in his arms and he carried me to my bed. Mother and Father used to carry me into my room like that, when I was very young and would fall asleep in the living room, listening to the radio or reading or watching Mother sew.

The Executioner returns for our bowls when we're done. She disappears for a moment and reappears with the same bowls. Inside each of them are slices of roasted meat. The Executioner leaves these with us and disappears again.

Hesitantly, I pick up the meat with my fingers and bite into it. In seconds I'm devouring the whole piece. It tastes even better than the boar. Gina watches me for a moment before digging in to her meal. We finish the meat in half the time we did the soup and then share the flask of water. The Executioner returns a few minutes after we've finished to take the bowls. She returns them to her makeshift kitchen and then passes us to go to the crates and piles in the left side of the room. I know I should ask her why she saved us and why she's taking care of us now, but the words stick in my throat again. She still terrifies me too much.

The Executioner pokes through a certain crate and then returns to us with thick white blankets. Icarii robes, stitched together in layers. She tosses me the blankets and then another two items she'd been carrying under her arms. It takes me a moment to process what's in front of me. Pillows. Small and crude and lumpy, but they're definitely pillows. Through the white fabric I can just see something darker below the surface. It takes me a moment, but then I realize she's stuffed them with screecher feathers.

When I look up, the Executioner's gone. I hear clattering in the makeshift kitchen. Beside me, Gina yawns. I quickly put the pillows behind us on the bedding and start arranging the blankets. Then I ease Gina down onto the pillow. She doesn't fight it, but she does murmur, "We gotta go back to Fates. Gus says never fall asleep anywhere but Fates."

"It's OK," I whisper in my hoarse, brittle voice. Whether Gina hears me or not, her eyes flutter closed as I pull the blanket up to her chin. With a glance back at the crates separating us from the Executioner, I lie down as well. As soon as my head hits the pillow I start to drift off. A part of me wants to stay up, to try and face what's happened to Felix, what Fates has done to us. A bigger, more exhausted part of me knows I'm not ready. All I can face right now is sleep.

When I wake up the next morning, the Executioner is gone. I try the door but it won't open. She's locked us in.

At least, for now, we won't starve. I find a pot of last night's soup over the hearth. It now contains pieces of the meat from last night. On the crate counters are a few matches and two bowls and spoons. I light the fire under the pot and wait. By the time the broth has heated and I've served up our portions, Gina's awake.

"Are we having breakfast before we go home?" she asks. I nod and hand her one of the bowls, then lead her back to sit on the bedding. The stone floor is cold on my bare feet, as it doubtlessly is hers. It's more comfortable to eat on the blankets.

"Why don't you talk?" Gina asks me. "Can you talk?"

I nod and start eating my soup.

"Why don't you talk then?"

I shrug, wishing she was a shy eight-year-old.

"It's silly not to talk," Gina says. "If you don't talk, you can't tell people things."

She starts eating after that. The broth is delicious enough to distract her for a good five minutes. When she's eaten her fill, however, she's back to the questioning.

"Gus says you can't talk because bad things happened to you in the lab– the laber– the maze. Is that true?"

I nod.

Gina's voice gets smaller. "Were the bad things bad like yesterday?"

Again, I nod, wishing more than anything I could do something to erase what she saw. Did she have nightmares last night, I wonder? She must have. I'm surprised I didn't. Actually, I slept better than I have in a long time.

But now that I'm awake it's like my mind is racing to make up for the nightmares I missed. Felix's death has started replaying in my head. My stomach turns and I have to lay down my breakfast, even though I know I need the food. But how can I eat when all I can think about is those monsters dragging Felix underwater?

I wish he hadn't stood up for me at dinner. I wish he'd hated me, like the others. At least then he'd still be alive. Instead, for a second time, I've watched a friend die. And this time it's all my fault.

Gina notices I've stopped eating. Frowning at her bowl, she stops eating too. When I start again, so does she. My stomach revolts against the food it wanted so badly moments before, but I make myself eat so that Gina will.

We finish our breakfast in silence. After I've put the bowls back, I'm at a loss. What do I do if the Executioner doesn't come back? What do I do if she does?

I find Gina picking through one of the piles of sticks. She finds two that are bent at funny angles and brings them back to the bedding. She starts playing with them like she does her horse and soldier back at Fates.

"I wish I brought my toys," Gina mumbles after a while, laying down the sticks. "They have faces and Gus made them just for me."

A couple of minutes after this, Gina gets up and collects more sticks, which she brings back to the bedding. She starts making cone-shaped houses out of the sticks. She seems content now to construct her village, so I get up and give her more bedding on which to build. This is as good a time as any to explore the room and the crates.

I find a door on the other side of the makeshift kitchen. It's the only other door in the room and it's unlocked. It leads to a small bathroom which, to my surprise, has a wooden seat constructed over the toilet pit. Back at Fates they just had holes in the ground. I close the door on the bathroom to keep the smell out of the main room. Still, it's nowhere near as bad as the smell of the washrooms at Fates.

Back in the main room, Gina's still content with her twigs so I turn to examining the piles. I go first to the pile of bronze feathers that caught my attention last night. Hesitantly, I pick one up. It's heavy and when I pinch the stalk it doesn't give. Running my finger lightly along the edge of the feather, I find it sharp. The tip, particularly, is very pointy. It could easily cut my flesh. I remember Addie telling me about the bronze beaks and their impenetrable bodies. Could these be their feathers?

I move on to the other piles. The piles of cloth are mostly rags or makeshift gauze. Hidden behind all the other cloth piles, I find another pile of Icarii robes. They're only pieces, not full robes, and every single one bears some sort of blood stain. I remember watching the Executioner collect and separate stained and unstained Icarii cloth. If she uses the unstained for pillows and blankets, for what does she use the bloodied cloth?

Not wanting to think about it, I move on. I can't make myself examine the bones so I begin picking through crates. I start with those open, where she deposited her weapons. When I look inside I have to keep from catching my breath. Each crate is filled with weapons. The one to the far left contains what must be a hundred black arrows. Some of them are chipped, showing silver beneath the black. I guess she does find a way to cover them. The next crate has an assortment of swords: short and long, thin and thick. The third crate has all sorts of other weapons, some of which I can't even name. Hesitantly, I reach for what seems like a long, thin cylinder. As I pull it I realize there's a slinky silver chain attached to one end. I pull it out until the chain catches. Carefully, I ease an axe out of the way and yank out the rest of the long chain. I'm surprised to find an object attached to the end: a small metal ball from which protrude sharp spikes.

I hear the front door opening and immediately slide the weapon back in place. I'm standing awkwardly next to Gina and her twig village when the door opens. The Executioner doesn't even look at me as she locks the door behind her. She deposits her rucksack by the weapon crates and grabs the same small medical box as last night. She goes right to Gina.

Gina makes a fuss when the Executioner starts to pull at her dress. Peeking over her shoulder I see Gina's wound has bled through the material of the dress. It must have reopened in her sleep, or at some point when she was playing. Either way, her bandages need changing.

Eventually Gina lets the Executioner take off the dress, but when the Executioner reaches for the bloody bandages around the wound Gina slaps her hand away. I tense, waiting for the Executioner to hit Gina. Instead, she tries to pull off the bandages and gets another slap, accompanied by Gina's high-pitched, "No! Don't want to!"

The Executioner stares at Gina for a moment, then pushes to her feet. She goes over to a crate behind the pile of bloody Icarii robes. She pulls a sack from the crate and returns. Kneeling in front of Gina again, she pulls something from the sack and offers it to the girl. It's a little wooden lion, carved in remarkable detail and painted black. Its eyes are red.

Gina can't get her hands on it fast enough. She's so enthralled with the lion she doesn't protest as the Executioner unwinds her bandages and applies more salve to her wound. After that comes the fresh bandages. Then the Executioner is struggling to pull Gina's dress back over her head and get the girl's arms through her sleeves. This is because Gina won't let go of the lion. It's almost a funny scene to watch, at least from behind, where I can't see the Executioner's face. The second she turns around I'm reminded of why I'm so terrified of her. It's not even the X-shaped scar over her mouth that makes her so scary. It's the look in her eyes that's the worst part. There's something about them that might be animalistic if they weren't so cold.

But when the Executioner looks at Gina, her gaze isn't as cold.

As I watch the Executioner with Gina, I can't help thinking about the tales Addie told me. Surely, if the Executioner were an insane killer, she wouldn't save us from screechers and then bring us to safety? She definitely wouldn't treat Gina's wounds.

And she's not only treating Gina's wounds; she's doing it tenderly.

While Gina's content playing with her new toy, the Executioner returns the sack and medical supplies, grabbing her rucksack in the process. She passes by me and heads to the makeshift kitchen, motioning for me to follow. I stand behind her as she produces three bags from her rucksack. Untying them, she leaves them open on the counter, then points from them to the glass bottles of herbs. Peeking in the bags, I find them full of green leaves.

The Executioner takes the pot of broth off the fire. Then she empties one of the bags onto a sort of metal pan with a long wooden handle. Holding the handle, she puts the pan over the fire. She stays like this for a while, steadily watching the leaves over the fire. Finally she pulls back, waiting a few minutes for the pan to cool. Then she deposits the leaves on the crate counter and lays the pan aside. She holds a crisped leaf in front of my face, then opens an empty glass bottle and crumbles the leaf into it. The little green bits that fall to the bottom are identical to those in the bottles at the end of her herb collection. She adds this bottle to the back of those with similar herbs. After checking to see I've been watching, she takes the bottle back out and hands it to me. Then she gestures to the crisped leaves and picks up another bag.

She shows me the purple leaves inside but she doesn't give them to me right away. Instead, she pulls out a pair of crude cloth gloves from her rucksack. She puts one on and picks up one of the leaves, twirling it in front of my face. Then she puts the leaf back and takes off the glove. She tosses the glove into a pot of water, which she sets to boil, then hands me a new pair of cloth gloves from her rucksack and sets two specific glass bottles in front of me.

The Executioner goes through several different sacks of leaves and, through her miming, I come to understand what each is for. The purple leaves, for instance, are some kind of poison. The various green herbs are for cooking, while others are for salves. There's a herb for sleep, and I recognize it as one of the herbs in our broth last night. No wonder I slept so well. I'm not sure if I should be grateful towards the Executioner for it, or wary that she would sedate us so easily. I'll keep an eye on our meals in the future.

Once she's done our lesson, the Executioner picks up her rucksack and leaves the makeshift kitchen. I get to work right away, grinding up the herbs and then drying the other leaves. This task gives me hope. If the Executioner's showing me how to do chores for her maybe she's thinking of keeping Gina and me around for that purpose. At least that way we'd have a roof over our heads and food over the fire. This could work out for us.

Later, after I've finished with the herbs, the Executioner returns to the kitchen. She pulls something out of a sack and it takes me a moment to process what's in front of me. She's holding a dead rabbit by the ears.

I'm so stunned I almost miss the first half of the Executioner's soundless instructions. I can't believe that this labyrinth full of monsters has rabbits. No one at Fates ever mentioned there being such a normal, innocent animal in the labyrinth. The fact there are boars is strange enough, but rabbits?

The Executioner starts showing me how to skin the rabbit. The instant she starts hacking off the feet my stomach rolls and I almost throw up into the hearth. Bottling herbs is no problem but I'm not sure I can stomach carving up and then gutting a rabbit. The Executioner lets the feet drop onto a cloth in front of her and moves her blade to its back.

I can't do it. Although there's not as much blood as I expected, it's more revolting than I could have ever imagined. I squeeze my eyes shut on the disgusting scene.

The Executioner notices I've stopped watching because she shakes my shoulder. When I open my eyes she's glaring at me, jabbing her dagger towards the rabbit.

There are stringy bits of pink flesh hanging from where the rabbit's feet used to be. They swing as the Executioner gestures.

Without looking at the Executioner I shake my head and push to my feet, hurrying back to the bedding, where Gina's constructed a twig fort for her lion. The Executioner doesn't drag me back. I don't see her again until she brings us supper: bowls of broth, like last night, but with small pieces of meat. There's only one piece of meat in mine.

Like last night, the Executioner collects our bowls and returns with slices of meat. Tonight, there's only meat for Gina. The Executioner gives me back my empty bowl to drive home her point.

I watch Gina eat her meat. She likes it even more than last night's meal and says as much. Apparently, this meat tastes different. She says it's kind of chewier but she likes the taste more. I realize halfway through her meal that it's the rabbit the Executioner caught. I've never actually tried rabbit before. It was always chicken or pork or beef back home. Sometimes it was turkey.

I go to sleep dreaming of the taste of rabbit.

The Executioner wakes me up. As I rub the sleep from my eyes she dumps a bundle in my lap. I sort through it and find a shoulder cloak and hood like the one she wears as well as a dark tunic and pair of britches. I don't know what's going on but, as she disappears into the kitchen, I start to change.

Gina's already awake. She, or maybe the Executioner, has pulled a blanket over to the pile of sticks, where Gina is recreating her village from yesterday. This time her inhabitants aren't oddly bent sticks but her lion and another new toy – a lizard, painted blue with black eyes – which the Executioner must have given her while I was sleeping. There's a half-full bowl of broth beside her and another bowl with chunks of meat, as well as a large flask of water.

When I pull the cloak over my head Gina glances over. She says, "You look like a scavenger!"

My fingers freeze over the cloak's clasp. What if the Executioner thinks I'm a scavenger from Fates and plans to have me help her in the labyrinth?

The Executioner returns with a bowl of gruel. It's not a welcome sight, but when I take my first bite I realize it's not like the gruel at Fates. It has flavour and it's thicker. There are chunks of meat mixed in with it too.

The Executioner dumps a pair of boots in front of me before I'm done eating. They're heavy black boots that reach to just below my knees and lace up at the sides. They have thick soles and seem to be made of durable material. My feet definitely won't get scraped in these.

After eating and lacing up my boots, the Executioner tosses a rucksack at me. It's exactly the same as the one on her back. She motions for me to open it. Inside I find two full flasks of water, dried, packaged meat, a small pack of matches, some folded cloth sacks, two pairs of cloth gloves and three sheathed knives.

I've barely closed the bag when the Executioner tosses me a belt, which I just manage to catch. It has two sheaths on either side and a pouch at the back. After I put on the belt she hands me daggers for the sheaths.

The Executioner grabs her bow and quiver, having all her other items already equipped, then heads for the door. When I don't follow she glances back at me and juts her chin towards the stairwell. It's the same motion she made when she tried to make me gut the rabbit last night.

I glance back at Gina. She has food and water, but can we really leave her here on her own?

Thanks to my hesitation, Gina notices us. She immediately abandons her toys and scrambles over. "Are we going home now?"

This time, I glance at the Executioner. A troubled look passes over her face before she nods me into the stairwell again. This time, I follow, although I'm terrified Gina is right. I know she wants to return to Fates, but if I go back I'm sure Collin will finish me off. At this point I'd rather stay with the Executioner, if she'll let me.

When Gina tries to follow me into the stairwell, the Executioner puts a hand on her shoulder and tries to gently guide her back to her blanket.

"Oh, right," Gina says. "I almost forgot my new toys!"

While Gina goes to retrieve them, the Executioner joins me in the stairwell and closes the door. I'm speechless as she locks it after her, barring Gina inside, but the Executioner doesn't even look at me as she heads up the stairs. Quietly, I try the door, but it won't open from the outside either. I don't want to leave Gina in there alone, but I don't know what else to do. I follow the Executioner.

In less than a minute, we surface into the early morning sunlight of the labyrinth. The Executioner takes off at a clipped pace and I trip over myself to keep up. I'm really out here again. A monster could kill me at any moment. The Executioner could kill me. Maybe that's her plan, but if it isn't, she's the only protection I have. I stay close.

The Executioner leads me through countless twisting passageways. She stops at one point, cocking her head to the side. Then she stares me down. I try to pick up on whatever it is she's heard, but I can't. Whether the Executioner's aware of this or not she presses on.

As we walk, I realize monsters aren't the only thing I have to fear. What if we run into someone from Fates? If Collin still thinks I'm alive, he'll probably have given the others orders to drag me back or even kill me on the spot. I doubt Andrea's team would hurt me, but if it's one of the other teams... if it's Collin's team...

We take a sharp left turn and come out in a small, square clearing. The Executioner motions me forward. When I'm standing next to her, she reaches over and yanks my hood down. I immediately reach to pull it back up but, before I can, she shoves me into the clearing.

I stumble and turn to her, moving to pull my hood back up again, but I find an arrow trained on me. When I start to move my hood higher she releases the arrow. It zips right past my head, embedding itself in the labyrinth wall somewhere behind me. She has another arrow notched in an instant. I let my hood fall.

That's when I hear it. The faint disturbance in the air that has nothing to do with the natural breeze. I look around and then see shadows on the horizon. A screech rings through the air.

I'm trembling all over. I have to run and find cover. I have to put my hood back up. As I start to move the Executioner shoots at me again, narrowly missing my leg. I freeze.

The shrieks are high and excited above me now. I don't dare look up. Suddenly, the Executioner turns her arrow towards the air and lets it go. There's a scream of pain and a thud behind me. The Executioner notches another arrow. The next screecher falls right in front of me, making me scream and stumble backwards. In doing so, I see another screecher diving at me.

I throw myself out of the way right before the screecher swoops. It never returns to the air, instead toppling forward and skidding against the ground, an arrow jutting out of the back of its skull.

I hear another screech and look up. My heart almost stops. There are a half dozen screechers in the air, all intent on me. Two of them dive.

The Executioner's arrow takes down one, but I have to roll away to avoid another. It pulls back just in time to stop from hitting a wall. Then it drops onto the ground, talons scraping against the stone floor before digging into it and cracking stone. The screecher shrieks right at me, so close that spit hits my face.

Suddenly the screecher's head is knocked backwards and it falls, an arrow jutting from its forehead. I'm still staring at the screecher's corpse when another falls.

I'm sure I'm going to faint by the time the last screecher is downed. The Executioner suddenly appears beside me, making me jump. She ignores my reaction and yanks my hood back up. Then she goes to the nearest screecher and pulls out her arrow.

My legs give way and I hit the ground hard enough to bruise my knees. I'm shivering all over and I can't seem to make it stop. I can't make the memories stop.

It's my first day in the labyrinth again. There are screechers everywhere. There's blood everywhere. The blue clip I gave Clara is on the ground. And Clara–

The Executioner hauls me roughly to my feet. When I just stare at her, she waves her arrow in my face. It's coated in black screecher blood, which drips on the floor between us. I almost throw up. Then I realize the Executioner is trying to give me directions. She wants me to help retrieve her arrows.

That would mean going up close to the screechers.

When I remain frozen, the Executioner abruptly wipes her arrow across my tunic. I stumble back but it's too late; the screecher's blood is smeared across my stomach. As I stare in horror, the Executioner grabs my hand and makes my fingers close around the arrow. I feel something slick and try to pull back, but the Executioner won't let me. She holds me there until I meet her eyes, then she juts her chin towards the nearest screecher. When she releases me, I don't drop the arrow.

I go to the screecher she indicated. It has an arrow in the back of its head. It takes me a moment, but finally I bring myself to put my foot on its head, keeping it in place as I yank out the arrow. It comes free with a spurt of black blood, which barely shows on the arrow itself.

After we've collected the arrows the Executioner takes out one of her daggers. She kneels by a screecher and starts cutting free some of its feathers. I watch her for a while, how she only cuts out the long, thin feathers in the best condition. Then I start cutting out feathers from the other wing. We put them in one of her cloth sacks, which she returns to her rucksack when we're done.

Next, the Executioner turns to the screecher's feathered legs. She pulls the foot towards her and digs her dagger into the base of the first talon.

For whatever reason, it's not as bad watching this as it was watching the rabbit. Even though there's more blood, this blood isn't red. It doesn't feel like I'm watching something innocent being cut apart. After carefully watching her cut out the talons on the left foot, I do the right myself. We add that to a separate bag, which we end up putting in my rucksack.

Although we only collect feathers from one more screecher, we collect all of their talons. Once we're done the Executioner heaves her rucksack back on her shoulders and takes the closest exit, opposite of the way we came. I don't hesitate to follow.

We walk for a while longer, passing another clearing in the process. This one is larger and scattered with several half-eaten screecher carcasses. I see the arrow holes in their heads and know the Executioner sent them down. I'd hate to see what ate them afterwards. By the size of the bites taken out of the screechers, it had to be big.

Eventually we come to another clearing that has moss covering a good portion of the floor and walls. There are vines as well but, unlike the dying ones I've seen in the labyrinth, these seem healthy. Some of them even sprout little, shrivelled white flowers. Withered as they are, something about them is incredibly pretty.

There seems to be some sort of hole in the corner of the clearing. I can't tell how far down it goes because it's full of water. This must be one of the rain-made ponds I was told about at Fates; the kind to which they actually send their water fetchers.

Remembering what happened last time I went to a watering hole, I keep my distance. The Executioner, however, goes right up to the hole and kneels down, scooping water into her mouth. Then she turns to the bushes growing against the wall. Digging deep in one of them she pulls out a handful of bumpy red berries. She shows them to me, then gestures to three bushes close to each other. Putting the berries in a sack, she moves on to a few bushes that are farther away. Here, she takes out and puts on her gloves before reaching into the foliage. She pulls out a handful of smooth yellow berries and shakes her head at me, then adds them to another sack.

I'm tasked with collecting the red berries, while she collects the yellow ones. Again, I wonder for what the Executioner uses such poison. Unable to answer the question, I shake it off and finish filling my bag. When we're done I go to the pond and drink, then rinse my face.

The Executioner sits beside me. She unhooks an empty flask from her belt and fills it with water. Instead of returning the full flask, she bends her head forward and empties the water over her hair. She scrubs her fingers through her wet hair and repeats the process. She then straightens up and offers the empty flask to me. As I fill it, she goes to inspect the bushes on the other side of the clearing.

My hands start shaking when I reach to untie my braids. I've tried not to touch my hair for a while now. It's disgustingly slick with grease and the texture always makes me nauseous. I can't imagine how bad it must smell to someone not used to such scents.

There's another reason I hesitate to untie my hair. It's been this way since my first day in the labyrinth, when Clara braided it for me. Her touch is still there, in my braids, hidden somewhere beneath all the filth. There's still a little bit of Clara left with me. After losing everyone and everything I can't lose this too.

Except in this place I'm bound to lose it eventually. It's better to let it go myself.

It takes me much longer to wash my hair than it did the Executioner. My hair is far dirtier and, besides, it's longer than hers. When I'm done I rinse the ties that were in my hair then use them to collect my wet hair into a bun, which I hide under my hood.

The second I'm finished the Executioner's ready to go. I don't realize we're heading back to base until we reach the sliding wall. Instantly, I remember Gina, and I feel horrible. I got so caught up in the day that, at some point, I stopped thinking about her.

I expect Gina to throw a tantrum when we come back, but instead she runs over and hugs me. That makes me feel even worse. She begs me not to leave again and when she says, "Promise?" all I can do is nod. It's enough for her, and from that moment on she won't let go of my hand, even when she brings me over to play with her and her village. It's different than how it was before and it's grown. She must have deconstructed and reconstructed it multiple times while we were gone. I notice Gina's also finished most of her food, and the flask is nearly empty. The Executioner brings Gina more food and water, but Gina outright ignores her. I may be wrong but I think, for a moment, the Executioner looks hurt.

Later the Executioner comes to retrieve me. Now Gina does throw a tantrum. Eventually the Executioner pacifies her by giving her another new toy: a wooden deer with horns made out of some kind of shiny material. It instantly becomes her favourite. Still, Gina makes me promise to come back and play with her quickly.

The Executioner leads me to the kitchen and motions for me to sit beside her by the hearth. She drags over a nearby sack and pulls out another rabbit.

The Executioner gets to work as she did before, first cutting off the feet. Then she makes an incision along the back and gets her fingers below the hide. I grind my feet into the floor and ball my hands together so tightly my nails dig into my palms. I have to make myself watch this time.

With a hard yank the Executioner pulls the hide on one end towards the neck and on the other towards the feet. The hide around the legs comes off and bunches around the neck. I almost throw up when I see the naked animal carcass. That feeling only gets worse when the Executioner holds the rabbit up by its hind legs and starts twisting the hide off around its head. She gives a final yank and it slips right off into a fleshy, furry heap in front of her.

Next the Executioner lays the rabbit carcass straight on the ground. She makes a small slit in the belly, then holds the carcass up again with one hand while using her other to insert two fingers into the slit. She digs around a bit and suddenly fleshy red mounds are falling out of the hole in the rabbit and onto the floor. I gag and start to shut my eyes, then force them open again, staring at the tiny, moist organs.

The Executioner collects the organs in a piece of cloth and lays them on the counter. She immediately fills an empty pot with cold water from a flask and starts rinsing the carcass. She kneads it with her hands, scrubbing it clean. Stray bits of fur and dirt start clouding the water. Leaving the carcass in the water, the Executioner dries off her hands and knife and pulls something else out of the sack. Another rabbit.

She holds it out to me.

I shake my head helplessly. It's one thing to watch but it's another entirely to do it myself. I don't want to know what it feels like to pull hide from flesh, let alone what it's like to stick my fingers inside an animal's stomach.

The Executioner turns from me and stretches the rabbit in front of her to start again. At this rate, I won't be eating meat any time soon. Nor will I be getting back to Gina as quickly as promised.

Before the Executioner can pick up her knife again I grab it. She looks at me a moment, then pushes to her feet, leaving the rabbit and the kitchen. I stare at the animal a very long time before sitting down. Its throat has been slit and blood coats its fur. She must have bled it out before coming back.

I've seen pictures of rabbits, but never a live one. I guess I still haven't seen a live one. In the pictures they looked so cute, with their giant black eyes and perky ears. I hate that this rabbit, even with a bloody throat, still has those eyes and ears. It makes it feel wrong, what I'm about to do.

Then I remember what the meat in Gina's bowl looked like, how tempting it smelled. My mouth waters instantly at the memories. I want to taste it.

It takes me much longer to skin and gut the rabbit than it did the Executioner, and I do a far messier job. Still, somehow I get to the point where I'm wrapping small, squishy organs in a cloth and then cleaning off a naked carcass in a pot of water. At this point I feel numb to what I'm doing, but when I finally finish my skin starts crawling again. I can still feel the rabbit's squishy insides against my fingertips.

The Executioner returns. She barely looks at my work at all before pulling out her rabbit carcass from the pot. She dries it quickly and takes another knife from the counters. This is when I realize our work is far from finished.

Later that night I don't think I'll have the stomach for supper. Not after I helped to skin, gut and butcher it. Our soup tonight is augmented with chunks of cooked rabbit organs. Gina knows nothing of the meal preparation and so eats blissfully. I stare at my soup. Gina's halfway finished hers when I finally decide to try it. If I want to survive out here it's not as if I can be picky about what I eat.

The soup is surprisingly good. My appetite returns and I finish my portion quickly. By the time the Executioner serves us our slices of meat I have no qualms about eating the rabbit. I'm actually rather excited for it.

The meat is delicious and I find myself more content than I have been for a very long time. I realize it's because, although the Executioner caught our meal, I helped to prepare it.

I'm a little proud of myself.

The next morning, after I've braided my hair, the Executioner pulls out the sacks of feathers and talons that we collected. From one of the weapon crates she retrieves a long dagger. The blade isn't silver in colour but bronze. The Executioner grabs several bones from one of her piles. All the bones are long and thin. Sitting in front of me, she picks up one of them and starts blunting both ends with the dagger. When she's done she lays it in front of me. Then she takes out three feathers and places them on the ground at the end of the bone. Next she takes out a talon. She carves it into a thin sort of cone, with the tip of the talon as the cone's point. She lays this at the other end of the bone and gets up.

As she does something in the kitchen I stare at the materials in front of me. In the way she's lain them before me it's obvious this is an arrow.

The Executioner returns with a bowl of paste and starts assembling the arrow. She lays it aside to dry and then passes me a new bone and the dagger. I get to work right away.

Gina comes over to sit with me and watch me make the arrows. She quickly gets bored and starts playing with her toys, which seem to be going on an adventure amidst my work materials. I'm glad Gina doesn't seem to link the black feathers with the monster that attacked her. Even the talons she simply glances at curiously before turning back to her toys.

As I work I'm reminded of doing this same task back at Fates. It brings me the same comfort as it did there, because this is something I can do to contribute to the survival effort. Except I didn't contribute enough back at Fates, did I? That's why so many of them hate me now. But if I'd known I wasn't pulling my weight, I would have. I would have tried to become like Cassie, proficient in every task inside Fates. Even if I couldn't do that, I could have learned to prepare meals or make medicine. The Executioner's already teaching me that much. I could have done it. It could have been different.

But it wasn't, and now Felix is dead, and Gina can't go home, and Collin wants to kill me.

I mess up the next arrow and have to take a moment to calm down. Thinking about Fates won't do me any good now. I just have to focus on whatever task the Executioner gives me, so that she'll see that I can learn, that I'll be useful and she should keep Gina and me around.

The Executioner comes for Gina a few minutes later, but Gina clings to me and buries her face in my lap. I glance at the Executioner, looking for the rejection I saw in her face yesterday, but her expression is as closed as ever. She gestures at Gina and motions to her own stomach. Realizing she wants to change Gina's bandages again, I carefully coax the girl to follow the Executioner. Finally she does, whispering for me to watch her toys as she goes.

From the kitchen I can hear Gina complaining. She shrieks in delight a moment later. When she returns, bandages changed, I find out it's because she's been given another toy. It's a wooden pig that has a strip of bristly fur pasted along its spine.

While Gina is distracted with her toy, the Executioner dumps the gear I wore yesterday at my feet. So we're going back into the labyrinth.

Gina throws another tantrum when we try to leave. She screams accusations at me, saying I promised I wouldn't leave her, that I'm horrible and she hates me. I want to tell her I don't want to go, that I'm doing this so the Executioner will keep us safe, but when I try to speak to her she just screams louder and starts hitting me. When red spots start appearing through her dress the Executioner whisks her away, to see to her bandages yet again. Gina screams all throughout the process, and even starts smacking the Executioner. I'm horrified but the Executioner doesn't flinch. Eventually Gina's screams dissolve into sobs, the same words over and over: "I want Gus! I want to go home!"

We leave Gina like that, crying on her blankets, toys scattered, forgotten, around her, and I hate myself even more than she hates me.

Today the Executioner has brought with her two bows. She stops at the end of a long corridor and slings the bows off her shoulders, handing one to me and keeping one for herself. Without notching an arrow, she makes as if to shoot, holding the pose for me to study. I try copying it, with minimal success. Even without an arrow to worry about I'm not strong enough to keep the string held back. The Executioner continues the lesson anyway, drawing an arrow from her quiver without looking. I try doing the same, with the quiver she gave me, but my arrow knocks against the case and it takes me a moment to slide it out. By the time I have the arrow free of the quiver the Executioner has shot an arrow down the corridor.

As I fumble with the bow, I remember my first day in the labyrinth, when Ryan shot the digger that was about to attack me. The digger seemed huge at the time, but now that I'm trying to use a bow myself, I can't imagine how Ryan could possibly hit it. If his aim had been off at all, he might have hit me instead. Not that I expect he'd have cared much.

This makes me think of the last time I saw Ryan, and most of Fates, at that horrible dinner. He left, clearly out of concern for Andrea. But if he was so concerned, why not support her when she tried to challenge Collin?

Because that was more about me than Andrea, and Ryan's never liked me. He thinks I'm weak. Useless. Most of them probably did, but because I was Collin's sister, they couldn't complain. Only Ryan and Addie ever said anything to my face. That was more than enough for me to get the general idea: I can't do anything on my own.

The bowstring whips across my arm, leaving a fiery trail. I'm sure I've skinned myself, but I hardly notice, because I'm staring at the arrow I just released. The one that, instead of clattering in front of me, flew down the hall.

The Executioner doesn't give me so much as a nod of approval; all she does is adjust my hold on the bow. But that's what I really need. Her advice. Her teachings. I can't be coddled any more.

I notch another arrow.

Our lessons last until the sun is getting low in the sky, at which point we return to the Executioner's base. Gina ignores both of us, but she doesn't ignore the food the Executioner lays down beside her. Later in the evening the Executioner shows me how to make a dark paste out of dried black leaves and shows me how to coat the arrows I made earlier. Gina comes over at one point, but still refuses to look at me. Before I can stop her she dips her hand in the paste. Then she starts drawing on the crates by our bedding. When she comes back for more paste I can't bring myself to stop her. At one point I catch the Executioner watching Gina. She doesn't stop her from drawing; instead, she disappears into the kitchen and returns a moment later, with another bowl of black paste, just for Gina.

Gina still ignores us both, but at least she's smiling now.

Later, after Gina's fallen asleep, the Executioner comes over to me with a dagger. I expect her to show me something but instead, when she crouches beside me, she grabs my closest braid and brings it up to her blade.

"No!" The word escapes before I can stop it. I pull away from the Executioner. She stares at me with those cold eyes, then reaches forward and grabs my braid again, pulling so hard that it hurts. I flinch but yank from her hold again, rapidly shaking my head.

The Executioner leaves the dagger in front of me and gets up. After collecting her supplies, she leaves. I stare at the dagger after she's gone, then abruptly kick it away.

This is the one thing I won't change for her. The one thing.

The next morning, Gina is in a better mood. The Executioner has made her pastes of all different colours and given her a pile of rags on which to paint. When Gina sees me changing into my gear, however, she grows sullen. I think she'll ignore me again today but, as I'm pulling on my boots, she asks in a quiet voice, "Will we ever go home?"

I don't want to lie to her again, like I did when I promised I wouldn't leave her, but I don't know if she'll get to go back to Fates. I know I never will, not willingly.

"Please can we go home?" Gina continues. "I miss Gus." It's not just Gus she misses. A moment later she starts listing everyone's names and then she starts crying. I hug her and stroke her hair, like I used to see Gus do, but it doesn't calm her down.

Again, we leave her crying, pining for Fates and the only family she's ever known.

As I follow the Executioner, I can't help thinking about how Fates had started to feel like a family to me too, before Collin found out I wasn't Clara. Andrea and Theo were always friendly, always trying to make me feel at home when they had the chance. Cassie was so sweet and patient. Felix was quickly becoming an important friend.

I even enjoyed learning about the labyrinth from Addie, despite her snide comments. Gus always had interesting stories to tell Gina and the other children, like the story about the Fey, which I couldn't help but listen in on. I was getting used to the food and, between my sewing and making the arrows, gradually feeling like I belonged. Even spending time with Elle was fun, especially at first, before she became so possessive. And there were moments, like when I arrived at Fates, and then just before I left, when Elle was a true comfort to me. I hope I was a comfort to her too.

But my favourite part about Fates was my time with Collin. He made me feel protected. Loved. He was the perfect big brother, the kind I now, after experiencing that, will always wish I really had. When I was with Collin, the labyrinth faded away, and it was just us. And Clara.

Now my memories of Fates are tainted, every moment riddled with pain and guilt and something deeper, scarier. It's a foreign feeling, something I've only ever felt in flashes, and always tried to suppress. Except this time, the feeling won't disappear and every time I think about Fates, it grows.

Is this what Collin felt when he found out about my deception, this hatred?

The Executioner takes me to a clearing, but doesn't pull down my hood. She unsheathes her short sword and motions for me to do the same with the one she gave me this morning. I'm a slow learner and I receive multiple cuts, all of which the Executioner immediately treats with salve she always carries. The bruises get no such soothing, and there are far more of those, but I don't care. I rush to learn, to get my next set of bruises, to cleave the air with my sword as if it could cleave my thoughts of Fates.

And as I sweat and pant and train, the memories of Fates scatter, as if I really can scare them off. Soon, all that remains is that dark feeling inside me. But I don't mind it so much now.

It's just fuel for the next thrust of my sword.

A week has passed since I started my training with the Executioner. Gina has grown accustomed to our leaving. At first she continued to ignore us, instead pretending to be absorbed with her paints or toys, but now when we leave Gina will grab my sleeve and say, "You're coming back, right?" I always nod, and take comfort in the fact that I'm not lying. Nothing in the labyrinth has killed me yet.

In truth, the Executioner and I have encountered very little. I've seen a flock of screechers, at a distance, but they didn't spot us and we quickly slipped away. With the Executioner's help, I'm learning how to listen for monsters, be they on the ground or in the air. My senses are still nowhere near as acute as hers, but I'm more aware in the labyrinth now, and less inclined to panic.

The Executioner and I are out most of the day, but before we leave and when we return Gina's bandages are changed. She must be nearly healed by now, but the Executioner insists on giving her fresh bandages. And more toys, when Gina decides to protest. So far, Gina has collected a small herd of cattle, their bodies painted white and their hooves gold, and a bird like the swans I have seen in pictures, but with black speckles on its back and neck and rusty red tint underneath its raised wings.

She also has a bull, painted to match the cattle but for its varnished black horns.

When we return in the evenings, I play with Gina before supper, unless I'm making supper. One night, just after I've finished skinning a rabbit, I hear Gina giggling. Checking on her, I'm surprised to see she's abandoned her toys. Her attention is fixed on the Executioner, who's making shadow puppets on the wall. I'm frozen for a moment, watching one shadow dog tease the other, nipping at it, then disappearing as its companion turns around. Before I know it my attention has strayed from the show, and I'm watching the Executioner watch Gina. When Gina giggles again, the Executioner smiles.

I'm struck by the expression. Before I can collect myself, the Executioner notices me watching. She drops her hands and seems about to approach me, perhaps even scold me in her silent way, but Gina says, "No, no! Keep going! The good dog has to catch the bad dog!"

With a final warning look for me, the Executioner resumes her post as entertainer. I return to preparing dinner, the Executioner's smile still flashing in my mind. It's the first time I've seen her make that expression.

I'm screecher bait again today. The Executioner shoots down the screechers very, very slowly. One of them almost grabs onto my arm at one point, but even then the Executioner doesn't shoot it down until I've dodged the attack. When there's one screecher left I see the Executioner lower her bow.

My heart hammers. Even if I've come to terms with my screecher trauma, I haven't come to terms with dying this instant. I've never taken down a screecher before.

I scramble for my bow but the screecher dives at me before I can notch an arrow. I drop the bow in my hurry to dodge and it clatters away, next to a screecher carcass. I hurry to retrieve it but the screecher drops between me and the bow. It screams at me.

I draw my short sword and swing. I'm panicked and my aim is off. The sword passes through empty air with a whistle. The screecher screams at me again and hops off the ground, powerful wings flapping, drawing it higher. If it gets any farther it's going to be out of range.

I slice my sword at the screecher's leg. It screams in pain as my sword embeds in its feather-covered flesh. It kicks with such force my hold on the sword slips and I'm tossed to the side. It screeches again and kicks its leg more, trying to dislodge the sword. While it's distracted I grab my bow and notch an arrow.

The screecher gives up on the sword just as I start to aim. Panicked, I release the arrow. It doesn't hit the screecher's forehead, but digs into the monster's chest, startling it into a fit. I've bought myself more time. Notch another arrow. Focus. Don't panic. Focus on survival.

The shrieks piercing my brain seem to fade into the background as I aim at its constantly moving forehead. It won't stand still. No target I really need to take down ever will, not in the labyrinth. My timing has to be perfect.

An arrow lodges in the screecher's forehead and it thuds to the ground. I whip my head around so quickly my braids slap against my back. The Executioner lowers her bow again, casting me a brief, cold look before moving to the nearest screecher to start collecting. I lower my own bow, letting the string relax before I put away my arrow.

The issue isn't just perfect timing, but quick timing. Even if the screecher didn't get me this time, I was too slow.

After I retrieve my sword and the Executioner has her arrows back, we start collecting feathers and talons. The Executioner leaves the talons to me, as she's been doing lately.

When we're done I'm surprised that the Executioner doesn't leave. Instead, she pulls out a bottle from her rucksack. The poison paste we made last night. As she pulls on her gloves I hurry to do the same. She hands me the bottle and takes out another for herself. Then she kneels by the nearest screecher carcass and starts spreading the paste in a thin layer over its bare flesh. I do the same, remembering the bites I've seen taken out of dead screechers. The Executioner must be trying to kill whatever it is that eats them. Is that because it's a monster too strong for even her to fight or is it because she's not going to take any unnecessary chances? If my time with the Executioner has taught me anything about her it's that, as well as being the most remarkable warrior I've ever seen, she's intelligent. She fights when she needs to and uses her tricks and tactics the rest of the time. It's probably how she survived out here long enough to reach adulthood.

If she entered the labyrinth as a child, that is.

Gina isn't feeling well that night – she says her stomach "feels funny" – so the Executioner slips medicine into her broth. The medicine makes her sleepy and she goes to bed much earlier than usual. After tucking Gina in, as she's been doing lately, the Executioner starts gearing up again. I'm not that surprised. We've never trained during the night, but I expected it to start at some point. Fear stirs in my gut at the thought of braving a dark labyrinth, but I bury it and take the axe the Executioner holds out to me. It's like the one I've been practising with of late.

Quickly grabbing my short sword and rucksack, I follow the Executioner into the stairwell. Once I'm in the hall she closes and locks the door, as usual. Then we're on our way through the corridors.

I'm not used to the labyrinth like this. It's so dark. For a moment it reminds me of my first night, when the bats attacked and I had to climb the wall. It seems silly when I think about it now. But, for me back then, getting over that wall was huge, and it really did mean the difference between life and death.

Even though the labyrinth is dark, the moon and stars provide enough light by which to navigate without needing lanterns. Firelight would make it much easier to see, of course, but we'd be spotted right away by the monsters prowling through the darkness.

I follow the Executioner and, although I know which way we're heading, I feel as if I've entered another world. I listen as we walk, searching for something, but the night is silent. No distant rumbles shake the earth and no shadows grace the sky. Rather, the entire labyrinth seems made of shadows. We too would likely seem as such from above.

The Executioner does something I don't expect: she pulls out a candle and lights it. She holds it high over her head and continues walking. I see her motion for me to fall back. I do so, staying just outside the candlelight.

After maybe five minutes of walking like this I hear it. A slight whooshing sound, like the screechers but different. It's slightly familiar. Where have I heard it before?

The Executioner stops. She sets down the candle in front of her and turns to face me. She pulls out her axe, holding it against her side so that the blade doesn't reflect the light. The whooshing gets closer. She kicks the candle so it falls on its side, extinguishing the flame. I blink rapidly, trying to readjust my sight to the darkness. I do so just in time to see them descend.

Bats. Three of them, all heading for the Executioner. I flash back to the story Ryan told me, about the head and the arms and the legs.

A bat dives at the Executioner's head. She swings her axe in an arc, aiming upwards. The bat is inches away when her axe meets its neck. In a shower of black rain the creature's head falls from its shoulders. Its wings flap a moment longer and its decapitated body flies over her head, crashing into the ground in front of me.

The next bat is already flying at her arms, its own outstretched. She continues the axe's arc, swinging it down so that it chops right through the arms coming at her. They disconnect and the creature shrieks, flying right through where she was standing as she steps back. She slams her axe into its back, sending both bat and axe to the ground. The creature screeches again but the Executioner's already drawn her sword and now brings it down against its head. There's a spurt and she draws out the sword. At the same time, she grips the hilt of her axe in her free hand and gives it a tug. It stays stuck.

The last bat flies at her legs and I know she'll be knocked off her feet. At the last moment the Executioner pushes her feet off the ground, sending her into a headstand with her hands still grasping the weapons stuck in the bat. The weapons pull free as she completes her flip, landing on the ground on the other side of the bat carcass. She spins around as the third bat pulls up from its failed assault, sending both her weapons into an arc with her spin. Her axe nails the bat's haunches first and it shrieks. Then her sword clips through the top of its wings and digs halfway through its head. The creature goes limp against her weapons as the Executioner releases them. Bat and weapons drop to the ground with a thud and a clatter.

The Executioner stands where she is for a moment and I realize she's catching her breath. I've never seen her have to do that before. Not that I'm surprised, after the show I've just witnessed.

When she's back to normal she pulls out the axe and sword. They're both still covered in fresh, dark blood. With the axe, the Executioner points to the bat that attacked her first, then gestures to her own head. Next is the second bat and a gesture to her own arms. Then the third bat and a gesture to her own legs. I understand what she's trying to tell me. They attack those areas, in that order. Although they attack in quick succession they don't attack all at once.

I nod at the Executioner and she turns from me, going to retrieve the doused candle. She picks off bits of melted wax and lets them fall to the ground as she returns to me. She offers the candle and a match. I take them.

The next morning Gina barely touches her breakfast. When we get ready to leave she doesn't speak to us. At first I think she's ignoring us again, but something about the way she just stares at the toys in her hands, without voicing them or wiggling them around, worries me.

The Executioner takes a spiked club with her instead of her axe when we leave. We go straight down our archery corridor without stopping. We pass several mossy clearings without stopping. It seems like, today, the Executioner is going to keep us walking forever.

I wonder why we haven't run into Fates. We never have, and I'm extremely thankful for that, but I wish I knew why so that I can continue avoiding them. If it's because the Executioner's territory is outside Fates' search areas, then I hope they never broaden their search in our direction.

The Executioner starts to slow when we reach a corridor with a dirt floor. The floor is bumpy and cracked in some places. We round a corner and I see, just ahead, a wide hole in the dirt. As we skirt it I glance down. I can't see the bottom.

We walk a while longer, slowly and silently. The Executioner has her head cocked, listening for something. I strain to listen as well. We keep walking.

Finally a sound reaches my ears. A distant, muted grinding. I can't tell from what direction it comes. The Executioner evidently can because she takes the right hall and starts moving forward, even more slowly. Then she stops, and I do too. She unhooks her club from her belt.

I can hear it without even trying now. Underfoot, the ground is shaking slightly, almost unnoticeably. The Executioner suddenly slams her club into the dirt in front of her. The sound immediately gets louder and the tremors intensify. The Executioner's grip tightens around her club. The sound's getting closer.

The Executioner slams her club down again. A split second after she moves, the dirt below where she first thumped the ground bursts open. Her club meets the head of a digger. Not even half out of the ground, the digger jolts against the hit and goes still. The Executioner lets her club fall to her side as the digger slumps over the hole.

It's larger than the one that attacked me on my first night, but not by much. Still, its mouth is large enough to easily devour my arm whole, even my leg if it surfaced right under me.

The Executioner holds out the club to me. I accept it. She juts her chin forward. I'm to take the lead.

I advance down the corridor much slower than she did. When I reach the end I glance back at her, waiting for her to indicate if I should go left or right. She doesn't. I go left.

By the time we've passed down two more corridors I'm afraid I've gotten us lost or led us in a circle. Then the Executioner stops. I do too. Her head is cocked to the side and she's staring at me with cold eyes. I haven't been listening.

I listen now and realize there's a digger nearby. The sound is faint, but still there. I try to pinpoint what direction it's coming from. I start walking down the right hall. The sound gradually gets fainter. I backtrack.

Finally, the sound starts to get louder, closer. I stop. I'm not sure if I've stopped too soon but I'd rather that than too late. I listen a while longer. It doesn't seem to be getting farther away, but it doesn't seem to be getting closer either. Is this when I'm supposed to draw it out?

I glance back at the Executioner but of course she doesn't let me know. Making a decision, I slam the club into the ground. The digger doesn't sound to be coming closer. I hit the ground again.

There. It's getting louder now. It's moving faster. It's coming. My nerves are on edge as I wait. How long do I wait? Will the Executioner let me know when to move? Will she let it eat my leg if I get it wrong?

When I feel as if the sound can't get any louder I slam the ground with my club. I don't hit anything but dirt. The digger's still coming. I wait a moment and slam the ground again. Still nothing. I start hammering the ground with my club, worried that in between my waiting the digger will shoot up. Then it does shoot up, right in front of the spot I'm hammering. It makes a disgusting hissing, gurgling sound something like the water diggers and dives at me, mouth gaping wide.

I swing the club at the digger, knocking it to the side. It slams into the ground next to me, but I haven't killed it. The digger gurgles at me as it starts to snap back up. I pound it down again, and then I keep hitting it over and over on the head until it slumps. By the time I stop, my shoulders are heaving with exertion and my breath comes in and out very fast.

I feel the Executioner's hand on my shoulder. Her grip is hard as she slowly backs us up, away from the digger body. She stops only when her back meets the labyrinth wall, then motions for me to stand the same way. I press against the wall next to her and wait. We don't move for a long time. Am I supposed to move first? Is this another test?

A distant rumbling reaches my ears. It's different than what I've been listening for today. It's louder, and it gets even louder more quickly than any of the other digger sounds. The ground under my feet starts shaking. The shaking gets more intense until the ground is rocking with tremors. I brace against the wall, fighting to keep my balance. The rumbling is close and sounds like thunder, except it's coming from underground.

Suddenly the ground at the end of the corridor spikes skywards. The spiking continues straight down the passage at an alarming rate, displacing the ground but not revealing what lies beneath. Whatever it is comes straight towards us. As the ground juts up in front of me I press against the wall as much as I can.

All of a sudden, dirt and grit explode in my face. A monster is surfacing from the ground just like the water diggers surfaced from the lake. Except this creature is a hundred – a thousand – times larger. It's almost as wide as the corridor and definitely as long. I can only see the top of it but its scales are the same colour as the digger's.

The creature opens its mouth and the sun glints off its first visible layers of enormous teeth. It crashes right through the dead digger, swallowing the carcass whole, and several loads of dirt along with it. The monster's mouth slams shut and it starts sinking back below the dirt.

The rest of its body follows behind it, half above the ground. I watch it slide past, flinching against the bits of rock and dirt that hit my face. After what seems like forever the ground starts to fall back into place behind the monster's body. Eventually the monster disappears underground entirely, leaving the surface a jumbled, jagged mess.

The Executioner doesn't move and so I don't either. We must wait ten minutes before the Executioner finally steps forward, head cocked to the side. She stretches and then takes the club back. We head in the direction opposite to the way the monster went, and we do so with extremely soft steps. We encounter no more monsters and finally reach a corridor that has stone flooring.

As we start the long walk back to the Executioner's base I'm still shaking. I can't get the image of that colossal monster out of my head.

I guess this is what it's like after you see your first adult digger.

The next morning Gina sleeps through breakfast. I can hardly eat my own soup as I sit beside her, waiting for her to wake up. She's pale and breathing heavily. When I dare touch her forehead I find she has an intensely high fever.

When the Executioner brings out Gina's breakfast and finds her like this, she quickly shoos me away. I watch from a distance as she pulls up Gina's dress and unwinds the bandages. Usually the Executioner sends me into the kitchen with some sort of task before tending to Gina's wound, but today she's forgotten about me and I see it all. Gina's wound, which should be nearly healed by now, is coated with yellow and green pus at the centre while around it her skin is covered in ulcers and splotches of bright red. My stomach rolls at the sight and I have to look away. When I do glance back, it's at Gina's face. I realize Gina can't see her own wound; the Executioner is having her hold up her dress at such an angle so that she can't see what's happening to her body.

The Executioner reaches into her rucksack and produces a jar of salve as well as a handful of turquoise leaves. She applies the salve to the grotesque wound and then presses the leaves in place. She wraps Gina in fresh bandages and then helps her lie down again. Today, she gives her a little wooden horse, stained red, and a wooden warrior, her armour shining silver. I expect Gina to love these most of all, especially the horse, but she just rolls them over in her hands, blinking at them as if trying to stay awake. The Executioner turns away and I see, for the first time, that her face is ashen.

I decide that if the Executioner tries to make me go into the labyrinth today, I'll refuse. But I don't have to worry because the Executioner doesn't try to leave at all; she doesn't even put on her own gear.

The Executioner spends most of the morning making different kinds of broth, each of which she brings to Gina, but Gina will only eat a spoonful or two before burrowing back into her pillow. I sit with Gina while the Executioner works, too concerned to leave her side. Eventually Gina stops burrowing into her pillow and snuggles into my lap instead. I run my hands through Gina's hair as she rests her cheek on my stomach. She reaches out to trace the figures she drew on the crates. At the centre there's a short stick figure wearing a dress, with a tall stick figure on one side and a stick figure horse on the other.

"I want a story," Gina murmurs.

So I tell her a story. I tell her every story I can remember Gus having told her in the past. I know I'm leaving out parts, forgetting the middle or the end, but Gina doesn't complain. She falls asleep halfway through some of the stories, but I keep telling them, in case she's just resting her eyes. In case, even in sleep, the stories give her comfort.

The Executioner has stopped trying to make something Gina will want to eat. Now she sits across from us, pretending to sharpen her axe as she watches Gina. When I run out of Gus's stories, I resort to some Addie has told, hoping Gus may have told them to Gina at some point.

I decide to retell the tales of the Executioner herself. When I talk about her brawl with the temple lion, Gina inspects her lion toy, then takes her warrior toy and makes the two clink together. When I speak of the Executioner defeating a flock of screechers, she does the same thing with her bird toy and the warrior. I leave out the Executioner's nickname, though I'm not sure Gina would have questioned it. She's just staring at her little warrior.

But the Executioner is paying attention, watching me while I tell the stories, her gaze unflinching, unrevealing. If any parts of these tales are true, she won't let on.

I don't tell the third story Addie told me, in which the Executioner supposedly slaughters a group of Icarii; I tell Gina a story about a hero who appears and saves all the Icarii.

I think Gina's asleep, but she asks in a small, brittle voice, "Does she bring them home?"

Somehow, my voice is even smaller. "Yes. She brings them home."

That night the Executioner makes us a decadent meal, in terms of food for the labyrinth. The soup not only has meat, but little sliced carrots and some sort of green vegetable with which I'm unfamiliar. Our sliced meat is of several different kinds, and it's been cooked in a herb water to give it even more taste than usual. Finally the Executioner brings out a bowl of bumpy red berries.

Gina can't bring herself to eat any of it, except for a few handfuls of berries. She smiles at the sweet taste and asks me, "Can I have more tomorrow, Gus?"

Despite the chill that runs down my spine, I nod. She smiles right past me, at the crates over my shoulder, her brown eyes unfocused. Soon after that she falls asleep and I tuck her in. All her toys are lined up on the floor beside her, except for the warrior, which she clutches in her hands. Afraid it may poke her in her sleep, I gently try to pry it from her hand.

"No," Gina mumbles, and I can't tell if she's asleep or not. "My hero."

I lie down beside Gina and, for hours, listen to her ragged breathing. Even in the dim light I can see the sweat on her forehead. Hesitantly, I move my hand there, to feel the heat. It doesn't seem as bad as earlier. The Executioner's salve must be working.

I repeat this thought over and over in my head until I finally fall asleep.

I shouldn't have fallen asleep.

I wake up to a distant noise that I can no longer pinpoint, but that doesn't matter. Gina's not lying beside me. Even her toys are gone. In their place is a cup, half-filled with liquid tinted the same colour as the Executioner's sedation herbs. Bits of the herbs float to the surface. I'm on my feet in an instant, calling for her in my weak voice. There's no answer. I'm the only one here.

That's when I see that the door is cracked open. I slip into the stairwell just as a distant light goes out.

I scramble for the closest alcove, finding a match, then a candle. The match won't light. I grab another, striking it against the stone wall. A seed of fire sparks above my fingers. I'm hurrying down the hall before I even have the candle lit.

We used to race up the stairs between floors, back home, when the lift was full or when we were bored. Clara would always initiate the races. I remember watching her blonde hair flying out behind her before she disappeared up the steps at an unbelievable speed. I always came in last, too late to see the moment Clara hopped over the final step. I was always too late to see her come in first.

I run up these steps faster than I ever have in my life. At the top I'm met with the flat brick wall that slides away. The brick at the centre gives beneath my hand and the wall moves, revealing the labyrinth and the Executioner, walking away. I see Gina's legs hanging over her arms. The candle falls from my trembling grasp and goes out.

I stumble after the Executioner as the door closes behind me. Then I'm running. She must hear me but she doesn't stop or even slow.

"What are you doing?" The question scratches my throat but I don't care. "Where are you taking–"

The words die on my lips as I reach the Executioner's side. Gina is curled, limp in her arms. There's a dark cloth over her neck. In the sunlight I see the cloth is moist, shining red. Horror consumes me and I can't move. The Executioner keeps walking.

"You killed her," I whisper. Suddenly I'm screaming, "You killed her!"

The Executioner falters. She starts walking again. I run after her, beating at her back and screaming, "Murderer!" until my throat is raw. I don't care if a monster hears me. I don't care if we're attacked. I'm sick of the labyrinth and all its death and pain.

I don't know when my screams stopped and the sobs started but I'm sobbing now. My voice is shaky. "She was only a child."

The Executioner is crying too, I realize. Silent tears are slipping down her cheeks. One catches on the edge of her scar, then slips in between the cracks of her X and drips down to the corner. It hangs there a moment, before falling from her lip.

I follow the Executioner and I don't care if I get lost or if she leaves me. We walk for so long I know my feet should be sore, but they aren't. We stop in a clearing overrun by dead vines. The Executioner sets Gina down by the wall. Then she starts breaking off vines, which she lays in a pile at the centre of the clearing. After she's built a waist-high pile, she retrieves Gina and lays her gently on the vines. Then she shrugs out of her rucksack and produces from it, one by one, Gina's toys. She lays them on either side of her, in the order in which they were given. Then she takes out a small sack, the same one from which she'd always give Gina a new toy. She lays this at Gina's feet.

The Executioner crouches by the pile as she pulls a match from her pocket. She strikes it against the ground and sticks it in between the vines, where she waits for it to catch. When she pulls back her hand, it's followed by a thin trail of smoke. More smoke rises from between the vines as the fire slowly starts to spread.

Standing, the Executioner pulls something from her jacket. It's Gina's warrior. The Executioner's hand clenches around the toy as she brings it to her mouth. She presses her lips gently to the warrior's head, then steps forward and carefully slips it into Gina's small hand. The Executioner stands there for a long moment, staring at Gina's face, while smoke coils around her legs and into the air. She brushes back Gina's hair from her forehead with such tenderness my heart breaks.

The Executioner turns her back on Gina and the pyre. She comes to stand beside me, but doesn't turn around again. She draws her bow. Behind me, I hear screeches.

I should be scared, but I'm not. I'm numb. All I can do is stare at Gina's small body among the gradually flaming vines. For the first time in my life, I managed to find my courage to save her from the screechers. Except I was too late. She'd already been wounded.

I was too late this morning, too, to stop the Executioner. Except even if I had made it in time, maybe I wouldn't have stopped her. Maybe I would have seen that it was best that Gina didn't suffer. Her wound was killing her slowly, painfully. What the Executioner did would have been quick. Gina was sedated, so she wouldn't have felt a thing. She would have slipped away dreaming of home.

Gina was just a child. I was right in saying that, but I realize now that I'm just a child too. I can't handle the terror and loss. Even when I thought I could, when I tried my best, it made no difference. I'm just a useless child in a labyrinth of horrors. That's what we all are. Everyone at Fates. Every Icarii sacrificed on Fallen Day. Useless, hopeless, fateless children.

We're all Fateless, like that girl in the Fey's story, because there's no way out of the labyrinth. There never was. Alyssia doesn't exist. The gods don't exist. Icarus doesn't exist. If he did, he would have protected us, like we were told.

The screechers are here now. The Executioner notches a black arrow. Lets it fly. Notches another. The pyre starts burning in earnest. Gina's pretty new dress catches fire and her toys are consumed. Her face blurs between the flames.

I'll never get out of the labyrinth. I know that now. I have no future. No fate. That must be what the Fey saw, when they looked into their own futures: nothing.

I'll become like them. I'll turn into mist and disappear into the labyrinth.

Another week of training comes and goes. The base is silent now, colder. Every trace of Gina is gone: her paints, her pictures, her clothes – even her pillow. All that remains are her drawings on the crates. The first few nights without her I stare at the one of her and Gus and her favourite toy horse.

Eventually I start sleeping on my other side, so I don't have to face the drawing. But this is just as bad. I'm facing the spot where Gina's bed used to be.

Now I sleep on my back.

The Executioner starts going out at night. She does it after she thinks I've fallen asleep. I try following her. The first few times I lose her right away. Lately, I've been able to tail her through a few halls, but I always lose her. She must have figured out by now that I'm following, but she hasn't indicated that she knows. She hasn't tried to stop me from following, either. The door remains unlocked whenever she goes.

This morning, when I'm ready to leave for training, the Executioner motions for me to sit by her on a closed crate. The moment I do, I feel her hands on one of my braids. Immediately I pull away. When I look at her she holds up her hands, showing no daggers. She reaches for my braid again and this time I don't pull away, although I remain tensed.

She does the last thing I expect: she unwinds my braid. For a moment I flash back to my mother doing my hair or Clara practising braids on me. I always loved it when Clara played with my hair. Mother, although she was usually sensitive, would brush my hair aggressively if we were in a hurry for something. She wouldn't ease through the knots.

The Executioner eases through the knots in my hair, even more carefully than Clara. She starts winding my braid back into being, but I realize she's winding something into my braid. When I try to peek she grips my chin to make me look straight ahead. I don't try to peek again.

When she's finished with one braid she steps in front of me. She grabs the other and yanks sharply. I wince and glare at her. Then she grabs the braid she just finished.

It's her turn to wince. She pulls back and shows me her hand. In several spots over her palm and fingers are little dots, sprouting blood.

Hesitantly, I touch the braid she just finished. I'm surprised to find it wound through with small spikes. I run my fingers over each one, lightly so as not to prick myself. They seem to be well hidden. My long hair has been turned into a weapon, rather than a weakness.

The Executioner sets to tying my other braid. This time she lets me watch as she does it. She shows me the little bands of spikes she's made and how she winds them into my hair and keeps them in place. Then she undoes both my braids and hands me the straps of spikes. As I start tying my left braid back together with the spikes, she stays and watches. When I do something wrong she adjusts my placing of the spikes or of my hair, making sure I watch as she does. After she's helped me with the left one, I find I can do the right on my own. When I finish she looks over my hair, nods once to herself, and goes to collect our quivers.

It's the first time she's guided me through anything so gently.

That night, an idea strikes me. After the Executioner sneaks away, I pull my gear back on and follow. But I don't try to track her; instead, I follow a route I've only taken once but could never forget.

I come out in the clearing of dried vines. The centre is burned black, but all the ashes have long since blown away. There's a pile at the centre of the charred stones. When I get closer I see they're little toys, like the ones with which Gina used to play. These, although as well-crafted as those given her by the Executioner, are not painted. On the top of the pile are three identical dogs. When I reach to pick up one of the dogs I realize they're connected at the heels, all carved from the same piece of wood and facing different directions. They're guarding each other's backs.

I've barely raised the toy an inch when an arrow whizzes past my head. It digs into the wall, breaking through and scattering dead vines. Turning, I find the Executioner lowering her bow, standing in the corner of the clearing. She isn't surprised to see me. If anything, it seems like she was waiting.

She crosses the clearing to retrieve her arrow, then comes to stand by my side, just like she did a week ago. We stood in these exact same spots, except she was turned around, shooting down screecher after screecher. Tonight, she doesn't turn around.

We stand and stare at Gina's grave for a long time.

The next day the Executioner is not in as much of a hurry to leave the base. That doesn't mean she isn't busy. She makes us a big breakfast and while I finish eating she packs multiple salves into both of our rucksacks, followed by more flasks and food than usual. I'm finished eating and sheathing my usual weapons when the Executioner hands me an extra tool from the weapons box. I recognize it right away as the chain and spiked ball I ogled my very first time going through the box. Could the Executioner have known? The box seemed a mess, in no particular order, but perhaps the mess *is* her order.

The chain is wrapped tight around the handle. The Executioner doesn't show me how to wield the weapon. She just helps me attach a new sheath to the front of my belt, above my left leg and a bit in front of my sword sheath. After putting away the chain I'm ready to go.

Once we hit the labyrinth the Executioner goes at a breakneck speed. However leisurely she seemed this morning, she's making up for it now. We weave through twists and turns all morning. By the time it hits noon we're into digger territory. I think we're hunting diggers today, in a different way for we don't have our clubs, but the Executioner continues over the dirt ground without breaking her pace. Eventually we arrive at stone ground again, in a section of the labyrinth in which I've never set foot. The Executioner clearly has because she doesn't hesitate at any turn, going faster and faster until I begin to get winded.

Abruptly we break into a mossy clearing. This clearing has darker moss than the ones I'm used to, and also seems thicker, more overgrown. The Executioner goes to the water at the centre of the clearing, peering into its depths. This pond is small and not very deep and it's easy to tell we have no water diggers to fear. The Executioner sits beside the water and pulls out a package of extra food. Apparently, we're taking a break.

Our break lasts long enough to eat, drink and catch our breath. We're up immediately after that and back to weaving through the labyrinth. The sun gets lower in the sky. I can't imagine how far we've gone, let alone where we're going.

The Executioner slows our pace to a brisk walk. She cocks her head to the side, listening. I do the same. Screechers. Up ahead, to the right, I think. The Executioner veers down the first left corridor, breaking into a jog. If I'm right about the screechers then, for once, the Executioner wants to avoid them.

The labyrinth becomes different. Moss covers more sections; living vines crawl along more walls. Some walls have crumbled to reveal not another corridor, but instead a physical hall, with floor, ceiling and walls. The Executioner hurries past all of these halls, not casting them a single glance. She doesn't slow down again until we're far away. Are they like the one in which we encountered the water diggers, or is there possibly something worse resting inside?

We finally reach one hall that the Executioner doesn't pass. Instead, she slows, then picks her way over the crumbled wall into the hallway. I follow her, wary of the darkness ahead. The Executioner produces a candle and lights it. The shadows peel back from the light, revealing a short hall ending in a heavy metal door with a small, barred window in the top. The Executioner passes the candle to me and approaches the door, at which point she pulls the chain around her neck from her jacket. The soundless bell sways as she fits the key to our base into this lock. The doorknob whines, then turns. The Executioner pulls her key back and returns it and the bell to the safety of her jacket. Then she shoves her shoulder up against the door. At first it doesn't budge, then it starts to grind open with a distressingly loud groan. It continues to groan, even deeper, as it opens to solid darkness.

Behind us, I hear a screech.

The Executioner slips into the darkness. Her hand appears, waving me in. I clear the door and hold up the candle to grey brick walls shining with moisture. The air smells and feels damp.

There's a groan behind me. Turning, I see the Executioner pushing the door closed. It takes a while but goes faster than the opening did. Moments after she gets it closed something slams against it. A screech follows, then another slam. This continues for a couple of minutes before silence fills the air. The screechers have given up.

Instead of taking the candle back, the Executioner produces and lights another. She starts ahead of me down the damp hall, her steps silent and measured. In the distance I can hear the drip of water and – even more faintly – gentle lapping.

I follow the Executioner down the hall, which begins to seem impossibly long. Suddenly the Executioner stops, cocking her head to the side. I do the same but can still only hear the water. Soon we come across the source of the sound. At the end of the hall is a set of steps, leading down to water. We turn down another corridor, but that isn't the last submerged hall we see. I'm wary of water diggers, but something about the steadiness of the current makes me think the water's empty. At least, as far as I can see.

Finally we reach a set of stairs that aren't submerged. Even the walls here don't seem as moist, the air drier. I'm surprised when the Executioner hesitates a moment before descending the stairs. Like always, I follow.

We go down so deep it starts to get cold. I have to wonder how far underground we are by now, and when these stairs will stop – if they ever do. Why are we here? It seems excessive for training and anything we hunt would be impossible to bring back after such a distance. As it is, I don't see how we'll make it back without camping somewhere. Even after all my training, that thought scares me. We could take turns guarding but, even with the Executioner guarding me, would I be able to sleep in the open air of the labyrinth?

I'm so surprised when we reach even ground I almost trip up. We advance down a wider hallway. When I hold up my candle I find the ceiling lower than those in the corridors upstairs. This hall is also surprisingly short. At the end of it are a pair of huge double doors made of stone. The Executioner holds up her candle as high as she can, lighting the words etched into the stone above the doorway. At least, I assume they're words. To me they just look like fancy scribbles. They remind me of passages in the Book of Daedala and in mosaics at the temple. Perhaps, like that, this is Ancient Daedalic.

The Executioner lowers her candle and faces the door. She stares at it for a long moment, then digs something out of her pocket with her free hand. She holds it out for me to see. A wooden lizard, something like the one she gave to Gina, except this one has long spikes all around its head and crude wings sprouting from its back. The Executioner abruptly drops it on the floor and stomps on it, grinding her heel in. When she pulls back the toy is destroyed.

I look at the Executioner and our eyes lock. She juts her chin towards the door.

Together, we push against one side of the massive double doors. It takes even longer than the door upstairs did but, eventually, it starts to budge. It groans inwards, and the sound echoes endlessly in the room beyond. How large must the room be to produce such an echo?

We get the door open just enough to slip in. The Executioner goes first, keeping her back to the door as she slides towards the wall of the room. Once there, she picks up something from the ground. As she straightens I see she's holding a torch. She turns to the wall and, as her candle turns as well, I see there's a sort of decorative urn attached to the wall. I think it's empty but when she dips the torch in I realize it contains some kind of dark liquid. The torch comes out dripping with the stuff. The Executioner presses the flame of her candle to the torch.

It lights right away, but the fire is nothing like candlelight. It starts out with that orange colour, but as it climbs higher over the black liquid it burns to pure white, then becomes tinged with blue, then green, until the fire is a mix between the two colours, with white at its depths. The Executioner blows out her candle and lets it drop to the floor. She takes a few steps more into the room, still hugging the wall. The torchlight reveals a sort of trench running along the wall, filled with similar liquid to that in the urn. The Executioner presses her torch to the liquid in the trench and, after a split second, it lights.

Suddenly green and blue fire lights up along the trench, travelling impossibly far into the distance. Then it takes a sharp turn to the left, lighting farther along the wall. The Executioner, meanwhile, has gone to the wall on the other side of the door and set alight an identical trench. The fire rushes along the surface of the black liquid, lighting up the entire wall, then the next wall. The two fires don't meet, however. They stop with only a thin strip of black in between them. I realize what separates them is a door.

The room is massive. It's larger than any open space I've ever seen and covered with dark, cracked stones. In places in the floor the stones fall away to darkness. Above us is a ceiling so impossibly high I can only see shadows. I try to think back to how far underground we've gone.

The Executioner starts across the giant room at a brisk pace. It soon becomes clear she's heading straight for the door. I look around the room warily as I follow her, but I can neither see nor hear any sign of the lizard monster we're supposed to destroy. Could I have misinterpreted such a seemingly obvious message?

We reach the door and the Executioner throws it open, speeding inside. She gestures for me to close the door as soon as we're in, which I do. Her torchlight and my candlelight reveal a small square room. There's a door in the back corner that's open and filled with rubble. The ceiling must have collapsed.

If not for the green and blue tint of the torch I think the floor and walls of the room would be white. I hold my candle up and find the ceiling is full of odd, bumpy panels. It takes a moment for me to realize why they're familiar and, when I do, my eyes widen. These look just like the full-panel ceiling lights back home, on the commercial floors.

But that can't be right. There can't be electrical lights in the labyrinth.

I'm in such shock I barely register when the Executioner takes my candle from me. She lays it on an off-white table. When I realize what's on the table, my shock triples. A computer. And not just one: the whole room is full of desks and ancient, broken computers. Some look bashed in, others have shattered screens, but there's no mistaking what they are. We had them in the library and a few at school, on which to do our homework or search the tower's database. There were also a few games that Clara used to love to play when we were younger, but claimed to have grown out of a few years ago. That's what she said in front of the others, anyway. When we were alone in the library she'd have us take turns keeping watch while trying to beat each other's scores on the game. I didn't enjoy the game all that much, and I usually lost, but it was worth it because sneaking around with Clara was always so much fun.

The memory is quickly overridden by my intense confusion. What are computers doing in the labyrinth? The supposedly *ancient* labyrinth?

The Executioner comes over to me. Behind her, I can see one of the desk drawers has been opened. She was looking for something and, evidently, she knew exactly where to find it. She shoves her torch into my hands, and ducks behind me. I feel a tug on my rucksack and realize she's opening it. She tucks something inside, as close to the bottom as she can get. I don't know what it is she came here to collect or why she's leaving it with me. I just hope that when we get back to base she has some way of explaining.

As the Executioner latches my rucksack closed, I realize the torch is reflecting off something in front of us: an observation window. Reaching forward, I wipe a hand across its surface and my palm comes away with a coating of dust. Where I rubbed I can see through to the large room we just left. As I peer through the window, there's a moment when I think I see something fall from the ceiling.

Before I can get a better look, the Executioner is pulling me back to the door. When she opens it, the air in the room beyond is clear. What I saw must have been dust in my eyes or a trick of the light.

We start back through the room, at an even faster pace than before. Despite our haste it feels as if crossing is taking us twice, three times as long. It's like a dream in which the corridor you run down keeps extending farther and farther, but this is all too real.

Something falls in front of my face, then hits my hood. I look up only to get a face-full of hazy material. My first thought is mist and I'm immediately reminded of the Fey. Then I start coughing and I realize the material is dirt. Dirt and rocks are falling from the ceiling. The Executioner spins around and starts running back the way we came, since it's closer than the exit. She must want to wait out the shower of debris in the computer room. I follow her but the dirt and rocks seem to follow us, then they seem to be falling all around us, just like rain. Is the ceiling going to cave in?

There's a resounding crack and the Executioner and I pull up short, spinning just as the ceiling caves in behind us. Except the massive form dropping to the ground isn't rock. It's moving – alive. And as it hits the ground a pair of giant wings flap out behind it.

The impact it makes when it hits the ground sends stones jutting up around the floor and causes such a tremor it knocks the Executioner and me off our feet. The Executioner's standing in an instant, but I can't get up. I can't even move. I'm frozen as I stare at the monster in front of us. It's the largest thing I've ever seen. I thought the adult digger was colossal but I was wrong. This nightmare, looming, breathing before me, is truly titanic.

Its body is like that of a lizard and covered in dark scales that reflect the firelight, casting it a bluish green. Huge, leathery wings are folded against its back while its massive tail flicks behind it, cleaving the stone tiles straight from the floor and sending them crashing into the wall. The worst part of the monster by far is its head, which is attached by a long, thick neck that reminds me of a digger's body. This creature's head, however, is far better defined. Horns jut from its temple, a pair sticking up and a thick pair curling around its jaw like tusks. It hardly needs tusks when its teeth are as massive as they are. I get a good look at the teeth when the monster opens its mouth and an ear-splitting roar echoes through the room. The ground shakes by pure virtue of the noise and more rock and dirt fall from overhead.

The monster before me looks like the pictures of dragons I've seen in old books, but a hundred times worse because, along with this one snake-like neck and head, there must be ninety-nine other snake-like necks that have no head. They all coil and writhe around the one head, like a mane made of tentacles. At the end of each of these tentacles are what, at first, I think are spikes, but I then realize are sharpened bones, stretching right out of the flesh.

Another roar shakes the room but is abruptly cut off when an arrow, flaming blue and green at the tip, hits one of the creature's spare necks. This breaks me from my stupor, at least enough to glance over my shoulder. The Executioner has backed up to the wall, where she's dipping an arrow wrapped in rags into the fire and black liquid. The tip coats with liquid and lights with the fire. The Executioner shoots the beast again. Although it seems to have minimal to no effect, it prompts the monster to let out another ear-splitting roar. I wince and cover my ears, but when I open my eyes again I see the Executioner looking at me with her cold gaze. She juts her chin forward and at first I think it's to the monster. Then I realize it's to the door. Our exit.

She wants me to escape.

I start shaking all over. Even if I wanted to escape on my own, the monster is blocking my way. If I try to run around, then it could easily crush me with its tail, if it doesn't spear me through with its spare necks first.

I hear running footsteps and the Executioner passes me, firing an arrow as she goes. Not just one flaming arrow, I realize. She's managed to notch and fire three at the same time. The monster roars at her, its spare necks convulsing when they're hit. The Executioner notches another arrow as she veers off to the right, running towards the side wall. The monster sweeps its tail at her. The Executioner runs right at it, jumping at the last minute and landing on the other side in a crouch. She turns and fires at the monster with her unlit arrow. The beast ignores this hit entirely, but still sweeps its tail back towards her.

She draws her short sword, which I realize is already

wrapped in rags. She dips this into the black liquid and it instantly catches fire. As the massive tail swings towards her she turns and throws her sword at it. The sword sings through the air and embeds in the fleshier part of the tail, right below the scales. The monster roars with pain, thrashing its tail up and down. The Executioner throws herself out of the way of the deadly writhing, quickly backing up out of reach. Her sword pops free from the tail, doused but still covered in black liquid that I realize isn't the fire starter but the creature's blood. Its tail leaks this same liquid but stops disturbingly fast. I watch in horrified awe as the cut flesh of the tail starts to weave back together. I shouldn't be as shocked as I am. When it comes to scale, the damage the Executioner dealt to this monster would be equivalent to a paper-cut.

Suddenly the monster lumbers forward, its spiked necks darting at me, even as its tail swishes again at the Executioner. I have to look away from her as I stumble to my feet, hopping back just in time. A bone spike embeds into the floor right where I was sitting, followed by six others. They pull back with such speed that I shiver. My shivering grows more intense when I see the destruction they dealt to the floor. A few seconds earlier and that could have been me.

And if I dwell on our situation a few seconds longer it *will* be me.

Pulling out my short sword I quickly back up, keeping my eye always on the neck spikes that seem set on skewering me. I wish the Executioner had given me a heads-up about the blue fire, or at least wrapped my sword in rags for me. I would have found it extremely strange, but I wouldn't have questioned her.

As the monster advances on us, driving us closer and closer to the wall, I begin to notice a pattern. It attacks with its seven longest necks, while the others make the attack motion but only ever make it to the ground immediately in front of the monster. Also, the seven necks seem only able to attack once before pulling back and stabbing again, as if they aren't able to pull back a little and re-stab. They need momentum for their attack.

I keep backing up and wait for all seven neck spikes to stab the ground in front of me, as they have every time. Then I duck forward, right after the seventh hits the ground and the first starts to pull up. I slash my sword into the seventh.

My sword bounces off its scales without leaving a dent.

I quickly hop back as the first neck spike snaps back at me, having recovered faster than I expected. Quickly sheathing my sword, I move to take out my bow. Then I remember how the Executioner shot at the monster's neck already and, even with flaming arrows, did no damage. If this monster is impenetrable, how can we possibly hope to fight it, let alone defeat it?

The spikes come at me again. On reflex, I fumble with my sword, only for my fingers to brush my chain. I haven't even uncoiled it yet, let alone practised with it. Hopefully when it comes to this I'll be a natural.

The chain uncoils with two flicks of my wrist, the spiked ball snapping surprisingly hard into the ground.

I yank and it tears out, just before a spike jabs into the ground in front of me. The other spikes follow. I flick the chain around them, thinking maybe I can catch them all. The chain wraps around the fifth neck. When the neck suddenly jerks back my chain is pulled with it. I hold tight and find myself pulled with the chain. The next thing I know I'm dangling from one neck spike in the mane of neck spikes. I squeeze my eyes shut, waiting to be skewered.

When it doesn't happen, I crack my eyes open. I realize the monster is confused. I've suddenly disappeared and the Executioner is nowhere in sight. I don't know where she is, but I know I need to get down before it realizes I'm in the opportune spearing location.

I give one heave, then another. I kick off one of the other necks for extra momentum. Soon I find myself swinging towards the creature's back. The neck to which I'm attached bows backwards as my feet meet scaly back muscle. I give the chain a hard yank, telling myself if it doesn't come free I'll let go. Luckily, it gives, half due to the neck's sudden shakes to dislodge whatever has attached to it. Now that I have the chain, I hold the handle in one hand and keep the chain collected in my other hand, spiked ball swinging in the air. I'm doing my best to balance on the creature's back when suddenly its head turns around and all the necks follow suit.

The monster roars at me and its back muscles tense, throwing me off balance. I tumble off its back, hitting the ground hard. My shoulder and right arm scream and I worry I've broken something. Then the monster roars in absolute pain and I look up, only to realize I fell just in time.

At least thirty of the monster's neck spikes are stuck in its own back, where I was standing. It tries to pull out the spikes and roars again when they break free in a shower of black blood. More blood drips down the wound and I realize it's not closing as quickly, if at all.

Even if it's impenetrable to everything else, it's not impenetrable to itself.

I haven't even picked myself to my feet when suddenly the head of the monster whips around to zero in on me. It opens its jaws and I think it's going to try and snap me up, but then I see something: a light at the back of its throat. A bluish green light.

I drop my chain and roll, and keep rolling until I find myself under the monster's draped wing. Behind me blue and green flames explode against the ground where I was lying. The flames get closer and closer until they hit the edge of the monster's wing, then abruptly stop. The monster roars in pain and flaps its wing, creating a gust that effectively hammers me into the ground. When it stops, its wings stay raised. The head levels at me again and I find myself staring into its black slit eyes as its jaw opens. The light comes at the back of its throat and I know this time I won't escape.

Suddenly the monster's main neck snaps back while the others start writhing. Flames spill impossibly high into the air, hitting the black rock ceiling right next to a massive hole. The flames fizzle into bluish green bits that rain around the room. Through the fiery shower I see the Executioner sliding from underneath the monster's stomach. Glancing at the monster's stomach shows it to be open, spilling black blood in a long line along the floor. The monster roars in pain, even as the blood flow slows. Looking back to the Executioner, I realize she's covered in the monster's blood, so that all I can see of her face are her eyes, blinking through the black liquid. She tosses her axe aside and pulls something from her jacket pocket as the monster turns its head and all its spikes on her. I can't see what she pulls out, but as she crouches and strikes it against the floor a little white flame sparks to life in her hands.

She looks at me and – in that moment – I realize her eyes aren't cold, but determined.

Just as she presses the flame to her liquid-drenched head, the monster's jaws close over her.

I scream. My scream echoes through the room as the monster stretches its head high and swallows. It hasn't finished swallowing when its jaws open wide. I expect a roar but what comes out is a horrible choking sound. Flames burst up from its jaw, but not like before. This isn't a flamethrower but an explosion, all blue and green and white. The monster's wings and spare necks all fall limp, leaving its main neck still stretched taut and frozen in the air. Its black eyes are wide open as the explosion of flame rains sparks around us. The scales on the creature's head and neck start falling away in charred pieces, as if peeling back on themselves. Flesh crisped black is revealed underneath, then also falls away. Soon all that remains is the skeleton of its neck and skull. Those charred bones hold their form for a second, then dissolve to dust that follows the rain of embers, coating the monster's ninety-nine limp necks.

No sign of the Executioner remains.

I don't move for a very, very long time. When I do, it's to go to the Executioner's axe. It's still drenched with the monster's blood, which, I realize now, is just like the liquid that creates the blue and green fire.

I stare at the monster corpse in front of me, then at the axe in my hand. She knew that the only thing that could destroy the monster was itself. That's why she used the fire to distract it, because it knew the fire was an actual threat. That's why she coated herself in its blood and set that blood on fire, to burn it from the inside. She destroyed herself so the monster could destroy itself.

All to save whatever's in my bag.

I fall to my knees, rucksack already in front of me. I dig everything out of it until my hands close around something foreign. I pull it out and find myself face to face with an old, faded red notebook, bound with a leather strap. Carefully, I open the strap and flip through the first couple of pages. It's blocked with writing. I squint at the cursive letters. My heart drops. It's the same as the writing outside of this chamber. Ancient Daedalic.

After binding the notebook again I return it to my bag, at a complete and utter loss. A notebook I can't read. We fought the worst monster imaginable and the

Executioner died for this and it's useless. With me, it's all useless.

As I put back the notebook my fingers brush something else. I pull it out and find myself holding a chain. On the chain is a key and, next to that, a large, silver, soundless bell. Without a moment's hesitation I pull the chain over my head.

The first thing I do when I step outside is take a deep breath of the labyrinth's fresh night air. Then I close the door behind me and lock it. I doubt I'll return but at least I know I have the key.

As I head back I keep my ears open for bats or screechers, though I'm still not sure if screechers actually hunt at night. Still, better safe than sorry.

I'm not scared. It doesn't even cross my mind to be scared. I'm just sort of empty. Now I truly am on my own and, even if I'm a hundred times better prepared to survive than when I first entered the labyrinth, I'm going to be doing it all alone. Despite the fact she tested me harshly and left me to fend for myself, having the Executioner with me was often enough to ease my mind while wandering the labyrinth. Now she's dead and I might not even make it back to base alive.

Yet I'm not scared.

I know now that the Executioner faced that monster prepared to die. Otherwise she wouldn't have given me her key and bell, the latter of which I couldn't even look at before without receiving a death glare. She seemed to be familiar with the monster, not only because of the wooden toy she showed me, but because of her wariness to and from the computer room, along with her quick execution of a plan that would kill the monster and herself both. Maybe it was always her plan to die down there tonight.

Despite the fact I've been on the move all day I don't let my exhaustion stop me. I press on until I reach a mossy area where we took a break earlier today. I spend the next few minutes drinking more water than I ever have in one sitting. Then I lean against the wall by the water, easing into the moss that clings to the wall and floor. It's so comfortable I feel my eyelids flutter shut.

I pinch my cheeks and blink rapidly to wake up, Gina's voice echoing in my head: *Gus says never fall asleep anywhere but Fates.* Fates isn't an option for me any more, but the point not to sleep in the labyrinth remains. It's not safe. Then again, it's not as if I'll be able to make it back to base without resting. Even after coming this far, I still have another six-hour journey or more ahead of me, and some of that is through digger territory. Night or day doesn't matter to them; I have to be as aware as possible. Right now, I'm practically half asleep.

Rooting through my bag I search for my extra food, thinking something in my stomach might help keep me energized. My fingers brush the notebook again. Even though I know it only holds disappointment, I pull it out and unlatch the binding.

I flip through the pages again, slowly. Like before, all they offer are unknown words and letters. I sigh and, at that same moment, something falls out from between the back pages into my lap. Two somethings, I realize.

Frowning to myself, I pick up the more tightly folded parchment and open it. The paper is incredibly thin and the page itself is actually quite large.

At first I don't understand what I'm seeing. Lines and boxes and circles and odd Daedalic notes and squiggles, all mashed together in no particular order. Then it dawns on me that their order isn't nonsensical but, in fact, very precise. My heart starts pounding against my ribcage and I realize my free hand has started gripping the bell.

I'm staring at a map of the labyrinth.

I scramble to open the other folded paper. It's a letter, written in my language. And it's from the Executioner.

*I do not know your name and you will not know mine. That makes this easier.*

*There has been no need until now for us to exchange words. Words are worth little in the labyrinth, but now they are all I have left to give you.*

*I know the Icarii tell stories about me. They say I was once one of them, but that is not true. I was sent here almost ten years ago, with others, from a world outside the labyrinth. Teams have been sent before. None have returned. My team was no different.*

*Half of us were killed within the first year. I deserted my group to try and escape the labyrinth. They caught me. They should have executed me, but I was with child at the time, so they cut out my tongue and branded the mark of a traitor across my mouth.*

*After I gave birth, they took the child and abandoned me, leaving me with nothing. I survived, for her, and followed them, for her. When monsters attacked them, I stole her away. They are all dead now. Only I am left.*

*I could not raise my daughter on my own in the labyrinth. I left her with a girl who led a band of children. They called themselves Icarii. The girl called herself Sybil.*

*Sybil taught me her language and I taught her mine. She called it Ancient Daedalic, but that is wrong; my language is older than yours, but in no way ancient. I taught Sybil of the labyrinth and she taught me of her city. We planned to flee the labyrinth with her Icarii when my daughter was old enough. But Sybil was killed. The Icarii fear me now, as you feared me when we first met.*

*There is a way out of the labyrinth. Not the way my team and I entered; that passage has been destroyed by a monster that killed three of my men.*

*Tomorrow I will lead you to a cavern which I once braved with part of my team. A monster trapped us in the observation room, and it is in that room where I left a map and a journal, documenting the labyrinth and all its terrors. They are written in 'Ancient Daedalic'. You will have to find a way to translate them. I know Sybil taught her fellow Icarii my language: go to them. You will need their help to escape. The path out of the labyrinth is treacherous. If you attempt to brave it without the knowledge in my journal, it will kill you.*

*I did not take the journal and map with me when I left the cavern because I was sure I would be killed; they were too valuable to be lost. Now, I will likely be killed retrieving them.*

*I know that to the Icarii I am the Executioner. Know that I have only ever executed a single man: the one who refused to lead our team out of the labyrinth, the one who carved these lines into my mouth, the one who took my baby from me weeks after she was born. That was my first and only execution.*

*If I have died, then I have successfully committed my last.*

*I will give you this letter no matter what happens, but if I am dead you must keep going. Escape the labyrinth. Reach my world and save those trapped here. Save your city and your fellow Icarii. Save the people that my daughter loved.*

*And know that, while there is no Alyssia, if there is a place like it, that is where I now go to find my daughter.*

I stare at the letter, then the map. Will it lead me to Alyssia, or is the Executioner's world something else entirely? Whatever it is, I hope there are others like the Executioner there, because I can't possibly save the Icarii on my own. I'm still learning how to save myself.

But with this map I could escape the labyrinth, and no one would ever know. Collin and the rest of Fates think I'm dead. I can just disappear, like the Fey. No, more than the Fey: I could become Fateless. I would be gone, my fate unknown, a secret to all but myself.

Except I'm not Fateless. Nor am I the girl who left the city of Daedalum. I'm not Clara or a member of Fates or Nameless. I'm not the Executioner. But I will take what all of them taught me and I'll use it to escape the labyrinth.

As myself.

As a child, Caighlan Smith loved to build and navigate pillow mazes. An adoration of Greek mythology soon followed. Canadian born and raised, Smith studied English Literature and Classics at Memorial University of Newfoundland. Her first novel was published when she was nineteen. The 'c' in her name is hard, the 'gh' silent.

For more exciting books from
brilliant authors, follow the fox!
**www.curious-fox.com**